W9-ATY-556

The Hurricane Conspiracy

Joan and Bob
Merry Christmas

The Hurricane Conspiracy

David and Nancy Beckwith

SeaStory Press
Key West, Florida

The Hurricane Conspiracy

© 2010 by David and Nancy Beckwith

Quotations from the following musical compositions appear in the text:

The Wind Is Gonna Blow, written by Howard Livingston, performed by Howard Livingston and Mile Marker 24

Yesterday, written by Paul McCartney and John Lennon, performed by Matt Monro

Detroit City, written by Danny Dilland and Mel Tillis, performed by Tom Jones

Bad Moon Rising, written by John Fogerty, performed by Creedance Clearwater Revival

Hooked On The Easy Life, written and performed by Terry Cassidy

Christmas In The Sun, written by Grub Cooper, performed by The Fab 5 featuring Grub Cooper

Welcome Home, written by Grub Cooper, performed by The Fab 5 featuring Grub Cooper

Put Jesus In Your Christmas, written and performed by Crazy (Edwin Ayoung)

Count Your Blessings, public domain, lyrics 1897 by Johnson Oatman Jr. based on Thesalonians 5:18, music 1897 Edwin D. Excell, performed by Rosemary Clooney

ISBN 978-0-9821151-6-9

LCCN 2010935253

SeaStory Press
305 Whitehead St. #1
Key West. Florida 33040
www.seastorypress.com

We dedicate this book to our daughter Aimée (A/K/A Lexie) who has brought endless sunshine to our lives. This book is also dedicated to the exclusive fraternity of hurricane veterans who share our goal to live in a tropical paradise.

Chapter 1

It is a dark and stormy night, Will typed into his computer. Indeed it was. A gust of wind hit, rattled the house, and a torrent of rain followed.

"Lord, I hope I get this finished and get this e-mail off to Lexie before the power goes out," Will said to his wife, who was squinting to see the storm's progress out of the one open panel they had left open in the accordion storm shutters.

Betsy frowned as rain hit the window again, "You better hurry. This thing is starting to look wicked. Good grief, Will, you should have seen that bottlebrush branch sway just now. They're saying ten more minutes until Peter comes on again with a storm update. Hope the cable isn't getting ready to crap out."

"I'm hurrying; I'm hurrying. I'm so flustered I keep making typos," Will replied, not bothering to hide his irritation. "Man oh man! Do you hear the avocado tree? It sounds like it's beating itself to death against the house."

"Peter's coming on the air," Betsy added. "You'll want to hear this!"

"Just keep your drawers on, and let me finish this. I'll be there in a second."

We're now feeling the feeder bands as the storm approaches shore. Winds are at fifty miles per hour, gusting to seventy. Most of you should have completed your evacuation; but if you chose to ride out the storm, stay where you are. It's too late to go anywhere now. Road visibility is extremely limited. All the shelters in the county report they are full. Stay tuned to the National Weather Center for updates.

Peter McCosh, the Indian River County director of emergency management, spoke calmly into the television. Peter McCosh was a big man, not athletic looking, just big. He was six feet four or so but did not fit the stereotype of a network announcer. In his brown polyester short-sleeved shirt, black wingtips and vintage necktie, he looked more like a scientist than a slick salesman with an agenda. His authoritative tone was one the public trusted. Peter's trademark was his necktie. People had known for years that when Peter removed it, disaster was imminent. As long as the tie was visible, he expected a nonevent.

"Peter's got his tie off. You know what that means?" Betsy continued again.

"Yeah, I know, I know," Will said. "I'm coming. The e-mail to Lexie is out of here."

"Will, that last wave really slapped the dock. Do you think the Grady-White is going to be okay on the davits?"

"If it's not, it's too late now. See what other channels are on," Will said in a worried tone.

"And now a report has just come into Channel 6 that the county sheriff's department has arrested two cars of revelers on State Road 60 when they refused to break up a hurricane party that was blocking the highway and preventing people from evacuating. Traffic had backed up for five miles."

"Idiots! Can you imagine such stupidity?" Will said. "Flip over to the Weather Channel."

This is Jim Corrolla, meteorologist for the Weather Channel. I am in the parking lot of the Seahorse Villa, a condominium complex near the Pelican Inlet. Nervousness continues to build as residents here listen and wait. As you can see behind me some people are still out on the beach, and there's even a surfer or two. Orchid Island has been evacuated and the bridge to the mainland is being patrolled. Orchid Island residents are being allowed to leave the island, but no one is allowed to return.

"Well, Will, I guess we still have time to bail," Betsy said.

"We decided we were going to ride it out," Will said. "This certainly isn't our first storm. Remember Amanda? I'm still convinced this house was built to take a cat 3 or 4."

"I hope you're right," Betsy mumbled.

"I know I am. Sometimes you just have to trust your gut and keep your head, especially when those around you don't. Something I've learned from my years in the stock market. Maybe we ought to call the Walshes while we still have a phone and see if they decided to stay put."

A sudden gust of wind brought the Norfolk pine almost to the ground. A band of rain pummeled the boat again.

"I hope I don't regret not having that boat trailered," said Will, looking through the Stygian darkness at their boat.

The lights flickered, and the computer went down. Lucy, the fox terrier, jumped into Betsy's lap and down again. UP! DOWN! UP! DOWN! The avocado tree branches scraped the eaves of the house. Lucy bolted and hid under the couch until Betsy finally dragged her out. Lucy jumped back into Betsy's lap, every bone in her body shivering and rattling. Coco, the family dachshund, whined in sympathy.

The wind howled again. Lightning cut the sky like a saber, and a deafening clap of thunder followed. Lucy jumped straight up.

"We probably should have left," Betsy said.

When Will and Betsy still had time to leave, the path of the storm was uncertain – was it going into the Gulf or move up Florida's east coast? They decided to stay and see the storm through at their house since their daughter Lexie was off at school and there was only the two of them and the dogs to worry about. The only place they had to go was Betsy's cousin's house in Naples. Besides they had no place to board the dogs. Public storm shelters did not allow animals.

"Maybe you're right, but we can't leave now so let's see what we can learn from the TV while we still have one," Will said.

"I'll fix one last hot, fresh dinner. We could easily be eating out of a can for the next few days," Betsy said. "I just know that I'm not going to have any plants left... and the yard was starting to look so good."

"It was a dark and stormy night... A perfect night for murder," Will murmured, giving his best Humphrey Bogart imitation.

"You've been watching too many episodes of 'Murder She Wrote'," Betsy said. Outside, another blast of wind bent the bottlebrush tree.

Chapter 2

*W*ill turned on the stereo while he waited for Betsy to start cooking. Mile Marker 24's smooth island, country rhythms could be heard in the background.

> *We all live on an island*
> *Some call it paradise*
> *The sun almost always shines*
> *and the weather is so very nice*
> *But there's a price you pay for living by the sea*
> *When the tropical depression becomes a category 3*

"You know how to pick 'em," Betsy said.

The power flashed off and on. The digital clock on the microwave started flashing. The stereo reverted to its default setting, AM radio. When the sky lit up, the boat dock seemed to move like it was highlighted by a disco strobe. Once again, Lucy bolted and jumped up on Betsy's leg, scratching it with her sandpaper-like paws before she started running around the room. A late arrival to this scene would have thought Lucy had been pinched by an invisible force that then began chasing her around the kitchen. Betsy almost dropped the stovetop griddle she had been cooking steaks on.

"Ouch! That hurt! Sometimes I hate that dog. Catch her, Will. You know what happens when she gets out of control. She throws up. That's all we need," Betsy said.

"Phone, I'll get it. It may be Lexie."

"It's probably a cold call, somebody wanting money. We can't even get away from solicitors while a hurricane is going on," Will said.

When Betsy hung up she looked at Will and said, "You're not going to believe who that was. Connie Tressler, Dave's wife. She's looking for Dave. Seems he hasn't come home from work."

"Funny. I'm pretty sure he was gone by the time I left the office today," Will said.

"She also said he'd gone off somewhere with Joe Bowen on his Harley," Betsy continued.

"So he went home and left again?"

"Apparently. I hope he's all right – not the kind of weather you want to ride a Harley in," Betsy said, shaking her head.

The storm-related news on the radio caught their attention.

Twenty Mile Bend on State Road 60 is starting to flood, hampering last-minute evacuation efforts. The line of cars on State Road 60 is now twenty-three miles long because of the gridlock caused by traffic that cannot make the right-hand turn to get onto the turnpike. Northbound traffic on the turnpike is at a standstill.

Evacuees who make it past the turnpike are facing yet another challenge in Lake Wales. A car containing an elderly couple has blocked State Road 60 for more than an hour. Their Ford caught on fire in the middle of the intersection of

State Road 60 and Highway 27. Fire trucks have been trying to reach the car. Smoke from the fire has reduced the already limited visibility in this area. Our correspondent on the scene has verified this heartrending story of the couple standing in the rain watching their car burn, their possessions in a pile on the soft shoulder of the road.

We have had our first reported death attributable to Clarice. A woman leaving her home on 43rd Avenue in Vero Beach has backed over her husband in her haste to evacuate.

A report is just in of a couple who have been broadsided attempting to cross an intersection after another motorist waved them through. A third motorist plowed into the passenger side of their car as he attempted to bull his way through the intersection by driving on the shoulder of the road. Police are now looking for this hit-and-run driver.

"I'm glad we didn't evacuate," Will said. "I'd rather face Clarice here than be out on the road with all those idiots. I swear some of these damned fools must have gotten their driver's license at Kmart."

"Will, turn off the radio and let's listen to some music on the stereo," Betsy added.

Will did not respond. Betsy wondered if he was tuning her out, but soon she heard Matt Monro's mellow voice drifting into the kitchen and had to laugh...

Yesterday
all my troubles seemed so far away
Now it looks as though
they're here to stay
Oh I believe in yesterday

Chapter 3

"*D*id you feel that gust rattle the hurricane shutters?" Betsy said.

"Aren't you glad we have shutters instead of plywood?" Will asked.

Betsy replied, "As long as I live I'll never forget that phone call I got from Bobby before Hurricane Floyd telling me you were stuck at the top of the bridge with plywood scattered from one side of it to the other."

"It's a miracle I didn't kill somebody that day with plywood flying everywhere, but you know I can't count the times I had used bungee cords to tie loads of lumber on the top of the van's luggage rack before and never had a problem. A gust of wind must have gotten up under the plywood just as I got to the top of the bridge. I shudder to think what would have happened if that stuff had hit someone. We'd have been in lawsuits for the rest of our lives. That's why I swore up and down never, never again. I didn't care what it cost. We were going to have shutters on this house during the next storm," said Will.

"Did you see that bolt of lightning?" Betsy asked.

By 9 p.m. Clarice was shrieking. Winds were over 70, gusting to 100. The rain pounded the side of the house. Miraculously, the power had flashed but not gone out altogether. They waited for the calm that would occur when the eye of the storm finally crossed over Vero Beach.

The power blinked again; this time it didn't come back on.

At times the house was engulfed in darkness only to be momentarily lit up again by a bright blue bolt of lightning, which was followed by an instantaneous slam of thunder. The house shook. Will stepped outside and peered to see the boat dock. The boat was still secure.

"Boat looks okay," he announced, the relief showing in his voice.

They looked again and saw a dead blue heron lying near the dock. It looked as if a wild animal had snapped its neck.

"I can use some help in the kitchen," Betsy said. "You better aim the flashlight at the dining room table so we can see to eat these steaks while they're hot. And turn on the battery radio. It's a good thing we both like rare beef since the power just went out. Help me get these potatoes to the table."

As Will came back in the house, the wind whooshed through the opening, fluttering the curtains in the family room. Lucy, who had followed Will outside, rushed through the door, almost tripping him in her haste to get back inside. They both jumped when a limb thumped against the roof several times as the wind rolled it over and over. One of the extra Styrofoam blocks blew out from under the Grady-White and rolled across the yard causing the boat to sway from a sudden gust of wind rocking it on the davits. The wind was driving the rain horizontally. Betsy held up her flashlight to the barometer hanging in the family room. It had fallen more. A white spray showered over the dock. The heron was gone.

As they sat down to dinner, Will said to Betsy, "Well, when we were dating, I promised you candlelight dinners. Is a flashlight dinner close enough?"

As they ate in silence, Will played with the radio dial. The station was taking call-ins.

They heard the frantic cry of an elderly woman. *I'm sitting at home in the dark. My husband is critical. My power is out, and his respirator won't work. You've got to come here and help me.*

You need to call 911. This is WANG radio station, the DJ tried to explain.

No, you need to help us.

Ma'am, you need to call 911. This is WANG.

We need help! You have to help us! He may die!

Ma'am, give me your name and address, and I will try to call 911 for you.

You have to help us! And then she hung up.

WANG, the DJ announced as he took the next call.

My power just came back on, but I can't hear my TV for my damned next door neighbor's generator, complained the caller loudly.

Sir, do you know how fortunate you are to have power, the DJ began.

Dead air again.

WANG...

I was just calling in to let your listeners know that now is not the time to trim your trees.

The radio DJ lowered his voice and said, *Uh...Thanks for the advice, sir.*

WANG...

I live over on the beach...on Cyprus Road. We really have a lot of trees down.

Yes, Ma'am. They are down all over town.

I have some Australian pines that were real pretty...

Yes, Ma'am, what's your point. I have callers stacking up.

Well, there's a motorcycle squashing my ficus hedge.

What kind of motorcycle ma'am?

I know nothing about motorcycles except fools usually drive them like maniacs.

Ma'am, couldn't it belong to one of your neighbors?

Nobody in this neighborhood has one of those things. We're all older people with more sense. My question, young man, is if no one shows up to claim it, who does it belong to?

"It's really starting to get crazy out there," Betsy said, cutting a slice of steak. "You know, Will, things were so normal on Monday when we first heard about Clarice."

Chapter 4

Monday, August 29, had been a utopian summer day. The cloudless sky was a deep, azure blue, the kind of sky that, had you seen it in a painting, you would have sworn it was the product of the artist's overactive imagination. An occasional breeze gently disturbed the palm trees' slumber. Gulls and pelicans circled lazily. The pelicans took an occasional calculated dive for fish. Everything for animals, birds, and people seemed to move in slow motion in the late summer heat.

Traffic was light, not a snowbird in sight. Residents could take left-hand turns onto A1A without any delays. Locals didn't have to plan their trips to Publix since the parking lot was only half full most of the time. Restaurants were running summer specials. Snowbirds in a few months would be creating lines everywhere as they competed for these same restaurants' services. Summer was the time of year that full time Floridians loved, the time when they knowingly told one another they had "gotten their town back." A myth perpetuated by year-rounders was that it was too hot to be in Florida during the dog days of summer. Full-time residents, however, knew better. They knew the summer weather in Florida wasn't much hotter than most other parts of the nation. They just didn't want the rest of the world to know.

This was also the time of year many businessmen closed for their annual in-depth cleaning or for renovation or remodeling or to just plain disappear for a few weeks of rest and relaxation before the beginning of the next winter season two months hence. Making it even easier to rationalize this calculated inertia was the approaching Labor Day weekend. It was hard to imagine anything could disturb this reverie.

The alarm clock had gone off at six thirty sharp that morning. Will stretched, jumped out of bed, let the dogs out, and went out to the front driveway to get the newspaper. Betsy in the meantime plugged in the coffee pot, got down bowls and spoons for cereal, and flipped on the TV.

Will always gave the local newspaper a thorough read as he listened to the early morning television news. Betsy would shower, apply her makeup, and work on her hair with another TV running in the bathroom. Since it was his profession, Will scanned the paper for any news that might affect that day's securities markets. He was also looking to see what was going on locally or if there were names in the obituaries he recognized. In Florida, it is prudent to never skip the obituaries if you want to be in the know. He would call out to Betsy any stories that might affect either of their jobs. The last thing either of them wanted was to start their week being blindsided by something they should have been aware of.

After Local On The Eights. The Storm Report shows tropical storm Clarice has moved over Anguilla. Its forward speed is five to ten knots, under the steering flow of a subtropical high pressure ridge. It is continuing west-northwestward. It is moving slowly toward the Virgin Islands and Puerto Rico. Pressure is 996 millibars. Sustained winds were reported by AFWA in Charlotte Amalie of 53 knots.

"Did you hear that, Will?" Betsy asked from the bathroom.

"Kinda. Something about a tropical storm called Clarice. The news media always tries to make these things seem bigger than they really are. By the way, I was listening to the earnings report on J and J. They beat the street estimates. The stock should have a good day. I've got a ton of shares on the books you know. I bet the analyst will be talking about it on the morning research call."

"I hope this doesn't turn into a hurricane," Betsy said.

"Not much chance of that. We're just talking about a little tropical storm way down in the Caribbean. They have to have something to talk about on the Weather Channel. Look out the window at the sky. It's drop-dead beautiful. Have you ever seen a more perfect day? I'm going to cut up some strawberries to put on my cereal. You want any? Then I gotta take a shower and get going. After the research call, I've got Dot Tuttle coming in to talk about her IRA rollover on her 401K. Did you know she's thinking about retiring?"

"I didn't know she was that old. Don't cut me any strawberries, Will," Betsy said as she picked up her curling iron. "They always have bagels at the bank for our Monday morning meeting. I'll call you if I hear more about the storm."

"Love you, sweet," Will's said as he tightened his tie, gave Betsy a quick kiss and headed for the office.

"Let the dogs out before you go. I'll let them back in before I leave" were the last words he heard as he checked to make sure he had his keys and glasses.

As he did most days, instead of taking A1A, Will drove to his office through an old Riomar neighborhood that ran parallel to the beach. The trees were mature, the houses were stately, and the drive was very scenic. People were out getting their newspapers or walking their dogs. There also was an occasional walker or jogger. It was peaceful and serene.

Once through this neighborhood, he came out into the central business district where he passed blocks of one-and two-story buildings. Very few were open this early. A few restaurants served breakfast – some indoors, others in outdoor locales overlooking the Atlantic. As Will drove down the street, he could see the ocean gently rolling. The early morning sun gave everything it touched a clean, fresh feel.

Early arrivals were sweeping up their small piece of sidewalk before putting out signs they hoped would attract customers later in the day. An occasional bicycle rider or exerciser could be seen. Will passed a city park and saw a few people reading as they sat around the picnic tables and looked at the tranquil water in the ocean.

Will pulled his car into a parking space facing the boardwalk. He did this most mornings. He wanted to be able to tell himself he had seen the Atlantic at least once each day. While he sat in his Jeep facing the ocean, he would note the strength of the wind, the height of the waves, and how high or low the tide was. He watched people leaning on the handrails on the boardwalk taking in nature's magnificent start to another day in paradise.

"We are so lucky," Will said to himself, before driving the final few blocks to his office. He could see the distinctive RST logo on the sign – Reynolds Smathers and Thompson – all the way from the street corner.

Will was just unlocking the outside door to the office building when his sales assistant drove into the parking lot. "Just another Monday in paradise," he said as he helped Barbara get her things out of her car.

"Maybe not just another Monday," she remarked casually. "Did you watch the weather this morning? The storm could hit Puerto Rico by Wednesday morning, the Dominican Republic by Thursday. By the weekend, it could roar toward the Keys."

"Yeah, I guess that's a possibility, but even if that happens, it'll probably never affect us," Will said. "There's a good chance it'll get sucked up into the Gulf. That's why they call the Gulf of Mexico hurricane alley."

"I wouldn't be so smug if I were you — we all know how unpredictable storms can be," Barbara said as she went to the office kitchen to make coffee.

Half an hour later, other members of the staff started drifting into the office. Will walked into the kitchen and all he heard was talk of a possible storm.

"Y'all are over reacting," Will said. "This is just a tropical storm. I'm going on UltimateCitrus.com and see what they have to say."

A few minutes later he came back into the kitchen and told the ones still there, "Ultimate Citrus says this thing is becoming more organized and conditions are right for it to be upgraded. But just look at the cloudless sky. Have you ever seen anything that looked less threatening? Guys, I don't have time to debate this; I have a client coming in at nine."

The morning flew by. Will spent about an hour with Mrs. Tuttle explaining IRA rollovers. He then started returning phone calls and working on operational matters. By then it was noon.

"Did you bring any lunch?" Barbara asked.

"I haven't thought about it," Will said.

"I've got enough tuna for two," Barbara said. "I'll tell you what, you buy the Diet Cokes, and I'll meet you in the conference room. We'll flip on the TV and see if the storm has gotten stronger."

"Be there as soon as I get this order in."

✦✦✦✦

By Wednesday the weather reports began to seem even more dismal.

And now the Channel 6 tropical weather update. Tropical storm Clarice has now made landfall on the southeastern coast of Puerto Rico. The observing site at San Juan Airport recorded a sustained wind of 43 knots and at the same time, the St. Croix Airport in the Virgin Islands reported a sustained wind of 45 knots. The highest reported storm total rainfall over the area was at Camp Garcia in Vieques, which recorded 23.75 inches. Generally, total rainfall amounts averaged from 5 to 15 inches with some locally higher amounts. Some areas have experienced heavy flooding.

The afternoon flew by. Later, as Will drove home, he couldn't help but note the day was ending about as perfectly as it started. "This sure doesn't look like storm weather to me," he said to himself. "I hear the Sirens calling. They are saying 'sun, bourbon, music, floatie, swimming pool... sun, bourbon, music, floatie, swimming pool.' I'm coming, you nubile nymphs. Hurricane, my ass!"

Betsy was in the kitchen when Will got to the house.

"Have you heard the latest?" she asked.

"I didn't know that there was a latest. I've been so busy it hasn't entered my mind."

"That's all everyone has been talking about at the bank," Betsy said. "I stopped at Publix on the way home. People are already beginning to stock up on provisions. Let's flip on the Weather Channel before we get in the pool."

✦✦✦✦

On Wednesday the storm continued to strengthen. Clarice moved away from Puerto Rico with maximum sustained surface winds reaching 60 knots. It then moved over the Mona Passage and inland at the eastern tip of the Dominican Republic. Clarice was briefly a hurricane while over the Mona Passage with 70 knot winds and during the Dominican Republic landfall but then weakened over the rough terrain of Hispaniola.

As they were pouring their coffee Thursday morning, Betsy said to Will, "I was watching Fox while you were in the shower. They said we have a fifty-fifty chance that Clarice will come up the east coast if it moves into the Florida Straits. It's hitting Haiti today as a category 1. If you don't have any appointments early this morning, why don't you make a run to Publix and get some water and canned food. You might also fill the Jeep with gas. I think I have enough batteries. I'll cash a check at the bank today so we'll be sure to have some money, and feed the hungry Hummer during my lunch hour. Another report is coming on. Listen."

Hurricane Clarice briefly weakened to a depression and moved over Atlantic waters just north of Hispaniola. In its weakened condition the low level center moved westward away from the deep convection and dissipated. A new center has reformed well to the northeast. Clarice's slow forward motion across the Caribbean is contributing to torrential rainfall. These rains and resultant fresh-water flooding and mudslides have caused thousands to die in Haiti. The loss of life was especially devastating in Gonaives.

"That does sound more serious," Will said. I'll leave the moment the market closes if the prognosis gets worse, and we can start planning on what to do with some of these plants. God, I hate dragging all those things in, but I sure don't want to lose them."

"Or have them act as missiles during a storm," Betsy quickly replied.

◆◆◆◆

By Thursday night when Will and Betsy got home from work, weather reports became even more serious. There were two storms to contend with.

Hurricane Clarice is not the only tropical disturbance in today's news. While Clarice is dumping rain over the Caribbean countries, a second hurricane, Hurricane Daniel, has begun to ravage other parts of the Caribbean. After passing Grenada, where it was briefly classified as a category 5 storm, Daniel moved across the central Caribbean Sea toward Jamaica. It passed by Jamaica in a weakened category 4 status. This weakening was in part due to an eyewall replacement. The combination of the westward turn and weakening kept the strongest winds from hitting Jamaica. Daniel then moved west-northwest after passing Jamaica and re-intensified for a second time to a category 5. This strengthening occurred since it remained in a low vertical shear environment. Daniel remains a category 4 storm and now threatens Grand Cayman Island. Governor Bush has said that if a threat to the Keys intensifies he will suspend tolls on the turnpike if necessary to assist evacuation efforts. Tourists are being ordered to leave the Keys immediately. Keys residents should stay tuned for possible upcoming evacuation announcements.

"We're closing the bank tomorrow at noon," Betsy said to Will. "What's your office doing?"

"We're still waiting for instructions from New York, but most of the brokers who don't have appointments will probably be just in and out. What do you want to bet some of the staff will call in sick as well?"

"Y'all better do something soon. I think this may be the one we've all dreaded. Everybody I talk to agrees that Vero Beach is overdue."

"Yeah, looks like hurricane season is getting ready to go into high gear. Could be a helluva September."

Chapter 5

*W*ill and Betsy were no strangers to hurricanes. Having lived on the Alabama coast in the northern Gulf of Mexico, hurricanes had become a regular summer event. In fact the Gulf of Mexico had been called "hurricane alley" for many years.

Will and Betsy met in 1979 in Mobile. He was a trainee broker. She was a Mobile native who had recently returned to the city after two years in Chicago working for the Gulf Mobile & Ohio Railroad. When Betsy returned to Mobile she resumed her former profession of banking where she started working summers while she was in college.

Will had moved to Mobile from the Mississippi Delta seeking in the port city what the Delta lacked – economic opportunity. The 1970s witnessed the continuation of an exodus from the Delta of talented young people seeking to escape what has been called "the most southern place on earth." The Delta had been dependent on massive cotton plantations since before the Civil War. Emphasis had been placed more on bringing economic benefits to agriculture than to building a well rounded economy. The older generation had done little to encourage industry, content with the status quo, even after it became obvious that this status quo was not in the long-range best interest of the region. Will harbored no hopes of ever returning to the Delta. He had carved out a life for himself that held the opportunity to achieve the American dream.

Betsy's original motivations for leaving her home in Mobile had been different from Will's. When she graduated from college she wanted to see a world different from the one she had grown up with in Mobile. She yearned to broaden her horizons beyond the Gulf Coast lifestyle. The G M & O Railroad was headquartered in Mobile but had a large office in Chicago, the largest railroad hub in the United States. Betsy excitedly moved to Chicago, but after a few winters the excitement waned and the languid Gulf Coast life style lured her home. She missed the ocean, the beaches, fishing, Mardi Gras, and all the other things she had taken for granted for so many years. Soon Betsy returned to school and got her MBA.

Betsy and Will had met in downtown Mobile, which was the center for the financial services industry and the legal profession. Despite the fact most people lived in the suburbs and retailing had long abandoned the downtown area, the financial services and legal professions viewed having a downtown location as a necessity to their being considered legitimate members of the Mobile business community.

Will worked for Reynolds Smathers and Thompson, a national security brokerage network. The national firms always have been the eight-hundred-pound gorillas of the brokerage industry. They had, for the most part, dictated industry trends and provided a full range of services to clients through a series of uniform offices nationwide. Being a risk averse person and industry neophyte, Will had chosen the career that provided him with the most job security and support — working for the giant national wirehouse, Reynolds Smathers and Thompson.

A traditional lunchtime retreat for downtown workers was Bienville Square, where you could sit on a park bench and enjoy watching nature and people. A favorite pastime was to buy hot roasted peanuts in the shell, have an inexpensive lunch, and feed the army of pigeons that flocked to the square for a free meal. It was the perfect break from a stressful morning in the office.

Will and Betsy had met in Bienville Square during this traditional pastime. They noticed they were both regulars, had the same lunch schedule, and immediately found it easy to talk to each other. Betsy was a petite blond with dark brown eyes and a golden tan. At least some part of every weekend was spent at the beach enjoying every type of water sport. In contrast, Will had fair skin, blue eyes and dimples, and was over six feet tall. His brownish red hair was beginning to recede slightly. Both were socially outgoing and loved to laugh – even at themselves. Betsy was instantly taken by Will's engaging smile.

Their discussions revealed they were both single, college graduates with advanced degrees, and had many of the same interests. Not long after meeting they went out on a date. A whirlwind courtship ensued, and soon they were inseparable.

One day as they were eating their peanuts Will told Betsy he had been offered a promotional opportunity. Reynolds Smathers and Thompson wanted him to move to Florida as part of the management team for their new office in Vero Beach.

Will wanted to marry Betsy and have her move there with him. Betsy returned to her office confused and unsure. She spent the afternoon pondering this move to a small town on the Atlantic side of Florida near Palm Beach. She then began a debate with herself about the adventure of leaving her hometown a second time. By evening Betsy had made her decision. She and Will were married within a month of his transfer to Vero Beach.

Betsy found Florida living much more to her liking than Chicago. She still had the ocean and the beaches, and the purchase of a boat brought fishing opportunities as well. Not only could she and Will enjoy the ocean, but the intercoastal waterway was their playground. In very little time Betsy had a good job at Florida National Bank, and she and Will soon began to discover the joys of small-town Florida living. Within a year, Will and Betsy's memories of Mobile had been reduced to nostalgia and both swore they had found the place where they wanted to spend the rest of their lives. A year later, their daughter Alexandria was born in Vero Beach, and their ties to Florida became unbreakable. Now as they looked at their tattered Vero Beach yard, memories of Mobile flooded back as Will and Betsy compared Clarice to Hurricane Frederick, the violent storm that both had survived in Mobile before they met.

Chapter 6

A ragged, hazy dawn finally arrived. Only the remnants of Clarice remained. The night had seemed like two or maybe even three. Will and Betsy both felt wrung out. Neither was sure if their dog-tired feeling was from the hours of tension or simply lack of sleep. Will thought as he peeked out into the rainy gloom, "I wonder if the storm has finally passed over."

Betsy roused herself from her stupor with a start when Lucy jumped on her lap. She had confined herself to one of the recliners in the dark, hot house for the last several hours as she tried in vain to sleep. She and Will had left the house completely dark most of the night so they might conserve the flashlight batteries, blindly listening to the howling, gusting wind and drenching rain. They heard nameless objects thump against the side of the house and other objects roll over the roof. Randomly, they would search the house with a flashlight trying to see if there were any leaks in the roof or around the doors and windows. So far, so good. They would take turns peering out the one partially open accordion shutter to appraise the storm's intensity before retreating to the safety of their recliners again. Then they would flip on the portable radio. Weather reports were sporadic and incomplete since the roof had blown off the headquarters of the county emergency service building. Reports were coming in that the sheriff's department's building had also been breached and filled with storm water.

Since the storm began Will and Betsy had closely watched a large gnarly live oak tree in the backyard to help gauge the wind's strength and direction. After this shaky reassurance they would then retire into the house and listen once again to the radio, their sole contact with the outside world.

News Flash! We have a report just in that a 911 call has been received by the Vero Beach Police Department concerning the Bay Federal branch on Citrus Avenue. A Press Monitor journalist has told WANG that the Citrus Avenue windows of Bay Federal have been riddled with bullet holes and the alarm wires have been cut. Thieves unsuccessfully tried to penetrate the building while the eye of Clarice passed over the city. As a result of the building being breached, wind and water have caused extensive damage. While police were investigating this attempted robbery, still other thieves attempted to remove and steal hurricane shutters from the rear of the police station.

In a separate incident, Indian River Sheriff deputies were called to rescue a man from a flooded house who was attempting to ride out the hurricane with his horse in his living room.

Sometime around midnight Will had looked into the back yard and could not find their barometer oak tree. Thinking he was merely suffering from reduced visibility, Will asked for Betsy's assistance. The tree had simply vanished. Both kept returning to look at the spot where the oak had been, but there was still no evidence of the tree in the blackness. When daylight ultimately broke and the rain slowed, they ventured out once again to look for the tree.

"I see it! I see it!" Betsy said.

The tree that once stood in their back yard had been deposited by the violent, raging storm in a magic-carpet-like journey into their neighbor's yard, flattening a portion of the wooden fence separating the two properties. It seemed as if a giant battering ram had been used to topple this entire portion of the fence.

They saw three-hundred and sixty degrees of destruction. Will and Betsy's once immaculate yard looked like a city dump. Unbroken trees were bent at odd angles. Some had been uprooted. Bushes and trees were stripped of their leaves giving them a prematurely barren, midwinter look. Will thought about a cemetery scene in a horror movie he remembered, leaving him shuddering as he drove his date home from the theater many years before. Limbs covered the lawn as well as the dock. The boat was hanging freely and awkwardly from the davits, swinging each time it was hit with a fresh gust of wind from the now receding storm. Water poured out of the Grady-White's drain hole. Grass and leaves had been glued by Mother Nature to the boat's side, partially covering the name: "Sundance." The Styrofoam blocks that the boat had rested on the day before had floated across the river, and were caught in the mangroves.

The screen enclosure to the pool had huge sections torn loose. The screen now flapped with each new gust of wind. The pool itself had several inches of debris. The water had turned an unhealthy shade of green. A raccoon floated face down, a crab riding his back like a miniature jockey. Fortunately, their house did not experience any damage other than wet, flying vegetation the wind stuck to its sides.

Will said to Betsy, "If the back yard looks this bad, I'm not so sure I want to see what the front looks like." There was no need to open the fence gate. There was a gaping hole in the fence where the gate had been one day before.

Will and Betsy waded through the muck and picked their way around the house, trying not to step on anything sharp or jagged. With every step the nasty muck tried to suck their deck shoes off their feet. The front yard was a repeat of the havoc they had seen in the back. Their showpiece traveler palm hung at a strange angle. The Norfolk pine had been broken about twenty feet above the ground. The broken portion had barely missed the house. Every branch on one side of the tree had been stripped, giving it an off balance appearance. Sea grape branches and leaves seemed to be everywhere. The swale in the driveway had over a foot of dirty, polluted looking water with nowhere to go. The water was already stagnating since the lawn surrounding the driveway was totally saturated with rain water; the water in the swale had nowhere to drain. Even the drier spots in the yard were mushy and sponge-like. Rain continued to fall in a steady downpour.

At last when the rain abated, with effort Will and Betsy climbed over the refuse and worked their way out to the street. The mailbox was open as if it were expecting a delivery. They looked in both directions. The street was impassable no matter which way they tried to go. More limbs littered the street than they had seen in the yard. These were interspersed with man-made objects like garbage cans, flower pots, yard lights, and lawn ornaments. Deep mounds of oak tree leaves seemed to be everywhere. The piles had been given a bit of color by hibiscus and croton leaves. Two houses down toward A1A, they saw the missing gate to their fence.

Around the corner it was even worse. Will and Betsy could not tell where the street ended and their neighbors' yards began. The entire street was like a Venetian canal that began at the edge of one house and ended at the edge of the house across the street. Some houses had been flooded; some had not. Mailboxes seemed strangely misplaced as they stood in the river of water surrounding them. Driveways had disappeared. A twelve-foot-high gristly mass of black soil had been ripped out of the ground by an uprooted forty-foot live oak tree. The mound was being held together by the tangle of tree roots from the one-hundred-plus-year-old oak now stretched sacrificially along the ground.

Will and Betsy looked at each other in disbelief and picked their way through the rubble of useless belongings and yard trash. For what seemed like a hot eternity, Will dragged large limbs out to the littered street. He finally created a path for him and Betsy to get back to their dark, damp, hot house. Since he was covered in sweat, Will dipped the dead raccoon out of the swimming pool and took its limp, waterlogged body out to the front yard, well away from where the dogs would be. He felt so grungy that he stripped down to his underwear and jumped into the vegetation-filled pool. When he did, he felt something move. Will looked, and about two feet from him was the land crab that he had seen in the pool earlier.

"Damn, I forgot about that thing," he mumbled. It snapped angrily at the floating thermometer Will used to swish it away from him. Coco barked madly at the strange intruder.

Will gasped and pointed to the riverbank adjacent to the dock. Betsy saw a throng of land crabs dotting the landscape. It was as if an army of them had risen from Davy Jones' locker and was invading the human race. The land crabs' large claws were raised like sabers being brandished in anticipation of the onset of a savage battle. Coco sounded a battle cry. Lucy lunged against her leash.

Betsy threw Will a towel, brought out the battery radio, and put the radio on the porch.

Along State Road 60 there are several locations totally flooded and impassible. State Road 60 between Yeehaw Junction and Vero Beach has been closed. All of the area surrounding Vero Beach Country Club is submerged. The concrete power poles along Indian River Boulevard across from the Vero Beach Book Center have broken off and are blocking the road.

Do not leave your home. The Vero Beach Police Department has ordered that until further notice only emergency vehicles will be permitted on roads. A dusk-to-dawn curfew is in effect. Violators will be arrested. Indian River County has been declared a disaster area by Governor Bush. Local law enforcement efforts will be supplemented by the National Guard. No one will be allowed across the bridge onto Orchid Island until the damage can be assessed. Residents will be informed when they can return to their homes. Looters will be harshly dealt with. Since there is no power in Indian River County, do not expect to find commercial establishments open. All Indian River County schools will be suspended until further notice.

Two additional reported deaths related to Hurricane Clarice have occurred. A couple on 45th Terrace died of carbon monoxide poisoning caused by a generator they brought into their family room during the storm to circulate water in their salt water fish tank.

On the mainland there are also reports of people Jet-skiing and reports of others dragging boogie boards behind cars on Bayside Avenue.

"Remember reading Herman Wouk's book, *Don't Stop The Carnival?*" Betsy asked. "This carnival is just beginning."

"I wish all I had to do with my time was boogie board down Bayside Avenue," Will replied. "I'm not sure how we are going to get off of this island or when. Hell, I'm not even sure how to get out of this neighborhood. Let me go see if I can raise our garage door by hand. Then if I can clear the street enough, maybe we can go exploring later today."

Since we're already on the island, I wonder if the curfew applies to us, Betsy mused to herself.

Chapter 7

*T*he next job was to open the storm shutters and try to somewhat ventilate and let light into the hot, stuffy, dark house. The rest of the morning was spent hauling limbs to the edge of the street, trying to leave a single lane wide enough for them to drive the Jeep through. The few neighbors who had chosen to ride out the storm in their homes were engaged in similar endeavors. Will saw neighbors he hadn't seen for a year. Tom Bradley, who lived a few houses away, had a chain saw. While Tom cut limbs into manageable lengths, Will dragged them to the side of the street. Soon the piles were head high or higher as far as either of them could see. The entire neighborhood began to resemble an out-of-control landfill.

Cypress Place, as well as their storm-ravaged yard, looked more like what Will imagined Baghdad to look like than the neighborhood he and Betsy had lived in for most of their married life. He also found it hard to imagine this abandoned looking dwelling was the house that had been the only home their daughter, Lexie, had known until she went to college.

About mid-afternoon Will and Betsy ventured in the Jeep to the end of the flooded street and worked their way toward A1A. The power line was drooping at the entrance to their neighborhood and resting on an uprooted tree. There was just enough room for the Jeep to squeeze through. However, when they reached A1A and looked north and south, it was apparent that even with four-wheel drive they would never get far. A1A was eerily deserted. Trees and power poles crossed and re-crossed the highway in an erratic pattern. A person viewing an aerial photograph of the area might have said the scene had been the creation of a mad giant builder who, once he had finished, had ripped up his creation in a fit of anger.

"We won't be going anywhere today," Will said.

"It looks like Mother Nature will be the curfew enforcer on the island today," added Betsy.

"Tom said he's been talking to everyone left in the neighborhood. People are dragging every gas grill they can find over to his house. The neighborhood's going to have an enormous cookout to barbeque the contents of everyone's freezer before the food goes bad. He said the beer may be warm but the food'll be hot. You know, Betsy, don't you think that it's five o'clock somewhere? Want a hot cocktail while we decide what food we're going to contribute to this must-attend social event of the season? We'll have black-tie t-shirt dancing in the streets."

"I'll check our social calendar to see if we're free tonight," Betsy said. "We better do our boogying before dark though. Otherwise we may hurt ourselves."

Chapter 8

*W*hen Will and Betsy awoke on day two after Hurricane Clarice, they were hot, tired and sticky. Betsy felt grungy after two days of cold showers in one of their formerly immaculate bathrooms, now musty and dark with only cold water. They had removed the cushions from the lawn chairs and slept on the back porch. The house was just too hot. An occasional breeze was their only relief. Frogs and crickets had an impromptu all-night jam session. The cushions were uncomfortable. Betsy fretted the entire night imagining snakes coming in the holes in the screen.

In the morning, Will jokingly asked Betsy, "Want your bacon and eggs sunny side up or over easy? Or would you rather have waffles? Would you settle for a delicious strawberry Pop-Tart?"

"Such a gourmet! That's why I married you."

"We can follow the scrumptious breakfast with a dip in our naturally green pool."

"You bringing the soap or am I?"

"I heard chain saws over on A1A. Maybe today is the day we can see some of the outside world again."

Betsy flipped on the radio as they ate their Pop-Tarts.

WANG AM. You're on the air.

How do you file a complaint with the OEC, a voice screamed at the announcer. *I have been to four goddamned stores. None of them will sell me a case of beer.*

Sir, Governor Bush has ordered a moratorium on all alcohol sales until we are through this catastrophic period.

Where does he get off doing something like that? A man has a God-given right to buy beer. I won't forget this at election time, I guarantee.

Sir...

Dead air.

WANG AM. You're on the air.

What's the phone number for Florida Power and Light?

Ma'am, they're doing the best they can to restore power.

I'm not calling about that. I want to know if they're going to pay for all the food I lost in my refrigerator.

Ma'am, I don't think they will assume the responsibility for the contents of your refrigerator during a general power outage caused by an act of God.

Well, it's not my fault. Someone has to pay.

WANG AM. You're on the air.

My power is still out. It's hot as hell. I have called all the way to Orlando. I can't get a hotel or motel reservation anywhere. They keep telling me they're filled with emergency workers. I just don't understand why these people can't just stay in tents.

WANG AM. You're on the air.

You told me to boil my water for forty-eight hours. I did what you said, but when I was finished there was nothing left.

The announcer laughed so hard he couldn't talk.

"I hope you're listening to all of this, Will," said Betsy, giggling. "This is just too much. God, the public can be stupid."

"Remember what I've always said. It's scary to think we have one man-one vote in this country."

"On a more serious note," the announcer continued. "We have a third report of a death. An Alabama Power lineman on loan to Florida Power and Light was electrocuted as he tried to reconnect the trunk line on Oslo Road in Vero Beach."

✦✦✦✦

Will and Betsy spent the rest of the morning hauling plants out of the garage. They stockpiled them on the boat dock. After a delicious canned-tuna-and-Ritz cracker luncheon, they decided to check out A1A again, this time on their bikes. A1A had come alive. Emergency workers hustled like worker ants. Will and Betsy saw bucket trucks, bulldozers, dump trucks, grappling hooks and cranes. Men in hard hats and leather gloves swarmed on both sides of the highway. What couldn't be loaded was simply being pushed aside. A path was slowly being carved out.

"Good God, Betsy," Will said. "I never realized there was so much vegetation along A1A. Can you imagine what it must be like on the side streets?"

They were stopped moments later by a sheriff's deputy, who courteously but firmly demanded to know what they were doing on the island. He wanted to see identification. Will explained that they lived on Orchid Island and had chosen not to evacuate before the storm. The deputy told them things were not safe, and they should return home.

"Other than emergency vehicles, no one is being allowed to cross the bridge unless they are checking on their place of business," he said.

"But my business is on the island," Will objected. "I need to check on it."

"Sir, may I ask the name of your business and its address."

After Will gave the officer the information, the deputy radioed in to confirm its validity. Finally, he gave Will and Betsy the go-ahead.

"Do you need an escort to your office?"

"No thanks, officer. We'll just ride our bikes on down there."

"Please be careful."

Will and Betsy were speechless as they gawked at the massive devastation. Debris seemed to be everywhere. The dense hammocks of oaks along both sides of A1A had been stripped of their foliage to where they looked like an eerie tropical Transylvanian forest. Standing water was almost everywhere. A four-way stop sign dangled from the top of an oak tree. Shiny panels in vinyl fences were blown out. Even chain link fences were down. At a gated community, the arm on the gate had been replaced by a fallen cabbage palm and a fallen power line. One house's gable had been reduced to trusses. Another house was now multi-colored, evidencing not only its present lime green color but the yellow, brick and gray that it had been at various times in the past.

A sign that read NO ALCOHOLIC BEVERAGES on the left hand side and NO ANIMALS EXCEPT HANDICAP ASSIST-

ED on the right had axed a cabbage palm. It was like new, but now imbedded three inches deep vertically into the trunk of the palm. The 7-Eleven's windows were covered with plywood, its parking lot flooded. The crude lettering on the plywood announced the obvious: NOT OPEN.

The balconies on one office building had been sheared off by the weight of a pool of storm water. The metal street lamp, now hanging at a forty-five degree angle, pointed at the building in a silent accusation. It seemed to be wagging a silent finger saying "I told you that it wasn't designed right."

A second building resembled the leaning tower of Pisa. It had been undermined when the land on the ocean side had been washed out to sea. Pine tree spiked roofs were common. All of the vinyl siding had been stripped off of a luxury condominium, leaving insulation flapping in the wind. The aluminum awning over a parking lot had collapsed, crushing the cars beneath it. The asphalt parking lot of an oceanfront pizzeria had collapsed into a giant sink hole, leaving the restaurant perched precariously on a newly created, contoured spoil island. A new river ran between the boardwalk and the eroded shore, leaving the boardwalk looking like a fishing pier accidentally constructed parallel to the bank instead of perpendicular. A condo was missing its exterior wall. Will and Betsy could see the furniture and appliances in the apartments. The remnants of the building reminded them of the open sides of Lexie's Barbie doll house.

Clarice's random path of destruction just seemed to go on and on and on, block after block. Nothing seemed to have escaped damage.

"Let's see if the Walshes rode out the storm at their house like they planned to," Will said.

"Lead on, Geronimo."

After an hour of alternately riding and walking, Will and Betsy finally saw the sign to the Walshes' street. The sign was twisted and leaned at a funny angle, pointing at A1A instead of at Seagrape Lane. The couple had to once again dismount and walk their bikes over and around limbs and other obstacles.

When Will and Betsy got to the other end of the block, they saw Guy and Penny Walsh sitting in their front yard in an empty circle of lawn chairs. A generator hummed. An ice chest sat next to them. Guy sat in a bathing suit, flip flops, and a Café Du Monde T-shirt. He was drinking merlot out of a stemmed crystal glass, smoking a cigar. A box fan blew hot air. Guy was running the fan off of an extension cord he had connected to the generator. Penny was bringing a tray out of the house with Vienna sausages, sardines and saltines. An open jar of Cheez Whiz with a knife sticking out of it was on the aluminum table. Guy was intently listening to his marine radio, cigar smoke wafting above him.

"Is this where you get a cold beer?" Will asked.

"Damned right," Guy replied, surprised to see them. "I've got the generator hooked to the Frigidaire."

"I haven't tasted anything cold for two days."

"Then pull up a chair. You're about to get a treat.

"Betcha a beer you don't know what the first named hurricane was?" Guy continued.

"No, I don't, but I've got a feeling I'm about to find out. I know some of the really big ones like the 1935 hurricane that hit the Keys or the butt buster that leveled Galveston didn't have a name," Will replied.

"George, 1947," Guy said. "Since a hurricane can last for a week or more and there can be more than one storm at a time, people would sometimes confuse one storm with another when they heard weathercasters talking about them. The U.S meteorologists in the Pacific began naming storms during World War II to try to eliminate confusion. It worked. So in 1947 the first U.S. named hurricane was called George. Number two was Bess, after Harry Truman's wife."

"I'll be damned! I can't say I went through the day without learning something."

"I'll give you another piece of trivia. In 1953, it was decided all hurricanes should be named after women. It stayed that way until 1979 when they decided to alternate women's and men's names like we do today," Guy said. "Lesson over for today."

"Spellbinding, but not as spellbinding as this ice cold beer! Now I remember why I come over here – to learn more about hurricanes and drink beer."

The two couples swapped war stories about Clarice and plotted a makeshift strategy they hoped would work for the next few days. After they had been at the Walshes about an hour, they saw a power lineman sizing up power lines on both sides of the street.

Will yelled across Guy's lawn at the burly lineman, "You look like you could use a cold brew."

"You ain't woofin'!" came the quick response, and he immediately walked on down. "You got any?"

Will reached into Guy's cooler and handed the lineman a can of Budweiser.

"Lord, that looks good. Put on a dress, and I'll marry you."

The lineman tipped his hard hat back, popped the top, and killed the beer with one giant chug. He wiped his mouth on his arm and said appreciatively, "Thank you, folks. That was awfully good. I bet you can't guess what my name is."

"Don't reckon I can," Will said.

"It's Gator. I'm from Clewiston, Florida. That isn't a nick-name either. It's my God-given name my mama gave me when I was born. If you don't believe me, I'll prove it to you."

Gator removed a leather glove and reached into his back pocket for his wallet. He pulled out his driver's license and passed it around.

"Proud to know you, Gator," Guy said, extending his hand.

"I'll tell you nice folks something. You may think you have it rough, but you don't know what hell is until you have to go through life with a name like Gator and work for Georgia Power Company."

Appreciative laughs went all around.

"So you're going to get our power going again today, Gator?" Penny asked.

"Nah! Doesn't look like it."

"Why not?" they all asked in unison.

"That fella that lives three doors down thataway won't let us come across his yard. His trees are caught in the power lines. We tried to explain we can't get in there to work unless we trim 'em. He said he'll be goddamned if he's going to let us make a bigger mess on his yard than's already there. He says that until he sees us bring a truck to haul off the limbs we cut, we can't come on his property. I tried to tell him the trees are on an easement and he doesn't own them anyway, but he is one bull-headed SOB. Hell, we've got too much work to do to waste time fighting with an SOB like that. I'll let the cops deal with him. I've got a lot of other streets we can be working on in the meantime."

"You mean this whole neighborhood could be getting power back except for one jerk?" Guy asked.

"That's right," Gator said and shook his head. "And I'm not sure when we'll be working over here in this neighborhood again. Thanks for the beer, y'all."

Guy and Penny just sat there, not knowing what to say or do next. Will and Betsy said their goodbyes. They needed to get moving on their bikes if they were going to get home before curfew.

Chapter 9

*W*hen Will and Betsy awoke the next morning there was still no sign of impending change.

I wish we could find a working phone or a spot where our cell phones could pick up transmission," Betsy said. "Lexie and our parents must be worried sick about us."

"Today, we'll try to get to my office, Will said. "Maybe by some miracle it will have a functional telephone. Surely they're about to open up traffic to the island."

Betsy flipped on the battery radio.

There was a report that the post office roof had been ripped off and all the undelivered mail had been damaged or destroyed. A second story concerned two floating docks at the Fort Pierce Marina that had disappeared along with the nineteen boats attached to them. Authorities had been conducting both air and land searches for them, but the boats seemed to have vanished. Two sink holes had opened on Indian River Drive between Fort Pierce and Stuart, isolating the residents who lived between them. Another sinkhole was blocking the northbound lane of I-95 at Lake Worth.

Frayed nerves had graduated to frazzled. There was a report of a water cooler being stolen off the back of an emergency truck as well as one about an irate person who had taken his rifle and shot the lock off an ice machine in front of a Mobil station.

A Wachovia branch manager returned after the storm to find his swimming pool filled with sand that was from a load that had been delivered to the golf course adjacent to his house.

Another story concerned a person who lived near a Realtor's office. He stole the Realtor's sign and used it to board up one of the windows of his home. He forgot, however, to turn the sign around backward so that the blank back of it would show on the street side. When the realtor returned after the storm, an altercation ensued when it became obvious where the makeshift hurricane shutter had originated.

Still another story was about a couple in Vero Beach who awoke to a hot house in the middle of the night, despite hearing their generator. When the husband went to the garage to diagnose the problem, he found the generator had been stolen. The thief had covered his tracks by leaving the couple's lawn mower running.

◆◆◆◆

Will and Betsy got dressed, piled the dogs in the Jeep, and took off. The roads had become a bit more passable.

They were not prepared for the appearance of Will's office. The backlit plastic face on the Reynolds Smathers and Thompson sign had exploded from its frame, leaving only the fluorescent bulbs. The parking lot was not navigable. Will and Betsy parked out on the street. Windows had been ripped from their frames; glass had shattered and lay on the parking lot. Jalousie windows that had not been broken had been forced open by the strength of the wind. To complete the picture, a water line had broken, and water spurted two stories up in the air.

Ocean Drive, the jewel of Vero Beach, had a bombed out, inner city look. All that was missing was graffiti. Entire walls were gone from the luxury hotel across the street from Will's office. Mattresses, lamps, and other hotel room furnishings had been unceremoniously deposited as far as a block down Ocean Drive. A decorative potted Christmas palm had speared the window in the lobby. The underground parking lot for the twelve story condo next to the hotel had become an exposed underground septic tank. Water rose to the tops of the doors of the abandoned cars remaining in it.

Pink fiberglass insulation blew up and down the street like cotton candy. From one end of Ocean Drive to the other, retail shop plate glass windows that had not had shutters or plywood covering had imploded. Expensive merchandise now looked like worthless rejects from a thrift shop.

Will saw a City of Vero Beach truck about a half a block away and ran down to ask the driver if he knew how to stop the geyser shooting from the office lawn. The driver reported the leak to his dispatcher. Will then returned to his office to finish surveying the damage. Betsy and the dogs waited for him to return and unlock the front door.

When Will and Betsy went in the lobby of the building, they were assailed by a sour mildewy odor. The heat that had been trapped in the lobby for three days rushed to equalize itself with the fresh outside air. The windowless lobby was dark and uninviting. The only dim light came from the windows inside the building. A quick search of the first floor revealed an avalanche of paper the wind had swirled like confetti when a downstairs window had broken. Pictures had been either pulled from the wall or left dangling.

Will and Betsy opened the door to the stairwell and, dogs in hand, climbed to the second floor. Will first went into his own office. He was pleasantly relieved. His windows had held and the door, which he had locked before the storm, had kept the wind out. He tried the phone. It was dead.

Most of the rest of the floor was an entirely different story, however. Many windows had broken. Office furniture had been overturned. Research reports seemed to be everywhere. Black fuzzy mold was already popping out of some patches of wallpaper. Shards of glass had knifed some walls in an extreme art-deco pattern. Large, jagged, dangerous looking hunks stuck out of the sheetrock. Betsy shut Coco and Lucy in Will's office so the dogs would not walk through the sea of broken glass. The handmade ceramic pencil holder on the desk of Will's sales assistant, Barbara, had been hurled at the tranquil acrylic beach picture that hung on the adjacent wall, smashing both before it ricocheted back, finally breaking the glass top on her desk.

They started on the west side of the building and examined each office. Some, like Will's, were in perfect condition. Others were in varying degrees of devastation. The roof over by the kitchen had been leaking, causing the acoustical tiles in that part of the building to bubble or sag limply. The refrigerator in the kitchen was filled with spoiled food. The icemaker had left a puddle that extended halfway across the kitchen floor.

As Will and Betsy worked their way toward the east side of the building, they were hit with a rotten odor permeating the offices. The wall between Phil Allen's office and Dave

Tressler's office was gone. All that was left were the steel studs that divided the two offices. Phil's "Bond Desk" sign waved at them like an upside-down banner.

When Will and Betsy stepped into Tressler's office they stopped dead in their tracks. This was the worst office yet. Nothing was where it should be. Every window looked like it had been hit with a sledge hammer. Shelves were over-turned. Dave's coat rack had been rammed through an opening where, before the storm, a wall had been. It was now half in Dave's office, half in Phil's. It looked as if a demonic base-ball bat had been taken to Dave's computer screen. This bat must have also been used to pulverize all the pictures of Dave's wife and children that Dave had kept in a neat arrangement on his credenza. The arrangement had once chronicled the story of the Tressler domestic life.

The back of Dave's desk chair was toward Will and Betsy. The front of the chair faced Dave's desk. Dave had positioned his desk so he always had a view of the ocean. This left his back toward anyone who came in his door.

Betsy noticed an arm dangling from one side of the chair.

"Dave, I didn't know you were here," Betsy said. "Why didn't you say something? I didn't see your car in the parking lot. Where'd you park?"

Dave said nothing.

Will waded through the rubble and gasped.

"My God! Betsy, he's dead!"

Betsy climbed over the wreckage until she got to Will.

"God in heaven. Will, I think I'm going to be sick!" Betsy gagged.

Dave was sitting straight up in his pedestal desk chair. His eyes were glassy, staring at the ocean. There was a swollen purple knot on his forehead. It appeared his nose and cheekbone had been broken. Dave sat, not in his usual business suit, but in a white golf shirt, chinos and flip flops. His neck and shirt were drenched with dried blood which had run down onto his chinos.

On the floor in front of Dave was the heavy crystal ball he always kept on his desk. It was about the size of a softball. Dave jokingly told all visitors he needed it as a market analysis tool since the whole world expected him to accurately predict the stock market. It had sat for years on a brass base containing a bull chasing a bear around an eternal circle, one always one step behind the other. The ball had to weigh at least ten pounds. Curious clients usually picked it up with one hand but then almost always grabbed it with their free hand to keep from dropping it.

"Do you think Dave was dumb enough to ride out the storm in his office?" Betsy asked.

Almost on cue Coco started barking, insistently demanding to be let out of his prison in Will's office.

"Sure looks that way," Will returned. "I can't believe what I'm seeing. What do we do now?"

"Better go find a cop. Don't touch anything."

Will and Betsy grabbed the dogs and ran down the stairs. They didn't even try to relock the outside door to the building. No cop or deputy was in sight. Not knowing what else to do, Will drove over to the Walshes' house a few blocks away.

Guy was working in his yard, unscrewing his hurricane shutters. Penny was holding a container for the wing nuts.

"Guy! Penny," Will gasped.

"Will, are you hurt?" Guy jumped off of the step stool he was standing on.

"It's not me! It's Dave Tressler."

"What?"

"It's Dave Tressler at my office!"

"Is he in your car?"

"No, at my office."

"Stop! Slow down! What are you talking about?"

"He's dead... At my office... Get in my car... I'll show you! Betsy, keep the dogs and stay with Penny until we get back."

Will and Guy backed out of the driveway and sped down the street. When they got back to Will's office they screeched to a halt and ran up the stairs to the second floor. Just as they opened Dave's door a damaged picture of the New York Stock Exchange crashed. Both jumped. The picture had been precariously hanging on a nail and had jarred loose when they opened the door.

Dave was in the same position he had been in when Will and Betsy had dashed out of the building. Guy gasped. The horror of seeing Dave again and smelling the stench made Will gag. Guy just stared in disbelief. They were both momentarily glued to the ravaged floor. Neither of them could take their eyes off Dave's body.

"Holy shit! We've got to find a cop – now!" Guy finally said. "I wish to hell goddamned cell phones were working again."

Chapter 10

"What do you mean a dead person?" the National Guard sergeant demanded.

"Just what I said, we found a dead person at Reynolds Smathers and Thompson."

The soldier radioed in, and Will and Guy headed back for the office. It was at least thirty minutes before the police road patrolman finally arrived.

"Now just what is the problem?" one patrolman asked abruptly in the parking lot.

After a brief summary of their findings, everyone rushed up the stairs.

"We have a signal 7 at 1500 Ocean Drive," the patrolman radioed his dispatcher. "I need an investigator."

"What were you doing in the building?" the other patrolman asked suspiciously. "No one except authorized personnel is supposed to be on the island."

Will and Guy began rattling their stories at once.

"Stop! I can't listen to you both at the same time. Now one at a time, please."

Will and Guy then gave a more coherent synopsis.

"Can you identify the deceased?"

"I've worked with him for the last nine years," Will replied. "His name is Dave Tressler. How long do you think he's been dead?"

"We won't be able to tell that until we have had time to investigate. Did you touch or move the body?"

"We just moved enough debris so we could get to Dave's office."

"We'll need both of your names and how to contact you."

They all waited together for the investigator to arrive. Guy pulled Will to one side.

"Will, remember the gaudy gold Rolex with all the diamonds Dave used to show off wherever he went? To him that was the proof he was a serious player."

"Sure, he never went anywhere without it. We used to joke around the office about it, saying he probably even took a shower with it."

"If we're permitted back in the building, glance at his wrist. He's not wearing it now.

"Also, did you notice one other thing that was kind of curious? Why was virtually everything thrown all over Dave's office while a pile of files on top of his credenza just sat there?"

"Maybe they had a heavy weight on them. We both know that winds are unpredictable."

"Yeah, I guess strange things can happen."

Chapter 11

*L*imited traffic will resume today on and off of Orchid Island. Only residents and authorized disaster relief personnel will be allowed onto the island until further notice. Residents will need to provide a picture ID to the soldiers who will be patrolling at the base of each bridge. Lines may be lengthy. We ask your patience. The curfew declared after the storm is still in effect. Residents will need to continue to boil their drinking water or use bottled water. Florida Power & Light is not giving estimates at this time on when service will be fully restored. There are still numerous power lines down throughout the county. Many areas are still inaccessible because of the excessive amounts of debris to be cleaned up. Cleanup crews are working seven days a week. It will just take time. Bottled water and ice are available on a first come first serve basis at the following locations...

"So the police think that Dave is a storm casualty," Guy said as he and Will sipped their beers.

"Or is this just a convenient conclusion since they have more on their plate than they can handle in the aftermath of the storm?" Will added.

"I forgot to tell you. The night of the storm Dave's wife Connie called our house looking for him. Seems like Dave left with Joe Bowen on his Harley."

"That's weird. Why would he be in his office during a major storm instead of at home with his wife and kids? And he was out on his bike? That's nuts! But the Harley wasn't at the office when we got there."

"Maybe the storm blew it away."

"Grab a cold one, and let's go see what some of the rest of the town looks like on storm damage. I haven't driven north yet. How about you?"

Will and Guy headed out in the Jeep. The sights on the north end of the beach rivaled those they had seen farther south.

Makeshift post-hurricane signs were starting to appear.

KEEP OUT DANGER!!

WALDO STILL LIVES WE WILL REOPEN

CLARICE I HATE YOU

SADDAM BIN LADEN CLARICE
WMD

I WANT A HOT SHOWER

NO POWER

FPL BROKEN POLE

RELIEF BATH $10

Mounds of household debris were starting to appear on curbs. Soggy mattresses, discarded furniture, appliances, lumber and limbs, black plastic bags filled with unidentified miscellaneous garbage that only a week before had been valued possessions. In some cases it looked liked the homeowner had chosen to set up house next to the street instead of indoors. One house had piled the chainsaw cuttings from his oak tree, some logs more than a foot in diameter, on the edge of the street. A spray-painted plywood sign by the homeowner informed the passerby humorously of the availability of

FREE FIREWOOD.

"Do you really think Tressler died in Clarice by just being at the wrong place at the wrong time like the police department is trying to say?" Will asked Guy.

"The whole thing just doesn't completely add up to me," Guy said.

"To me either. You know Dave played fast and loose with the rules sometimes. Just between us, my manager's secretary confided in me there have been some complaints filed against him from time to time."

"So he wasn't the most ethical person who ever lived. That wouldn't get him killed. Things like that just happen in the movies."

Chapter 12

*T*he following day Will and Betsy went over to Connie Tressler's house to pay their respects and to find out if there was any way they could help her. The Tresslers lived in a restricted neighborhood on the mainland. It took them over an hour to get there because of the hurricane damage. The sound of chain saws and generators seemed incessant and deafening.

The municipal power plant loomed in front of them, a tall, stark, boxy building made from sheet metal. Sheet metal now hung in bent, ragged sections from the upper portions of the building. In some places there were gaping holes. It looked like the scene of an industrial accident. Some patriotic soul had raised the American flag on the pole adjacent to the building in the storm's aftermath, and it waved as the only undamaged sight on the horizon.

"This is the first time I've been over the bridge since the storm," Betsy commented. "It's as bad over here as it is on the island. Let's drive over to 10th and see if my bank is damaged. I bet it will have power and maybe even telephones, since it is right next to City Hall."

"Good idea," Will said. "If their phones are working, we can call Lexie and our family. It took me three days to call my folks after Frederick. They were frantic."

As Will and Betsy approached the large stone building, it appeared to have no structural damage. A large oak tree was down in the drive-thru banking lanes, but it had not struck the building. Letters were missing in the sign. Tree limbs and downed signs covered the once neatly landscaped lawn and flower beds. Since there were a few cars in the bank's lot across the street, Will and Betsy decided to try and see if they could get in the building. Will banged on the side door.

Betsy was surprised to see one of her fellow workers who waved through the door.

"Have you ever had so much fun? Come on in and get to work," Kathryn said jokingly to Betsy. "Have you even been able to get on the island to see how you fared there? Rumor has it that it's a mess."

Betsy explained they had never evacuated and asked about Kathryn's home. Kathryn happily replied, "Except for some downed trees in our yard, one of which hit Tom's boat and trailer, we were fortunate to have very little to report."

"You have power? That's a miracle," Will said.

Betsy and Kathryn both replied at the same time, "No, just auxiliary power for corridors and stair wells."

Betsy inquired if there was a working telephone, and Kathryn said only the emergency phone in Joseph's office.

"Well, that's a blessing – thank God we can call Lexie and our families and let them know we are OK," added Betsy.

Will and Betsy followed Kathryn upstairs to the president's office and notified Lexie and their relatives that they were alive and well and experienced very little damage.

Betsy and Will told Kathryn about finding Dave Tressler and their plans to visit Connie. Kathryn said the bank's corporate headquarters was sending ice, bottled water, batteries, and other items to Vero Beach the next day, but she had not been able to reach many employees because most of the town had no phone or cell phone service.

After leaving the bank, they rode by the county Republican headquarters on U.S. 1. It had been a retail store before being rented by the county politicos. Most of the plate glass windows had been blown in. The one remaining window had twelve inch letters.

REP

Over the remnants of the canvas awning was a hand lettered sign. "WE SURVIVED & WE SHALL PREVAIL it announced to all passing motorists. Below it another sign waved in the breeze.

THE BUSH TEAM LET FREEDOM RING

One side of the building was missing. The only things intact inside were counters which still had red, white and blue banners hanging from them. The floor was covered with mounds of insulation and sheetrock and the remains of the sparse furniture that had furnished the storefront. The acoustical tiles had been ripped from the ceiling. A fluorescent fixture hung vertically from the ceiling, dangling from the electrical cord on one end. Even part of the brick fascia had been torn from the building's exterior.

"This must be what political headquarters look like after you lose an election in the Middle East," Will wisecracked.

They drove on through blocks of devastation. The steeple had been ripped out of a church roof on 27th Avenue leaving a gigantic hole too large to be covered with a blue tarp or plywood. There simply were no joists left to attach anything to. It was as if the giant fist of the Lord had hammered one end of the building. Another church had an endless series of blue tarps covering the entire roof. The steeple stuck up through the sea of blue untouched.

"Even God was no match for Clarice," Betsy said, shaking her head.

They stopped to allow a John Deere tractor to drag the trunk of a huge oak tree across an intersection. It was driven by a fully bearded, stocky middle-aged man dressed in scruffy overalls. He was shirtless and wore a sweat-stained brimmed straw hat. As he bounced by, he waved and smiled at Will and Betsy in an unassuming manner. He acted like this misplaced scene should be just another common everyday urban occurrence.

A creosoted power pole on the far side of the intersection had been snapped. Holding it parallel to the ground was a piece of galvanized conduit and the oak tree that it was resting on. A sign announced what was clearly evident.

BROKEN POLE

Will and Betsy passed a trailer park. The sagging chain link fence contributed to its junkyard look. Pieces of aluminum from some of the double wides hung at Picasso-like angles. Laundry decorated trees. Huge hunks of a trailer sat on the branches of an oak like a poorly designed tree house.

Down the street the remnants of a stucco fence guarded an unfinished subdivision. Sections of the fence had the stucco stripped revealing the Styrofoam core. This core alternated with sections that had been blown away completely, leaving only the posts and acorn shaped finials.

Handmade signs started to appear.

IT'S STILL PARADISE

CLARICE...
A WMD

A service station with the roof over the gas tanks tipped over proudly announced

FOR SALE

PRIME LOCATION

Will and Betsy finally arrived at the Tressler residence. Connie was in the yard dragging limbs toward the street. She seemed frazzled but glad to see them.

"Come on in. I need an excuse to take a break anyway. Lord, do you think we'll ever get back to normal?'

"We were worried about you. We're so sorry about Dave."

"I'm still trying to get over it. I could imagine life without Dave, but not this."

"Where are the kids?"

"They are spending a few days with the Henderson family; they have a large ranch west of town. Davie and Elizabeth go to Saint Edwards with the three Henderson children. Because of the hurricane damage school's out anyway. You heard anything about when we're getting power back? God, it's hot."

"I saw lots of FPL crews on the way over here. I hope we're getting close to getting it back. You don't realize how much you depend on something until it's not there.

"Connie, we're so sorry about Dave. Anything we can do? I guess you know we're the ones who found him. I can't imagine why he was still at the office," said Betsy.

"I guess it won't be a secret around town much longer. Dave and I had been having a rocky time of it off and on."

"No, we didn't know that. He never said anything at work, and I guess we haven't seen you since the Christmas party over at Karen's house last year."

"Well, you know how Dave loved to feel like a big shot. It seemed like the more he made, the more he would spend to try to impress people. We argued a lot about money. You probably already know Dave never went to college. He survived off of moxie and nerve. He always felt like he had to show all those college graduates he was as good as they were."

"It did seem like he was everywhere we went around town," said Will.

Connie continued to tell Betsy and Will the details of her marriage to Dave as if she was compelled by some unknown force.

"We've struggled to stay even ever since we've been married. He gave money to every charity that asked for it. He spent money over at the club like it was water. He would tell me I worried too much about money. Dave always said you only go around once. His favorite saying was 'Life is not a dress rehearsal.' His defense was we were young, and he could always make more. It seemed like I was always juggling past due bills until he got paid again. I can't tell you how many huge credit card bills I used to get in from him treating half the town at happy hour. I'd just pay the minimum and hope to catch them up when he had a big month. "

"I'm sure sorry to hear that. We didn't know. That had to be nerve wracking," said Betsy.

"It did seem to get better recently. He must have had some really good months so far this year. There seemed to be more money to go around even though Dave was spending more than ever."

Connie appeared tired and defeated. She gazed in the distance but proceeded to talk about Dave as if in a confessional. Betsy and Will listened to the personal disclosures in shock.

"We had a fight earlier in the month because he lost a lot of money in a golf game. Dave always said sporting events were twice as much fun if you had a vested interest. Football, basketball, baseball – it seemed like he was always betting on something. The golf game kind of sent me over the edge. I got so upset he moved in with one of his old high school teammates waiting for me to cool down."

"See, Betsy, and you jump on me when I forget to take the garbage out," Will said chidingly and winked at his wife. "Speaking of garbage, is there anything heavy that I might help you get out to the street while we're here?"

"Would you, Will?" Connie asked reluctantly. "There's huge broken pieces on the bird of paradise. I was wondering how I would ever get it to the street to get it picked up when FEMA gets to our neighborhood. They're around back."

"No problem, ma'am," Will quickly replied. "I'll have them out to the street in a jiffy. You girls visit until I get done."

When Will was out of sight Connie misted up. "You don't know how lucky you are, Betsy. I wish Dave could have been more like Will." Connie paused as regret apparently filled her thoughts.

"Dave was never here with me and the kids. During the week he worked all day, hit the local bars by night and spent every weekend at the country club. I really don't know how I will be able to make ends meet now Dave is gone. I know my parents will help but I just hate to ask them – they never liked Dave – Dad in particular. They used every family gathering to remind me what a mistake I had made in marrying Dave. Of course, this drove Dave more over the edge and he would stay away from home even more. Dave used to attend the kids' school events. But over the past few months, he never even showed up for any of Davie's little league games or Elizabeth's swimming meets at school." She wiped her eyes when she saw Will coming back around the house dragging a huge limb.

"I'd cut it up," he offered, "but it's not necessary. FEMA will pick up the big pieces of debris with a mechanical claw."

"Just look at me snifflin'," Connie said as if to provide an alibi to Will. "The pollen in the plants must have gotten to my sinuses."

"Connie, like I said, let us know if you need us to do anything," Betsy replied. Will and Betsy left. It had become awkward.

"Boy, I think we learned more than we wanted to know," Betsy said to Will after they drove off. "I can't believe she told us all of that. That's probably the longest conversation I've ever had with her. Oh, and by the way, Connie's sinuses weren't bothering her. She almost started crying when we were alone."

"I should have guessed, I reckon. Betsy, do you remember when we used to see them at cocktail parties? Connie usually just stood there while Dave dominated every conversation."

Will and Betsy drove out of the subdivision in a subdued mood. Finally Will broke the silence. "I'm sure though everything she confided in us was going to come out eventually anyway. It seems strange. You think you know someone, but then I guess you never actually know what's really going on behind the scenes. It's strange for her to say they had had more money recently. Rooney posts the production figures on the back of the kitchen cabinet door at the office every day. I'm positive Dave's production is about the same as it was last year. The only reason he's not behind is he landed a big insurance ticket a couple of months ago. But the only result was to offset the loss of one of Dave's big accounts, Bud Green, who died. Bud's son lives in Chicago. Dave told me he took his inheritance and bought an apartment on Lakeshore Drive."

Chapter 13

Guy and Penny came by Will and Betsy's the following morning. Will showed them the damage around the yard, and they retreated to the dock to talk where it was cooler.

"I still haven't been able to find out any information as to when the power will be back on at the office," Will said with a sigh. "I guess I can scratch any commission business off for this month. At least I have my fee based revenues. It's times like this that make me glad Betsy has a good salary and we have some savings."

"At least wirehouse employees don't have rent and a payroll to worry about like I do. I guess that's the price I pay for my independence," Guy added.

Will then proceeded to repeat to Guy the conversation he and Betsy had had with Connie Tressler.

"I bet Dave and Connie didn't have any savings to fall back on. That wouldn't be surprising. I'm sure you remember that Dave used to work for Smith Barney before y'all recruited him," Guy replied.

"I was told we didn't recruit him as much as he came looking for us," Will said.

"I've never told you this, but when we were both at Smith Barney, Dave pulled one of the ballsiest moves I've ever seen. I guess it's OK to talk about now," Guy continued. "Do you know how he got on at Smith Barney? You know he never darkened the doorway of a college."

"Connie told us that yesterday. I always thought he went to Florida. He had Gator shit all over his office, and he was always the most vocal person in our office on football weekends. Every week he aggressively pursued everyone in the office to take bets on the outcome of any Florida game and even rented a skybox at Florida Field. You wouldn't believe how much money he spent the last time the Gators were invited to the Sugar Bowl. He rented an RV and hired a driver. Dave presided over an open bar all the way to New Orleans and back. I heard he paid for the hotel rooms as well as most of the tab for his guests to go down to the French Quarter."

"A diehard Gator wannabe," Guy continued. "You know Mike Pollard? He has been Chairman's Club at Smith Barney for a zillion years. He is Connie Tressler's father. They are very close. Mike has always been very supportive and protective of her."

"No shit! I knew he was their big hitter, but I never connected him with Connie," Will said.

Guy and Will were distracted by the sight of a school of dolphin swimming by the dock.

Finally Guy said, "He's the reason Dave's in the business. Normally Smith Barney wouldn't even interview someone who only made it through high school, but since Mike was number one in the office and Dave had played ball for Vero Beach High School, Mike pressured the manager to give

Dave a chance. Dave was floundering as a trainee at first, but Mike opened the right doors for him by taking him on as a junior partner. Smith Barney began catering to Dave because they assumed he would inherit Mike's book someday when he retired. Mike made sure Dave was given favorable treatment when accounts were assigned after a broker left the firm. They also looked the other way at some of Dave's questionable trades. Some of these trades were pretty bad. The rest of us in the office never knew if the trades resulted from a lack of ethics or just inexperience and insufficient education. Whatever it was, Mike always protected him. Once Dave was accused of unauthorized trading and Mike smoothed it over."

"Well, I'll be damned. I never knew that. We just heard around town he was an up and comer," said Will.

Guy pressed on with experiences he had working in the same office with Dave Tressler.

"You would have no reason to since you didn't work there, but as you know, there's no secrets in a small office. Dave was one of the reasons I left and went out on my own. Some of his stunts were so blatant I simply couldn't believe them. I would have gotten sacked in nothing flat if I had tried half the stuff he got away with. But now he's dead and I don't work there anymore, I can tell you a story you're not going to believe."

"Smith Barney dirty laundry. This should be interesting," said Will.

"You remember Skip Turk don't you?"

Will nodded.

"Skip had a client who owned 400 shares of Pepsi Cola. She wanted to give it to her grandson. She signed an LOA to journal the stock to his account, but Skip's sales assistant accidentally transposed a couple of digits in the account number. The stock hit one of Dave Tressler's accounts – a woman who lived up in Grant. Dave saw the stock hit her account and questioned the cage to see if she had sent in a certificate. The ops manager told Dave she didn't see where the lady had either mailed in or brought in any Pepsi stock, but she'd get to the bottom of it when the cashier got back from vacation. The next day Dave sold the stock. By the time the cashier got back the following week the stock sale had settled. Dave's client immediately wrote a check for the proceeds. By the time anyone smelled a rat the check had cleared. The branch manager was livid, but Dave played dumb. He denied the conversation with the ops manager and said he had merely put the wrong account number on the ticket. He claimed he was selling Pepsi for another one of his accounts."

Will stared at Guy in disbelief.

"Pollard pulled rank on the manager. The trade got moved to the error account, but it was way too late to reclaim the money. The woman had bought a boat with it. The office left the debit in her account while they tried to think of what to do next, but she didn't have any margin papers on file. It was the biggest damned mess in the world."

"Why didn't they fire Tressler? Sounds like he was not only a crook but a stupid crook. They had him dead to rights!" said Will.

"It almost got to that point. Regional office was raising hell, but Mike Pollard kept jumping into the fray and defending Dave. Since Mike was over a third of the office's production, the powers that be were afraid to piss him off. Without Mike the office would have been losing money. Mike tried to put an end to the whole thing by agreeing to make the firm whole."

"It figures the firm would try to take the easy way out. Especially since Mike was willing to absorb the hit," Will added.

Guy said, "But then it got worse. It turned out that Dave was seeing the broad from Grant on the side. He had met her on one of his happy hour forays to the Village South. Mike had agreed to make things good after Connie's mother, his wife, cried on his shoulder. She convinced Mike that if Dave lost his job it would be fatal to Dave and Connie's marriage. She told Mike he needed to do it for the grandchildren."

"Jesus!"

"But this story ain't over yet."

"What else could happen, for God's sake?"

"Before Dave found out Mike had bailed his sorry butt out, he panicked and cut a deal with a headhunter to move over to Legg Mason. Legg Mason was trying to get the Vero Beach office started and offered Dave some big front money if he would move and bring some of Mike Pollard's clients with him. Dave called in sick on a Friday and then spent the weekend calling Mike's clients to test the waters to see how many of them would go with him. Before the weekend was out he knew very few were willing to leave Mike and transfer their accounts. Hell, a lot of these people had been with Mike for over twenty years. So on Sunday Dave panicked again, called the recruiter to tell her he had misjudged the situation and volunteered to give the front money back if Legg Mason would let him out of his contract."

"What a scumbag. How could he be so stupid not to realize what Mike had done for him," Will added.

"He showed back up for work at Smith Barney on Monday morning acting like nothing had ever happened. But then some of Mike's clients started calling him, telling him about Dave's activities over the weekend. Dave lied through his teeth and tried to deny the whole thing. Mike got so pissed he threw his laptop at Dave, crashing it into the window to his office. Mike had to pay for breaking the window. There was a little old lady in the hall who almost crapped all over herself when the window broke. And you want to hear about nerve? The bimbo in Grant called Connie because she thought the bastard was really in love with her. Tressler had to hide out for days until Pollard cooled down."

"So that's when Dave moved over to our office," said Will.

"I was told that we didn't pay Dave any front money, and now I know why. Without being able to raid Mike's book, he had nothing to sell. He was just damned lucky to find a job away from Mike."

Guy agreed.

"You hit it right on the head. Don't you know Thanksgiving dinner is exciting when the Tresslers get invited over to the Pollards?"

"Guy, he never was my favorite person. For God's sake, he tried real hard to make me his friend. But something seemed two faced about him; it was one of those things you couldn't quite put your finger on. Until now, I didn't realize what a complete shit he was! Maybe there's more to Dave's demise than the police think. You know the old saying, 'Mess with the bull and you get the horn'."

Guy and Will watched a flock of pelicans glide in the wind. Will finally broke the silence when one dived for a fish.

"Ever dream about being a private eye? Since the cops obviously aren't going to pursue this, it might be fun for us to look into this cesspool and see what kind of turd floats to the surface. Besides, since neither of us knows when we'll go back to work, it'll give us something to do. Maybe we can help Connie out. I really feel sorry for her. Connie took Lexie under her wing when she was working at Saint Edwards during the time Lexie was struggling through the pain of new braces on her teeth. You probably don't remember but she was the receptionist at the lower school office before she and Dave got married. And who knows? If the story turns out to be interesting enough we might even want to write a book."

Chapter 14

Will repeated his conversation with Guy to Betsy. He could have predicted her response.

"I always said the brokerage industry sure attracts a bunch of bad apples. You wouldn't see someone like that at the bank."

"Don't hand me that sanctimonious bullshit, Betsy! You remember the trust officer you had a few years ago who was diverting money from inactive trust accounts to pay for his boat. He ended up doing hard time. What I couldn't believe about him was he was a polio victim with a withered arm and still took that kind of chance. A desk job was all he was ever capable of doing. Now he'll never get another white collar job as long as he lives. Probably ended up working in a convenience store.

And remember the loan officer y'all had who was taking kickbacks on loans?"

"OK! You win! You're right! I guess we've had them too," she acknowledged. "But we've had fewer renegades than you have," she quickly added.

He laughed.

"I was just thinking about when Tressler almost got canned at the office about five years ago. The human resources person came over from Tampa and swore us all to secrecy. She told us it would cause irreparable damage to the office if we told anyone in Vero Beach about Dave's antics."

"On top of that I remember your manager also threatened disciplinary action if he heard any of you gossiping about Dave all over town," said Betsy.

In a retrospective tone, Will continued. "As if we were the ones who should get in trouble. Dave was the one backing up to broker's offices, dropping his drawers, and shooting them a moon."

"But that wasn't anywhere near as bad as when he sneaked up behind the receptionist while she was answering the phone and beat on her with his talliwacker. Patty almost jumped through the phone the first time he pulled that stunt. Then he jumped up on the counter and started beating his chest."

"Remember how everyone at work rationalized his behavior by just saying 'Well, that's just good old harmless Dave. You know how he is.' Like that made all his antics forgivable," Betsy continued.

"Yeah, good old life of the party Dave. You either loved him or hated him. No in between. It seemed like every time Dave did something erratic there was always somebody who would say you should look the other way because he was supposed to be such a good father or some other reason."

"Yeah, I guess he identified with his kids since he had never grown up himself," Betsy added.

"Remember when Dave's driver's license got suspended after he kept getting picked up for speeding. He sneaked to work for months taking a different route each day so the cops wouldn't pick him up again. If the police had caught him driving with a suspended license he would have had it revoked for good. Connie must be a saint to have put up with him as long as she did. They're so different. She's so quiet, so straight. She hardly ever seemed to say anything when they were out. She always just kind of melted into the background while Dave bounced all over the room glad-handing everyone."

"Will, I just remembered something. Dave has a brother here in Vero Beach. Tommy. Yeah, that's his name. His youngest son was one year ahead of Lexie in school. I used to see him when he took the kids to school in the morning. He might be able to shed some light on this whole thing."

"Good idea. Tommy used to live one street over from the Walshes. Why don't we see if he's still around?"

Betsy looked in the phone book and sure enough Thomas E. Tressler was listed. Later that day they passed by his house and saw a car in the driveway.

"Let's stop," Betsy urged Will.

Tommy Tressler looked like a balding, older version of Dave. He had the same prominent nose and florid complexion. Tommy was sitting under the large oak tree in his front yard, obviously taking a break from yard work. He was sipping a bottle of Gatorade. Will parked the Jeep, and they negotiated around the debris piles in Tommy's yard.

"Tommy?" Will said, holding out his hand. "I'm Will Black, and this is my wife Betsy. I used to work with Dave. We were in the neighborhood and thought we'd stop by and tell you how sorry we are Dave was killed. Dave and I worked together for nine years. Betsy and I were the ones who found him after the storm."

"Oh, sure, Will. I remember you. Your daughter was one grade behind Tommy junior wasn't she. I used to see Betsy when I dropped Tommy off in the mornings. We also shared the same table at the benefit one year with you. Where's your daughter going to college?"

"Lexie's at the University of Miami."

"A 'Cane! Tommy got a scholarship to Stetson."

"Lexie loves Miami. Does Tommy like Stetson?"

"He loves it so much we never see him except on major holidays."

"That certainly sounds like a familiar experience."

"We were so shocked when we found Dave after the storm," said Will.

"I'm still trying to get used to the fact that Dave is dead, but I expected him to get into some kind of trouble a long time ago. Even when we were kids he always stayed in trouble with Mama. She'd tell us what to do. I'd mind, no questions asked. Dave would obey only when he thought he'd get caught if he didn't."

"I guess Dave must have been a rambunctious child," said Betsy.

"It was more than that. He was self centered and sneaky even then. I haven't had much to do with him for the last five years. Not since he laid the wood to me after Mama's death."

"We're sorry to hear that," said Will.

"Shortly after he joined your office he sold our mama half-a-million-dollar-insurance policy. Daddy had died back in '95. While he was alive daddy took care of the family's finances.

Mama was overwhelmed with it all after he died and started depending on Dave more and more. She thought since he was a broker, he should handle her finances. Dave told her she needed some life insurance. I'm sure she never read any of the paperwork. She just trusted her son to do right by her. He had the premiums taken automatically from her checking account. Knowing her, she never gave it another thought. She told me afterwards that she had bought it because she wanted to leave us something more than just her house. When Mama died five years ago I found out Dave was the sole beneficiary of the policy. I never got a dime of that money. I'm sure she didn't know Dave set it up that way. She always told us that everything she had was going to be divided right down the middle. That's what her will said. She showed it to me.

"But when I asked the lawyer about it while we were probating the will, he told me that an insurance policy was not governed by her will, that the beneficiary form attached to the application determined who would get the money at her death."

Will and Betsy shared a glance of disbelief.

"When I called this to Dave's attention, he tried to tell me Mama had set it up leaving it all to him on purpose. He said she had told him this was her way of paying him back for helping her with her finances after Daddy passed away.

I knew that was a lie. Everything else was divided down the middle like she had been telling me all those years. I raised hell about it with Dave for weeks, but there was nothing I could do. What was done was done. Mama would turn over in her grave if she knew Dave had figured out a way to get the whole thing. So I decided if that's the way he was going to be,

I was just not going to have anything to do with him ever again. We haven't spoken for over five years now. I don't know if I'll even go to his funeral. I guess it'll look bad if I don't."

Will and Betsy said goodbye and left.

"Boy, boy, boy!" Betsy said as they drove away. "Like I said y'all sure know how to pick 'em. I can't believe Dave screwed his own brother to the wall."

Chapter 15

On the way home, Will and Betsy noticed a convenience store with the door open and cars in the parking lot. They could not see any lights on, but it seemed to be open for business. Plywood still covered the windows.

"Let's stop and see if we can stock up on some provisions," Betsy said, pulling on Will's arm.

Will turned the Jeep into the crowded parking lot and found a place back by the dumpster. They went into the store. There was no electricity. It was dark and humid. Shelves were mostly bare. They had not been restocked since the storm. The store had mostly staples there had been no demand for before Clarice. Now it appeared their customers would buy virtually anything.

The Indian clerk was calculating people's bills on a battery-run calculator. Since there was no electricity to scan bar codes, the clerk was guessing at the price of items. An irate customer checking out two gallon jugs of water was berating the tired, frazzled man.

"What do you mean you don't have a twelve pack of water? Not only do you not have what I want, but it's apparent you're in business to gouge me. Do you realize that a gallon of water is more in here today than it was yesterday?"

The sweaty cashier looked at the long line behind the complainer and replied, "Well, I guess you just got a deal yesterday," and continued to check out the more appreciative people.

Will looked at the empty shelves and the long line and told Betsy, "I don't see anything here we can't live without, let's get going."

As they were going back out to their car, Will noticed the familiar face of Ralph Ness. Ralph was a client of Dave's Will had known since he had moved to Vero Beach from Tampa. Will had met Ralph through a referral when Ralph and his family had first moved to town. Ralph had transferred his account to Dave, however, after Dave had regaled him with tall tales of his stock-picking ability and had convinced Ralph he had inside connections not normally found in Vero Beach. Ralph had never worked since he graduated from college, content to live off his wife's inheritance. He had been a receptive audience to Dave's arrogant and unprofessional claims and saw him as a way to impress his wealthy wife. Dave also convinced him he could break Ralph and his wife into Vero Beach society. Since that time Ralph and Will had maintained a cordial but distant relationship.

"Will! Will Black!" Ralph waved when he saw them. "They got anything left in there?"

"Not much!" Will crossed the parking lot to shake hands with Ralph. "How'd you make out in the storm?"

"Could have been worse," Ralph said. "I had a tree spike the roof over the garage. Everything in it was pretty much ruined. I had too much shit in there anyway. I've been meaning to clean that thing out. I guess now I'll have to hire someone to come over and do it. You know anyone cheap I might get?"

"Good luck!" said Will. "Labor is going to be at a major premium around here for a long time. By the way, haven't seen you in the office recently."

"You won't either. That damned Tressler nailed my ass to the wall."

"What do you mean?"

"That son of a bitch talked me into playing the options market. Told me it was like taking candy from a baby with his know-how on my side. We started out buying options. When that didn't work out he told me to sell options on my wife's stocks. When we didn't make much on that he told me the easy pickings were to be had by selling naked options. He said there was almost no chance the things would ever get exercised – that the odds were eight or nine to one in our favor. He said it was like picking up money off the streets. I thought there was almost no risk."

As they stood on the asphalt in the hot sun, Ralph was almost hyperventilating as he told Will his Tressler experience.

"We really loaded the boat on International Securities Exchange. The stock was trading at 48. He sold the 65s. These things expired in three months. He said there was no way in hell that the stock could go up 35% in three months. Well, remember when they got bought out at 67 ½. The stock opened up, my options got called away, and I lost over half of my wife's investment account. Almost caused me to get a divorce, and I've had to get a job selling shoes at the mall to make ends meet. My wife, Jinx, had to take a job as a receptionist at school so we could qualify for a scholarship to get the school tuition down to where we could afford to leave the kids there. Our marriage will never be the same. If I had any money left I'd hire a hit man to get that bastard. It was the worst day of my life when I met him. I took what was left and put it in some CD's at the bank. I can't afford to play around any more." Ralph's face turned red as he relived the horror story.

"God, that's awful," was all Will could think to say. "I'm so sorry."

"It's not your fault. I guarantee you one thing, however. If I had a windfall tomorrow I wouldn't put a dime of it in the stock market. You sorry bastards have seen the last of this sucker. Y'all don't care if the customer wins or loses. You get paid either way. If I ever get any money again I'm going to buy property. I can see it, feel it, touch it, smell it. Nobody's ever lost any money on land. You know, they're not making any more of it."

Will and Betsy told Ralph goodbye and drove away.

Betsy looked at Will and shook her head. "Why didn't you tell him Dave was dead?"

Will shrugged and replied, "Why should I? What good would it have done? Did you see how mad he got when he told us the story? I'm sure learning more about Dave since he's been dead than I ever knew when we worked together.

"And besides that, old Ralphie may have been the one who just flipped out and killed him. Sure sounds like he could have been tempted to."

Chapter 16

"*D*on't forget about Dave Tressler's funeral," Betsy said.

"Did you really want to go to that?" Will replied. "It's scheduled for eleven in the morning. I really need to be in Stuart tomorrow morning. By the time I get down there I'll just have to turn around and drive right back to Vero Beach. I'm going to waste the whole day on the highway. It just doesn't make any sense. You think we could just get by going to the wake tonight?"

"I've got a problem tomorrow too," Betsy said. "I have a lot of work to catch up on. Besides, the bank has another truck of ice and water coming tomorrow for employees. I volunteered to help them again at noon and planned to get some ice and bottled water for us. Let's just go to the funeral home tonight. There'll be so many people at the church tomorrow Connie will never even know if we're there anyway."

"Then we've made an executive decision," Will said. I'll take off early so I can get back and change clothes before we go tonight. I'll tell the people at my office what we're doing so they won't think we just skipped it. Maybe we will grab a bite after it's over."

Will picked up Betsy after work, and they went over to The Blue Horizon Funeral Home. There were probably thirty people coming, going, or visiting. The casket was open. The mortician had done his job well. Will and Betsy got some coffee while they were waiting to talk to Connie. Dave's children were sitting in metal folding chairs that had been lined along the wall.

Finally they were able to catch Connie's undivided attention.

"How's it going, Connie?"

"Not so well I'm afraid. I'm finding out what it is like to be a single parent. Dave was a generous father in spite of his other public behavior – the kids are really taking his death very hard. Even though Dave was gone a lot, the house still wasn't as empty as it seems now. And so many things to take care of! Thank goodness my parents are local and have been helping out with Davie and Elizabeth. How do people do it if they don't have any family? Plus it just seems like the kids and I can't shake this depressed feeling."

"Connie, I can't say that I know what you're going through because I don't," Betsy said. "I sure hope I never find out or don't find out what it's like not to have Will until I'm too old or too senile to care. I know I've asked you this before, but is there anything we can do?"

"No, there really isn't. If there were, I'd tell you. Would you excuse me for a second? I hope you don't think I'm rude, but there is someone over there I really need to speak to."

"No. Do what you have to do," Betsy replied. "We'll have time to talk later."

Connie made a beeline across the room to where some swarthy middle-aged men in business suits were impatiently standing near the refreshment table. They weren't talking to any of the other guests but seemed to be sizing up the remaining people in the room. They had positioned themselves so they could see new arrivals as they signed the register.

Will whispered to Betsy, "Those Hispanic guys don't look like they belong here. I wonder who they are."

Betsy whispered back, "They do look out of place. That one looks especially tough, and notice how he caters to the shorter one. It's almost like the short one is in charge."

"Yea, but in charge of what?"

The Blacks went back over toward the refreshment table to refill their coffee cups. They weren't trying to spy; they just didn't know what else to do since everyone they knew seemed to be engrossed in conversation.

One of the Hispanics seemed to be looking at the body in the casket as if he were trying to verify it was dead. It wasn't a compassionate look, more like he was assessing damage. He even reached in and felt Dave's hand.

Betsy felt a chill run through her.

Two other Latinos then quietly entered the room without signing the register. One man had acne scars. The first Hispanic group looked at them with disinterest but apparent recognition.

Connie seemed to be under stress as she too recognized the new arrivals. She looked back and forth as if trying to decide which group to speak to. She made a decision and worked her way over to the short man and his companion.

"Miguel," Connie said hesitantly. "Thank you for coming."

"I thought I would just drop by and see how my money was being spent," Miguel replied quietly but condescendingly. He sneered at his associate who seemed to return the smirk on cue.

"I should hear something about Dave's life insurance soon. I don't expect any delays. Dave's death was determined to be accidental."

"That is good information. Once again – my condolences."

"If you will excuse me now, I have other guests to speak with. Thank you for coming."

Connie shook hands with both and started to try to move toward the most recent group of Hispanic well-wishers and quietly acknowledged the man with the acne scars.

"Adolfo asked us to come by and check to see that things are well with you," he said. "He sends his condolences, Señora. He said you would understand why he could not offer them to you in person."

"Tell Mr. Soltero I appreciate his concern." Connie seemed to shiver slightly. "If Dave were here he would also appreciate the friendship that Mr. Soltero has always shown to our family."

"Let our families stay in touch," the man with the scars replied without compassion.

"I think we should get going," Betsy whispered to Will. "I'll tell Connie we're leaving."

Will and Betsy threaded their way toward the door, zigzagging through small groups of guests. As Betsy looked up to say "excuse me," she noticed the people she was trying to negotiate around were Connie's parents, Mike and Constance Pollard.

Constance started chatting with Betsy while Mike talked to Will.

Will shook Mike's hand. He felt obligated to try to express his surprise and horror at Dave's unexpected death.

"Mike, I never know what to say in situations like this. Everything always sounds so shallow and trite, but believe me when I say Betsy and I are so sorry about Dave's accident."

Mike grimaced and said, "It's tough on my daughter right now, but I think she'll be better off in the long run."

"I'm sorry to hear that. I thought you and Dave were not only in-laws but friends."

"I never talked about it because I didn't want to hurt my grandchildren's father, but Constance and I never approved of that marriage," Mike said. "In fact, Constance was absolutely distraught when they became engaged. She wanted me to try to talk Connie out of it, but I didn't want to interfere in my daughter's life. If I hadn't let her marry Dave I would have been the heavy in her eyes for the rest of her life. I discouraged a boy she met in college because I thought she was dating below her station. I wasn't up to doing it again, even to appease my wife. I'm sure not telling you anything you don't already know. The whole town knew he was wild as hell before Connie married him." Mike seemed to almost grind his teeth as he talked.

"Since you helped him get started and y'all were partners, I just assumed you had a good relationship," Will said.

"You do things for your children...you'll find out one of these days," Mike said. "I hope your daughter makes a better choice. I didn't see much of Dave. Constance sees Connie and the kids all the time. I see Connie when she brings the kids by on weekends, but the last time I was with Dave had to be when we treated them to lunch at the club after the Easter egg hunt... By the way, I would appreciate it if this talk didn't go any further. I'm sure I wouldn't have brought it up if I weren't upset and I didn't know you found him and you worked together."

"Mike, Betsy and I just want to help Connie if we can, and I know gossip isn't the way to do it. But let me know if we can do anything."

As their car pulled out of the funeral home parking lot into the evening traffic Will exhaled loudly, "Whew! Man, oh, man! I know it may be politically incorrect to say this about a minority group, but that bunch gave me the creeps, and wait'll I tell you about my conversation with Mike Pollard."

"Dave was certainly prospecting a different clientele than you have," Betsy said.

"Makes me appreciate some of my old crabs a little more."

"Speaking of crabs, you remember the customer who is an insurance agent, Tom Harmon? I introduced you to him last year at the bank's picnic. Well, he showed up yesterday at the distribution center while we were giving out water and ice. He said he wanted some ice. I told him it was only for bank personnel, but if he wanted to wait until 3 p.m. and there was any left, he was welcome to it. Being the obnoxious soul he is, he made one of his usual caustic comments and apparently looked around for another option. A few minutes later I saw him offering to help Susan Gossett – You remember her, she retired from the bank – carry four bags of ice to her car. I had already asked John Newton, one of the volunteers, to help carry her case of water. Susan is getting pretty frail – she has rheumatoid arthritis – her husband is also very ill, and she is raising two of their grandchildren."

"Isn't she the lady whose daughter was killed in the car accident on I-95?" Will asked.

"Yes. Anyway, I didn't have time to monitor Mr. Harmon's activities. I got busy and lost track of his helping Mrs. Gossett even though I figured his motives were self serving," said Betsy.

"Yea," said Will. I remember what an offensive jerk he made of himself in the food line at the picnic – breaking in front of people again and again before others had gotten anything to eat."

Betsy continued, "How well I recall. Anyway, the next thing I saw was John Newton walking toward me, laughing so hard I thought he was going to fall. When he regained his composure, he told me that Tom Harmon had gotten his just desserts."

"You mean he didn't con Mrs. Gossett out of some ice?" asked Will.

"Hardly," said Betsy. According to John, he put Mrs. Gossett's case of water in her trunk and then Tom Harmon put her ice in. Tom, showing his true character, then told Mrs. Gossett that since he had been so nice to her, she should give him a bag. With that, Mrs. Gossett slammed down the trunk and said, 'Fuck you, buddy.'"

"I love it. I wish I'd been there to see it. It couldn't have happened to a nicer person," said Will. He and Betsy laughed all the way to dinner.

Chapter 17

*F*riday arrived. It had been a week since Hurricane Clarice had displaced the populace of the Treasure Coast. If you just looked at the sky you would think nothing had happened. The weather was once again hot and summery. The sun shone brightly with daytime temperatures climbing into the nineties. The sky was an eye-popping blue. Not one cloud had the nerve to spoil this perfection. Birds glided sluggishly through a light breeze, landing in the massive nests of brush and mangled trees that dotted the ground below. Squirrels darted everywhere. Geckos sprang at insects and sunned. Their lives had returned to normal. As far as all of nature's creatures were concerned, there had been no disaster.

The lives of the often-pampered humans who shared this island with these creatures had been anything but normal. It had now been a week since most people had felt the refreshing chill of an air conditioner or been able to switch on a light. It was difficult to remember how long it had been since one had been able to cook a hot meal or reach in the refrigerator and grab a cold drink. It seemed like more than a week since their garbage had been picked up. It sat out by the street surrounded by mountains of yard debris, growing more pungent each day. In fact, people had learned to take it for granted because of this constant presence. It had been a week since they had been able to jump into a hot shower or doze through some mindless TV program. The computer junkies hadn't been able to have their Internet fix. Most missed receiving messages from or sending messages to their friends or laughing at the often inane jokes others routinely had e-mailed to them. People's schedules had been totally disrupted. No longer was their focus on going to work, looking forward to and savoring the company of their fellow workers, and finally returning home at a regular time each day. Instead people had become isolated. Life had become one long weekend without weekend pleasures – a weekend that found most of them stranded doing sweaty chores they would dearly love to hire out – if only there were workers available. Despite both high span bridges on and off of the island now being open and clear, the resident existences were anything but orderly.

Will and Betsy had learned earlier in the week that Saint Edwards School, the private school on the island, was planning to hold its regularly scheduled football game on Friday afternoon. Saint Edwards was Lexie's alma mater. Until Lexie had gone to college she had spent her entire academic career there, earning the "diehard" designation. Diehards were those students who had attended Saint Edwards from pre-K through the twelfth grade. Friday's impromptu social event was surprising since the school had no electricity. Rubbish covered most of the campus. Most of the classroom buildings had been severely damaged. The auditorium and library were considered total losses. The doors to the gymnasium had been blown open, allowing water to buckle the basketball court. Most of the letters had been plucked from the sign at the entrance to the campus. It had now read SA T E School. No one was sure when the school year would resume or where. By some miracle the football field, other than missing stadium lights, had not been damaged. The goal posts were standing.

Dr. Potter, the headmaster, told the members of the staff that he had been able to locate that they were to spread the word that on Friday afternoon the school would host the football game that had been scheduled for Friday night with Orlando Catholic. Dr. Potter told his staff, in a meeting under an oak tree adjacent to the school parking lot, the people he had been able to reach would be pleased to bring gas grills and ice chests to make the affair a success. The school staff raided the cafeteria storage room to get drinks and fill ice chests. It felt good to be doing something together. Arrangements were made with Betsy's bank for ice to be donated.

Dr. Potter further solicited eager volunteers to cook the free hot dogs and hamburgers he and his wife had driven most of a day to the Orlando area to purchase. The word spread quickly of this coming out celebration for both the current and former Saint Edwards community. It was agreed a social gathering on the ravaged campus would be the ideal symbolic gesture to signal life was returning to normal to these unsettled Floridians.

And for once the experts were correct! On Friday afternoon the campus was packed.

Will and Betsy and others jumped at the chance to participate. It was a relief to be able to go somewhere and do something social as well as constructive. It didn't matter that it was just as hot and sticky at school as it was at home and the volunteers would be working in the hot sun. Will and Betsy wanted to see, empathize with, and swap storm stories among their friends. Will helped to cook hamburgers and hot dogs; Betsy distributed the food and drinks. People saw people they had not seen for months or even years. It was like Christmas in September. Everyone babbled stories concerning the hurricane. Every armchair quarterback had an opinion on how various elected officials had handled the tragedy. It was all Will could do to stay ahead of the noisy hungry crowd. Football quickly became all but irrelevant except for the parents of the players. Folks were hungry for food and camaraderie. Some wanted nothing more than a sounding board or to hear someone else was worse off than they were. Others just wanted to get advice on how to deal with insurance adjusters and where to try to find construction workers. Everyone seemed just glad for a change of scenery for a few hours.

Once the initial rush had died down, Will shed his smoky apron and took a break to savor an ice-cold Diet Pepsi. As he stood watching the boisterous crowd he heard his name being called.

"Will! Will Black!"

Will turned and saw a familiar face. "Wally Beach! Long time, no see! How'd you make out in the storm?"

Wally Beach was one of those rare creatures that most Florida residents read about but only see occasionally – a Florida native. Most people meet Florida natives with about the same frequency as they see manatees. Wally worked for a citrus bird dog. A bird dog is an entrepreneur who buys and sells fruit. Wally was also a local sportscaster and color commentator for area ball games. He had once been touted as one of the top high school football players in Indian River County. He had been featured in *Parade* as a high school all-American. This seemed to ensure Wally would be offered a scholarship to a major college. He was highly recruited and even Bobby Bowden had visited him to try to persuade him to go to Florida State. But a knee injury his senior year in high school ended his promising career before it started. Without the crutch of athletics Wally would never be able to get into college and luckily got a job in the local citrus industry. Wally would always be the hometown boy the old-timers to this day nostalgically said should have been one of the best players Vero Beach High School ever produced.

"My house came through the storm fine," Wally responded, "but there's no fruit left to sell. It's all on the ground. We had a damned good crop on the trees too."

"Boy, that's got to be tough," Will said. "Y'all just can't seem to win for losing. It seems like the last few years you've either had canker, greening or droughts to contend with every single year. And now this hurricane."

"Yeah, this was going to be the year we were all going to make up some ground and make some serious money for a change. I guess there's always next year. Dick Young over there was just telling me that you found Dave Tressler dead after the storm."

"Betsy and I found him together. One of the biggest shocks of my life. We found him deader that a doornail in our office two days after the storm..."

Wally interrupted. "Son of a bitch had it coming. I hope he got his balls cut off. I wouldn't be selling fruit if it hadn't been for that dirty bastard."

"What do you mean?" Will asked.

"He's the one who took the cheap shot that took my knee out when I was a senior. If it weren't for him I would have gotten a college scholarship. I might even have ended up playing pro ball. Hell, the sky was the limit for me, and it all ended because that dirty bastard clipped me in practice. It wasn't an accident either. He would do anything to make himself look good. I've always wanted to see him get what was coming to him, and by God, it finally happened. I've always said what goes around comes around."

Betsy was excitedly waving at Will from across the field. So Will scooted over to see what Betsy wanted.

"What's up?"

"Bess Nagle just told me that Pelican Bay on north beach got power back," Betsy said excitedly.

"Please, God! Let us be next," Will said.

Chapter 18

*W*ill and Betsy woke up the following morning with greatly improved frames of mind. It was still hot and sticky. The news about Pelican Bay had given them new hope. After his morning bath in the swimming pool, Will couldn't wait to run over to Guy and Penny's and give them the news. He ate his Pop Tart on the way.

When Guy heard the news he decided to check the status of power at his office and invited Will to join him. Guy's building was on Ocean Drive several blocks south of Will's office. He had owned his suite for the last eight years. Clarice ripped the air conditioner from its mounting on Guy's building and the tenants had hired Denton Electric to reattach it to the roof. Once the task had been completed Denton had certified that the building was safe and could be reoccupied. Guy waited impatiently through the weekend for the city to "flip the switch." It never happened.

"The buildings on both sides of us have power, but I'm still dead in the water. I guess a visit to the city would not be out of order," Guy said after Will told him about Pelican Bay. I don't see where it could hurt anything. This is really starting to bind. I've still got all my employees on the payroll. I desperately need to get revenues flowing again. Want to take a car ride?"

"Sure. Why not?" Will replied. "I don't have any place else to go. My office doesn't have power either, and we won't for a while since the windows got blown out and, in my opinion, it's a possible crime scene. As long as we're going to town why don't we stop at the police station and see if they'll tell us anything about Tressler?"

"Good idea! They're right next door to each other. We'll talk to Lieutenant Mallette. I know him through United Way."

Guy and Will climbed in Guy's Explorer and headed for town. Reminders of Mother Nature's recent assault were everywhere. A private marina on Highway 1 had mangled, twisted sheets of galvanized aluminum dangling awkwardly from both the walls and roof of the building. The ribs of the building protruded showing where sheet metal had recently been attached. Yellow crime scene tape surrounded the carnage. All they could see were chest high mounds of rubble piled on the shoulder of the road. The American flag was suspended from a crane. One large sail boat sat on the remains of the metal roof of the Mobil gas station next door.

Graffiti on the hurricane shutters at the paint store said

CLARICE GO AWAY NOW

GO GATORS

Another homemade plywood sign announced

CLARICE CAME AND WENT...
THE GABLES WILL BE BACK

A head high mound of rubble had a sign propped up on top of it hand stenciled on plywood. It read:

NO POWER

Will smiled, looked at Guy and said, "No Power! No shit!"

On Highway 1 they passed a former bait shop and restaurant. The sides of the building looked like they had been hit with a wrecking ball. Orange cones surrounded what was left of the building. Boldly spray-painted in three-foot-high letters was the word

OPEN

Next to it was the regular sign

LONGPOINT BAIT & TACKLE and RESTAURANT

Below it was another homemade sign informing all passers-by of a

COOK-OUT

10-3

$5.00

COME AS YOU ARE

After stopping for a cold soft drink at this cookout, Guy and Will finally got to the police station. As they went in the front door they heard box fans being run by a generator. The lady behind the glass petition asked, "May I help you?"

"Is Lieutenant Mallette in?" Guy asked.

"May I tell him who is here?" she replied.

"Guy Walsh and Will Black," Guy answered.

Moments later, the door opened and Lieutenant Mallette came out in the lobby.

"Tom, I'd like to introduce you to my friend Will Black," Guy said, shaking hands with the policeman.

"Come on in, guys. It's too hot and dark to stand out in this lobby. What can I do you for?" Tom Mallette asked.

"Tom, Will and his wife were the ones who found Dave Tressler dead in his office at R S & T where Will and Dave worked together for years. Will is the assistant manager there. Have y'all found out any additional information about Tressler's death?"

"My gut instinct is the medical examiner's going to declare his death as accidental, and I don't think anyone will pressure him to say anything different. Fellows, it's been assigned an investigator. I'll tell both of you off the record. With everything that's going on we're going to be hard pressed to have the luxury of investigating this case to the extent we normally would. We're running with a skeleton staff. Until the power comes back on and the traffic signals start working, pretty much everyone we have is being used on traffic control. Also you wouldn't believe the number of domestic violence calls and all the crank calls we get when people's nerves get frayed. It's all we can do just to stay ahead of day-to-day crises. God knows when things will be normal again. If there were clear-cut evidence of a homicide we'd sure make it a priority item, but since there hasn't been we've had other fires to put out."

"Tom, could it have been a robbery?" Will asked. "The day we found the body Guy noticed Dave wasn't wearing the Rolex he normally wore everywhere. Also his files looked ransacked. The files weren't blown all around the office like you would expect the wind to do. Some folders had been taken out of their drawers and piled on top of the credenza. If they had been left out before the storm, they would have been scattered everywhere. Instead they were just sitting there damp but piled neat as hell under a rock paperweight."

"I'll note those things for the investigator," Tom replied. "But honestly would you wear your most expensive piece of jewelry out into a hurricane? I wouldn't!"

"He would," Guy said.

"As far as the papers go, he might have left them there and the paperweight might have just held them down. Thanks for coming by. Good to meet you, Will."

Knowing there was little else they could learn from Tom Mallette, Guy and Will thanked him and left the station.

"Well, you have to say this, at least he was honest," Will said as they walked to City Hall. "I guess if we're ever going to find out more about Dave we'll have to play junior detective ourselves. So what do you think? Think the storm killed Tressler, Monsieur Poirot?"

"I'm certainly starting to wonder," Guy answered.

At City Hall they asked to speak to someone in Code Enforcement. They were told to go to office 212 on the second floor where Guy politely tried to explain to that clerk a licensed electrical company had certified that his building was safe and could be reoccupied. He also told the clerk of his inability to get power restored. After a fifteen minute wait, the clerk returned to say that the department would not allow power to be restored until each suite within the building was deemed safe. Guy asked to speak to the clerk's superior but was informed it would do him no good because, "This is city code."

Guy and Will reluctantly returned to Guy's house to tell Penny and Betsy the disappointing news.

"Well, I guess I'll have to get hold of Denton Electric," Guy said. "Surely, they won't give me any trouble. After all they did do the work, and I paid them promptly."

Guy called the company and said, "Mr. Denton, your crew reattached the air conditioner on my office on Ocean Drive last week."

"Yes, I remember. Is anything wrong?"

"Yes. The city won't turn our power back on because your safety certification was for the whole building, and they need you to certify that each suite is safe."

"But we didn't inspect each suite," Denton said. "I can't certify what we didn't inspect, and I don't have time to revisit a job site twice. I'm short on men. We're running 24/7 just trying to catch up on other jobs. I hate to cut this short but I'm late for an appointment." And he hung up.

Guy slammed down the phone. "I can't believe that son of a bitch. He hung up on me. If I could stop payment on the damned check I gave him I'd do it. He basically said too f'ing bad; he didn't have time to mess with me."

"Certainly not the way I run my business," Will agreed.

Tuesday, after several unsuccessful calls to the city utilities director, Guy decided as a last resort to try to visit the city manager, and Will agreed to come along.

When they arrived at City Hall, Guy and Will were informed by a receptionist that the city manager was in a meeting. So they waited.

They thumbed through magazines for almost an hour. Still they saw no sign of the city manager. Guy thumbed through an internal directory he found in the magazine rack and noticed that it listed the city manager's direct line. He dialed the number and the city manger answered. When Guy identified himself and tried to explain his problem, the phone went dead. Then to Will and Guy's shock a police SWAT team burst into the room.

"Sir, I have been told you are creating a disturbance in a public building and refuse to leave," the SWAT team leader barked.

"Up until this moment no one has asked us to leave the building. How am I creating a disturbance? We've been sitting here quietly reading magazines," Guy replied.

"It's obvious you are here to create a disturbance or you would not be breathing heavily," barked the SWAT team leader.

"You'd be breathing heavy too if an armed person in a bullet-proof vest was threatening you for an unknown reason," Guy said, his face turning red.

"I warn you. One more word and I'll have you arrested," the policeman shouted back.

"On what charges?" Guy added.

"I demand to see your ID."

"Not until I know what charges are being brought against me," Guy shrieked.

Another policeman intervened. "I would suggest that you both calm down before this escalates into an incident you both will regret."

Things calmed down from that point. As Guy and Will drove home, Will said, "That city manager certainly has a unique management style."

The humor was wasted on Guy, who was still pissed. "I'll get even with that bastard if it's the last thing I ever do," he said.

"No, you won't," Will replied. "One glorious night we'll all get a big laugh as we tip a few and rehash this war story."

Chapter 19

*F*inally the lights flickered on.

The refrigerator started running!

The dishwasher leaped to life.

Air started coming out of the air conditioning vents.

The ceiling fans whirred.

"Will," Betsy said as she ran out of the house to find him. "The power's on!"

"Glory hallelujah! Thank you, God!" Will whooped. "Let's close the windows and doors and see if we can get this place to start cooling down and get some of this damned humidity out of here. Check and see if the TV works."

The house quickly cooled down. Betsy stripped the moist sheets off the bed, and gathered dirty towels to run a load of wash.

For the rest of the day the Blacks concentrated on returning their house to something resembling normal. They made a run to Publix and bought fresh food so they could celebrate that night with a feast. For the first time in a long time, Will and Betsy felt sure there was light at the end of the tunnel.

While Betsy was shopping at Publix Will bought a newspaper. Later, as she prepared a dinner of liver and onions, Will read highlights from the paper.

UNINVITED GUEST: CLARICE CRASHED MY WEDDING DAY

AFTERMATH OF CLARICE: "THINGS ARE A MESS" ACROSS THE TREASURE COAST

HURRICANE MAY FLATTEN FAMED CELEBRITY CHRISTMAS PARTY

FILTH AND MUCK LATEST CLARICE HEADACHE

STORMS BRUISE CITRUS INDUSTRY

COUPLE WELCOME NEIGHBORS FOR DAYS INTO THEIR POWERED HOME

Then Will noticed another story on page 5A.

MEDICAL EXAMINER RULES DEATH ACCIDENTAL

The Indian River County Medical Examiner has determined the death of securities broker David G. Tressler was accidental and related to Hurricane Clarice. Tressler, a prominent local businessman, was found dead in his office by a colleague two days following Clarice's rampage through Indian River County. Wilson and Elizabeth Black discovered Tressler's body in his 1500 Ocean Drive office as Black inspected their office for hurricane damage. Tressler was a native of Vero Beach and a member of the 1985 Vero Beach High School state championship football team.

Tressler is thought to have chosen to ride out the hurricane in his office and appears to have been killed by flying debris when the windows of the building gave way.

"Well, scratch an aggressive police investigation," Will added. "Mallette as much as told me so. What do you think?"

"I think from just the little bit we've gotten involved with so far there could be more to it than just being at the wrong place at the wrong time during Clarice, Betsy said. "I don't completely buy into the theory that a rational person would choose to stay in their office which is only across the street from the beach instead of being home with his family during a major storm. The official version just simply doesn't add up. Maybe Dave didn't have the perfect marriage, but gimme a break!"

Will and Betsy got out TV trays so they could watch the news while they ate. The announcer opened the broadcast.

Tonight we have one report of an inebriated woman who tired of branches hitting her townhouse. She reportedly started pulling oak tree limbs down by hand, sometimes swinging from limb to limb like a chimp. One of the branches broke off. Another limb broke her fall. The limb hit a power line, blowing a transformer. Immediately after the power went out, the woman told other residents of the complex who came streaming out of their apartments that she was an apartment manager of an adjacent condominium. She claimed to have a secret apartment manager "code" that could restore power to their building. People were at first impressed, believing the story, until witnesses began to tell them the tale of the drunken "Jane" who had swung from limb to limb until the unfortunate limb broke and subsequently crashed into the transformer. I can only say God must love drunks and fools. Jane reportedly not only avoided electrocution but survived the experience with only a few scratches and bruises.

The other announcer jumped in.

I don't think I can top that, but I'll try. The Vero Beach Fire Department was called out on an emergency call the afternoon Clarice was scheduled to make landfall. A Rock Ridge resident in his attempt to secure his metal shed ruptured a gas line with his boat anchor. Emergency repairs to the gas line took three hours and were finished only shortly before the storm came ashore.

"Ain't life wonderful?" Will said to Betsy.

"Weird is more like it," she said. "By the way, now that the power is back on I can set the alarm clock. It is exciting to think I will be able to see to put on my makeup before I go to work."

"Yeah," Will yawned. "The bank will be back to business as usual. That's more than I can say for my office. I'm going to take another run down to the Stuart office in the morning and touch base with my clients. Greg Smith, the manager, said we are welcome to continue using their empty offices. I'm sure I'll spend the day swapping storm stories with more clients, but who knows, someone may actually need something important – like money. Since the Vero Beach office has been closed, people who don't have checks on their accounts haven't had any way to get to their funds."

Chapter 20

Betsy was the first one home the next evening.

"Hi, honey," Will greeted her as he gave her a peck on the cheek. "I know what a road warrior feels like now. You wouldn't believe the traffic and how many traffic signals are still out on Highway 1. If this is what the wholesalers who come in our office have to fight every day I'm going to start being nicer to them when they drop in."

"I poured you a bourbon on the rocks when I heard the garage door going up," Betsy said as she kissed him back. "I figured that you were going to want one. By the way, I talked to Lexie this afternoon. She got an A on her Spanish test last week."

"Guy called me at the bank today. They finally got power at his office. He was teasing me that perhaps the bank would not have to foreclose."

"I told him, no chance."

Will plopped in his recliner and kicked off his shoes. "That's great! You know, I really miss that kid. Mix yourself a drink and let's chill for a few minutes. I've got a couple of things tell you."

"Sure you don't want to go back on the porch?" Betsy asked.

"Not only no, but hell no. Give me air conditioning. After the last week I may never go back on that porch again," Will replied.

Betsy joined him in their air-conditioned atrium.

"You wouldn't believe the phone call I got today," Will said. "I was in charge of managing our bunch today since Rooney wasn't there. He's still out of town. They stayed with his aunt in Sarasota during the storm. Anyway, the receptionist put a call through to me from a woman asking for Tressler. She was worried what effect the storm was going to have on a real estate limited partnership Dave had sold her. When I asked her what partnership, she said the one we were selling last year with the hotel in it. I finally dragged enough info out of her to figure out what was going on. Can you believe that asshole Tressler was selling units in a partnership that was not sponsored by the firm and telling people it was one of our approved products? It's a good thing no one found out before now. If the storm hadn't killed him our lawyers would have. That's outright fraud and misrepresentation. If he had been caught he would have been fired and also sanctioned by the SEC. Why would you risk your license and your career over something like that? I wonder how many of these LP investors are out there."

"And the roux thickens! And it's getting darker all the time. Old Dave was a real sweetheart, wasn't he? What hotel was it?" Betsy asked incredulously.

"I don't know. I was afraid to ask too much until I can see Rooney and report it to him. If I had set off bells and whistles today I'd have spent the rest of the day talking to a lawyer. I had too much to do. Rooney should be in tomorrow. I'll let him decide how he wants to handle it. Let's face it. There's nothing any of us can do now. One day's not going to make a lot of difference. I'm sure he'll take it to compliance. In the meantime I'll duck by our office before I go to Stuart tomorrow and see if there's anything in Dave's filing cabinet that will fill me in more on this matter. If I find anything I'll take it with me."

"Poor Connie and the kids! I guess they could cut her out of everything! She might not be able to collect on his life insurance or even keep the group medical policy! My God, if all this comes out what's going to happen to them," Betsy continued.

"Damned if I know! Messin' with fire like he was, let's hope somebody had enough sense to make other arrangements. Surely, Mike Pollard will look after her. After all she is Mike's daughter, and she's not the crook. It also isn't the first time. Dave was involved in some questionable limited partnership sales a few years ago. He often played a little fast and loose with the suitability issue when his commission was right. Remember the time Dave put that amputee assembly line worker in the aircraft leasing deal? He passed this guy off as a high net worth, sophisticated investor. The client didn't even have a high school education. The only reason he had any extra money at all was because he got a workman's comp settlement when he got his arm caught in a piece of machinery. It's a good thing the poor slob died before he found out what Dave had talked him into buying. GIGO – garbage in, garbage out. Good old Dave could make that computer sing when he wanted to make it project something – anything. Unethical, yes! Illegal, probably! But I never thought he was stupid or ballsy enough to put together his own deals and pass them off as legitimate syndications. There had to be someone else involved. The Dave Tressler I knew was not smart enough to structure something like this without help."

"I'm sure you're right," Betsy agreed.

"In all the excitement I almost forgot to tell you my other story," Will said.

"Remember Dick and Wanda Jeffries?"

"Of course! We were invited to a Christmas party at their house on the river two years ago. They're the ones who live out in the middle of nowhere. Do you still have an account with them?"

"Oh, yeah! Remember their house had double front doors?"

"How could I forget them? When we went over there for the Christmas party they had two gorgeous handmade wreaths on those doors."

"Well, when Clarice came on shore those showcase doors blew open into their living room. Dick and Wanda wrestled the doors back to a closed position. They then shoved furniture up against them. They rolled up a rug around the base of the doors and wedged the rug between the doors and the furniture.

"About forty-five minutes later they noticed water was coming under the doors and into the house. Soon they were standing in three feet of water and decided this was not going to be a good place to ride out the storm."

"Well, they live right on the river," added Betsy.

"Anyway, Dick decided they might be safer in their boat. It was trailered in their flooded yard. Dick held Wanda's hand, and they fought their way out to the boat only to find out it wouldn't float. Because Dick had taken the bailer plug out of the boat before the storm began, the bait well that Dick had put the plug in was flooded. Dick finally found the plug and managed to get it snapped back into the hole.

"It gets worse! They swam from the boat back to the house and went out into their garage to get some buckets to try to bail out the boat. They found a couple of mop buckets and swam back out to the boat. About the time the boat started to stabilize, Dick told me he and Wanda heard what sounded like a gunshot. It was one wall of their house collapsing. With the front doors open the storm waters had penetrated their entire residence."

"Oh, my God," Betsy said.

"Dick and Wanda watched their expensive furniture float down stream and out of sight.

"The water continued to rise, and when it did the nose of the boat dipped. The boat had floated off the trailer, but the bow was being pulled down since it was still attached to the trailer. Dick climbed out of the boat and started diving in the black, swirling water to try to free the boat before it became completely swamped. It took him three or four dives, but he finally managed to detach the line so the boat could float freely."

"This sounds like a scene out of a movie," said Betsy.

"Dick climbed off the boat a second time and towed the boat through the gash in the house. He hoped to secure it to what was left of a built in book shelf.

"Suddenly Dick said they were deafened by the scream of an alarm system. With limited visibility through the torrents of rain they saw both of their cars floating and then vanish into the darkness. The screaming noise was the protesting of the

SUV's burglar alarm system that had short circuited the car's electrical system, setting off the car's alarm systems."

"What else could happen?" Betsy asked.

"Dick managed to secure the boat. It tossed and turned wildly in their living room for the rest of the night but never capsized, giving Dick and Wanda the ride of their lives. They were found shivering and wet by rescuers about eleven o'clock the following day."

"Good grief, I can't imagine," was all that Betsy could add.

"Oh yeah! I almost forgot to mention. The built in china cabinet in their dining room? Not one piece of china or crystal in it was broken. Go figure."

Chapter 21

*T*he following morning when Will left the house he detoured by his Ocean Drive office. Two signs were on the door. One was from a general contractor announcing that they would soon begin to secure the building; the other from a company that had been hired to clean up mold. Black splotches of mold had started to form on both the walls and ceiling.

Will threaded through the junk to Dave Tressler's office. In his mind's eye, he still saw Dave's bloody body staring toward the ocean.

Will dragged a secretarial chair into Dave's office and sat for several minutes just looking around.

I wonder, he thought, *should I start with his desk drawer or one of his filing cabinets? Now if I were Dave Tressler where would I keep my sensitive files and what would I file them under?*

He went through the desk drawers first and found the usual stuff – old messages, confirms, an old calendar, membership rosters to various organizations and clubs, a Hershey bar, Tic Tacs, toothpaste, Dentyne, phone books, spare scratch pads, a ruler, pens, pencils, paper clips, an old *Playboy*.

Will began to sweat in the hot, humid office. He walked over to the broken window for fresh air before tackling Dave's credenza, which yielded old prospectuses, unframed sales awards and certificates, attaboys, stationary, research reports, Christmas cards, promotional goodies from both wholesalers and past obscure "deals of the month." Will moved on to the filing cabinet. He looked at the stack of files on top of the credenza – nothing unusual.

The top three drawers of the filing cabinet contained client folders arranged in alphabetical order. Will thumbed through the names to see if anything set off any bells. Nothing did. The bottom drawer contained more odds and ends. Just as he was about to call it a day, Will noticed a blue unidentified hanging file. He pulled it out. The thin file had a post-it on the top sheet of paper that said Spoonbill Partners L.P.

"Bingo" he wanted to yell. "I got you dead to rights, you SOB."

Will's heart raced as he thought about how he better grab the folder and haul ass. He didn't want to risk anyone walking in on him. He locked the building, jumped in the car, turned the air on high, and headed for work at his temporary office. No one would ever know he'd made a side trip by Ocean Drive on the way to Stuart.

When Will got to Stuart, Rooney was already there. He found a vacant office, pulled Rooney aside, and told him about his phone call with Tressler's client, Marcia Smith, the day before. He *forgot* to mention the file he had scarfed up in Vero Beach. He'd decided he wanted a chance to read it first. He could always put it back that night and then let the powers that be find it.

Rooney was at first in shock but not denial. After thinking for a moment, he told Will they'd better report the incident. What Dave had been doing was illegal, immoral and, if he were alive, grounds for dismissal.

Will retreated into his temporary office and started to examine his contraband. The first few pages were nothing more than names. Will didn't know if these were prospects or people who had actually invested in Dave's scheme. Halfway down the second page he recognized the name of Marcia Smith. She had a check mark and a date beside her name. Will wondered if this identified her as an investor. She had the initials SBPI written after a date. Other names had the code SBPI or SBPII written after them. Another group was identified by the notation MPI and MPII as well as dates. What the devil could these stand for?

He kept digging into the ambiguous file. When he saw no one around the copying machine he made a copy of the list. Finally, Will saw some scratch notes written to Dave from an "Adolfo". There were others written to him from an "Al". One note mentioned Spoonbill Partners. Another acknowledged Macadamia Partners. The notes had no useful information in them other than referring to these two vague, mysterious names, but they confirmed that Dave definitely had been involved in unauthorized outside business interests.

A light suddenly went off! SBP – Spoonbill Partners. Spoonbill Partners one and two and Macadamia Partners one and two. Off course! But what were Spoonbill Partners and Macadamia Partners? And who the hell was Adolfo or Al? The handwriting looked the same. Were they the same person? Will's motivation was renewed. He felt challenged to get to the bottom of the whole dirty mess.

His fist shot into the air as he put the list back in his brief-case.

"Will Black," he gloated to himself. "In my former life I was the great Boston Blackie. In this life I'm Vero Beach Blackie. Not BB - VBB."

"See, Dave," he chuckled at his own bad joke, "I can use obscure initials too!"

Chapter 22

*W*ill could hardly wait to leave Stuart that afternoon. He stayed until he felt like he could prudently sneak out about mid afternoon. He scooted up US 1 back to Vero Beach using the vague excuse he had some things to do. The mysterious blue file had fired his imagination. He felt compelled to go back by Dave's office and search it again. Surely there were other files. He just had to find them. Will hoped Dave hadn't kept his other files at home, but this time he had one leg up. This time instead of conducting a blind search Will had some clue as to what to look for.

Before Will left, he had poked his head in Rooney's office and made a vague inquiry to find out if Rooney had heard anything back from compliance on the Tressler issue.

"Not a word," reported Rooney. "I guess since he's dead and no one's complained he's not a priority item. You know how these things go."

"See you in the morning," Will responded, content to let the matter officially drop. "I've got some stuff I need to do."

Will flipped on the Jeep's radio. Tom Jones' baritone voice boomed.

Last night I went to sleep in Detroit city
and dreamed about those cotton fields and home

When it got to the chorus, Will couldn't help but do a duet with Tom

I wanna go home

I wanna go home

Ohh how I wanna go home

When Will got back to the office there was no one there or any sign that anyone had been there since his morning visit. He let himself in and went to Tressler's office. He ransacked the filing cabinet again. Nothing. Just packed with every assortment of stuff.

What a packrat! I never throw anything away either until the place gets so cluttered that even I can't stand it anymore. Now where in the hell would I store overflow files if I were Dave?

"Of course! How could I be so stupid? Those empty filing cabinets on the back stairwell! Rooney said we could use them as long as the office didn't need them," he said out loud.

Will waded through the jumble to the back stairwell. The stairwell door opened easily enough, but with the power still out, it was pitch black and radiated heat like an oven. Will went back to his car and got the flashlight Betsy always insisted he carry in the glove compartment.

He returned to the building and started searching the stairwell. Some filing cabinets had no identification. Others were labeled such that they were obviously daily work from the cage. Overflow was in dusty cardboard storage boxes. Old sales posters and banners had been thrown on top of some of the cabinets. The top of one cabinet had been used as a depository for a box of IRA applications that had been sent to the office during tax season to support a rollover campaign. Another had a box of 403b brochures. Another for leftover sales material and out-of-date prospectuses for an annuity that Will hadn't heard a whisper about in years. A pile of prospectuses from the New Horizon Delta Global Agricultural Fund. The firm treated Tressler and his family to a weekend on Marco Island as a reward for selling that piece of shit. A sure enough doozy! Will sneezed from the dust he had stirred up. Or was it the memories of campaigns past?

The first row of filing cabinets yielded nothing of value.

He started on the second row. A business card had been scotch-taped to the front of a drawer. The card said "David G. Tressler, Reynolds Smathers and Thompson, Vice President." Eureka!

Will held the flashlight in one hand and started rooting through the drawer with the other. A stuffed looking red hanging folder first attracted his attention. He pulled it out. Spoonbill Partners! He laid it aside and kept looking. A hunter green hanging folder was his next find. Macadamia Partners! Soon he found the files for Spoonbill II and Macadamia II. Mission accomplished! Will couldn't wait to get home and read the contents.

Chapter 23

*W*ill ran in the house. Betsy wasn't there yet.

He let the dogs out, got a Diet 7-Up out of the fridge, and spread the files out on the dining room table. *Which one do I want to read first?*

Will chose the Spoonbill file since it was the one that had started this whole thing. When he opened it, brochures and marketing material spilled out. There were glossy pictures of mature couples golfing and playing tennis or hanging out in a luxury bar laughing with other couples. Another elegant couple was enjoying an extravagant meal with their *GQ* handsome friends. An attractive, suntanned couple was enjoying the boating experience of a lifetime. Will read and reread the brochures. He couldn't wait to share them with Betsy. There were glossy spread sheets, with alluring projections. Everything implied this is how people were meant to live and effortlessly make money. Spoonbill certainly looked more glamorous than selling Aunt Nellie a hundred shares of FPL.

Betsy walked in.

"As soon as you get comfortable come into the dining room," Will said enthusiastically. "Do I have something to show you!"

After Betsy joined him, Will asked her, "Do you know what Spoonbill is?"

"I guess I'm about to find out. Isn't a Spoonbill a bird?"

Will proceeded to tell her about his amateur detective work and where he had found Dave's file on Spoonbill. Then he showed her the sales brochures and spread sheets.

"Spoonbill is a limited partnership in a proposed condo hotel resort complex. It's the old property Holiday Inn used to manage on the inlet."

"Didn't Holiday Inn break their management contract on that property about five years ago?" Betsy asked. "There was also some talk about it possibly being condemned or foreclosed on. Wasn't everybody involved suing everybody else involved in that property? Didn't everybody who was in on the original deal lose their ass?"

"The one and the same! Well, guess what? If Dave and his buddies have anything to do about it, it's about to become the Spoonbill Ocean Resort. It is now the showcase property of Spoonbill Limited Partnership. A few lucky limited partners have the-once-in-a-lifetime opportunity to buy a room or suite for a $400,000 to $700,000 reduced pre-renovation price. Then because the complex is in its construction phase these fortunate few will have their unit leased back from them by the general partner for two years at a lease price that will guarantee them a fifteen percent return on their investment and provide them with the cash flow to pay their mortgage payment while the construction proceeds."

"What a deal," said Betsy.

"The partnership claims to have a special relationship with a lender who will provide permanent financing at very attractive interest rates."

"I know it's not my bank," added Betsy.

"The brochure says these initial investors are buying into a five-star resort at *wholesale* prices. Investors two years from now will easily pay $600,000 to $1,100,000 for what you can get today for only four to seven hundred thousand. It further claims the project will appreciate at 20 percent per year and provide a double-digit income to the investors."

"Nothing like conservative projections. Do you get a toaster, too?" Betsy asked. "Did they happen to mention permitting issues? I read in the paper that area is considered to be environmentally sensitive and there are problems with property improvements being over the dune line."

"The only mention of that topic is the general partner does not anticipate any permitting issues."

"You've got to be shitting me! The underwriters at our bank discovered years ago that property is a hot potato. We turned down the Sinclairs when they requested just a small loan to buy that same property."

"Hey, I'm just quoting the brochure. Everybody knows if something is in writing it's got to be true," Will laughed.

"Yeah, right! By the way, who's the general partner?"

"Someone I never heard of – a Superior Holdings L.L.C."

"New name to me," said Betsy.

"I also found some notes in some of Dave's files from an Al and an Adolfo. I can only assume they're one and the same."

"I would say that's a good guess, Charlie Brown."

"Are you ready for the next tale?" Will teased.

"You mean there's more?"

"Let me tell you about Macadamia Partners."

"What the hell is that?"

"Wonder boy's other once-in-a-lifetime opportunity. Per the brochures I found squirreled away in the stairwell, for only $100,000 per unit you can own a piece of a newly established macadamia plantation in Guatemala. The sales piece describes it as a very compelling opportunity to invest in a medium which until now has been only available to super wealthy smart-moneyed investors. The general partner asserts that macadamia nuts are the prime edible nut in the world, bringing twice the price of cashews. It goes on to say that until now sixty percent of the macadamias in the world have been produced in Hawaii, giving them a stranglehold on this lucrative market. It also claims that until now there have been high barriers of entry for new macadamia growers since a macadamia seedling takes five to nine years to start producing and even longer to reach mature peak production."

That's feasible," said Betsy.

"The partnership alleges to have made some significant breakthroughs that will change the face of the macadamia industry. First it states that the general partner has determined the soil conditions in Guatemala are ideally suited to macadamia trees, but land is much cheaper and more available than land in Hawaii. The brochure states that with advanced grafting techniques on Beaumont rootstock, they have shortened the amount of time it takes for a tree to produce from five years plus, to two years. Per their projections, this new variety of macadamia is capable of producing with aggressive fertilization programs instead of fifty to one hundred and fifty pounds of nuts per tree annually, possibly as much as two hundred pounds per tree. This increased production efficiency should enable them to undercut prices charged by Hawaiian farmers while maintaining their profit margins. It is their expectation buyers will rush to buy Guatemalan nuts. It goes on to say the partnership will become a cash cow since macadamia trees live sixty to eighty years. And as if that weren't enough, the brochure claims the Beaumont is more vertical than other varieties enabling the grower to plant more trees per acre."

"Is there any downside to this wonderful investment?" asked Betsy.

"Very little," Will replied sarcastically. "Only that eating too many nuts may be fattening and a tree produces more than you want to eat."

"Like you have said before, more fun than selling a hundred shares of FPL to Aunt Nellie."

Chapter 24

Will had some time on his hands Friday afternoon and began to call some of the names on Dave Tressler's investor list. He pretended he was one of Dave's associates and asked what he thought were innocuous questions about investor satisfaction. He never acknowledged Dave's death. He wasn't even sure why he was calling. He just wanted to see what would happen. Will spoke to a wide variety of people. While they seemed a little different from the investors he dealt with each day, their knowledge was very limited when it came to both Spoonbill Partners and Macadamia Partners. All seemed to have high hopes for their investment. Most didn't even seem to remember Dave Tressler's name. He was just that nice young man "who got me units of this hard to get, tightly rationed private placement." They all just seemed to be ordinary investors who thought they knew a good deal when they heard one. Finally he got to the name Omar Perillo.

"Hello."

"Señor Perillo, my name is Will Black with Reynolds Smathers and Thompson. I am just giving you a courtesy call to see if you have any questions about your investment in Macadamia Partners."

"Who did you say this is?"

"Will Black, an associate of Dave Tressler's."

"How did you get my name?" came a gruff response.

"From Dave Tressler."

"What the fuck? He's not supposed to give anyone my name. How'd you get this phone number?"

"As I said – from Dave Tressler."

"Don't hand me that shit. The cocksucker's dead. If you know what's good for you, you'll lose this number and forget this name. Comprende? And a piece of advice. Whoever the fuck you are, I'd suggest you learn how to mind your own business."

"Ouch!" Will said after he hung up. "I wouldn't want to meet that guy in a dark alley."

Will didn't call any more names on Dave's list that afternoon.

✦✦✦✦

Garbage pickup had still not resumed, but the city allowed garbage to be taken to several city parks where it was transported daily to the landfill. On Saturday morning at Betsy's insistence Will loaded their garbage into the back of his Jeep and took it to the park.

The line was lengthy. The stench of raw garbage filled the hot air. Flies buzzed around garbage bags of spoiled food. People were edgy. Everyone wanted to drop off their waste and get out of there.

After waiting more than thirty minutes Will finally got to the front of the line. Behind him was a burly middle-aged Hispanic man with an acne-scarred complexion. The man was driving a half-ton pickup truck. Will paid him no mind.

This was a stranger who he was sure he would never see again. When his turn finally came Will got out of his Jeep, opened the back, and started to unload his black trash bags. Suddenly as he bent over to grab his last bag the truck behind him eased up to his car. It was so close that if it had moved forward a couple of inches Will's legs could easily have been pinned between the two bumpers.

"Watch what you're doing, Mister!" Will yelled angrily at the driver. "You almost cut my legs off!"

The rough looking man stared back at Will silently.

"Did you hear me?" Will repeated as he wiped the sweat off his brow. "You could have really hurt me."

"I guess garbage disposal could become hazardous," the man said with a deadpanned look. "There's lots of other ways a person could get hurt too."

"What did you say?"

"I said Omar told me to tell you that people minding other people's fucking business can get hurt and put out like garbage."

The man ground his unfiltered cigarette into the dirt. He then climbed back into his truck without having unloaded the first bag of garbage, backed his truck up a few feet, and without another word or glance back, drove away.

Chapter 25

Will was shaken. The man had quietly sent a strong message: "I will and can hurt you." He drove home in a daze. Just whose toes had he stepped on? All he had done was make a few phone calls. He hadn't even learned anything useful except that a partnership named Macadamia Partners existed and that Dave Tressler had been involved with it. Was he in something way over his head? Had Tressler gotten in over his head with these threatening characters? Just who was Omar or Omar's henchman, and why had his blind inquiries been received in such a hostile manner?

When Will got home, Betsy was on her computer. Lexie had excitedly sent them an e-mail about the new salsa class she had joined. It was called Salsa Craze. The class was sponsored by the Cuban Students Association. Lexie had infected Betsy with her enthusiasm.

"Will, I'm so glad that Lexie is getting involved with affairs at the university. She seems so happy. We're so blessed to have a well-adjusted daughter."

Will sat quietly letting Betsy finish her message to Lexie before telling about his encounter at the park.

"I don't know how to describe this guy to you. He just exuded evil. It wasn't as much what he said as how he said it. He looked right through me like it wouldn't bother him one little bit to grind me to dust. I don't know what I've done to incur these people's wrath. I don't even know who they are."

"What did you say the partnership's names are – Macadamia Partners and Spoonbill Partners? Let's see if I can find out anything about it on the Internet? There's a Web site named sunbiz.org. It will give you information on LP's and LLC's. Let's see what we can pull up."

Betsy soon found filings for both. Both used a principal address in Miami and had a common registered agent – Superior Holdings L.L.C. In addition each showed a common officer, Adolfo Soltero. She looked at the annual reports, but they shed very little new light on the mystery.

"I guess we know a little more than we did. There do seem to be some common parties involved. Print out what you've got. Let's take the boat out this afternoon. We need to do something fun," Will said.

"Good idea," Betsy replied. "Let's see if Guy and Penny want to go."

Guy and Penny met the Blacks at their house a couple of hours later. Guy and Will swung the davits out and launched the boat. They were all prepared for an afternoon of fun.

"Let's cruise the river and see what the hurricane damage looks like from that perspective," Will said.

The trip revealed riverfront houses that looked perfect. Others showed various degrees of calamity. Boats had been swamped. Some back yards had palm trees toppled on the docks; others leaned against houses. Blue tarps covered some roofs. Some docks were intact, others all but destroyed.

As they cruised, Guy said, "By the way I forgot to tell you about our roof. Yesterday, when Penny got home from the grocery store there was a roofing company at our house. A Mexican crew was ripping shingles off our house. Penny called me and told me she didn't know I had hired a roofing crew. I went ballistic. There was nothing wrong with our damned roof. I rushed home and tried to quiz the crew. Naturally none of them spoke English. The foreman had gone to check on another job. When he got back I demanded to see his work order. Turns out they were at the wrong address. They were supposed to be working at the Walkers one block up. I screamed and yelled so they started tacking on tar paper and the Walkers' shingles on top of the area they had pulled off. I was livid. The shingles they put on don't match ours worth a damn. The whole thing looks like total shit. Now I've got to go fight with the roofing company about making things right. On top of everything else they're not even a local company. It's some roofer out of Texas somewhere who came here chasing the storm. In case I can't get anything out of them, does the insurance company pay? You know, my shingles have been discontinued. You can't even buy them anymore."

Guy was starting to turn red in the face.

Suddenly, he almost lost his balance as he stood and banged his knee on the console. Will had to hang onto the wheel. The girls were sitting down but grabbed the munchies as the boat suddenly pitched. When they looked up again they saw the thirty five-foot Baja Outlaw that had almost capsized them. It had red and black vertical markings and a sharp bow made for speed. The twin 600 SCI's rumbled as it idled near them. The boat had ripped around the spoil island so fast they had not even realized it was there until their boat rocked violently from the Baja's wake. Will started to say something but refrained when he saw the passenger in the boat. The captain was a Latin-looking hoodlum wearing a white guayabera; the passenger was the same pockmarked man who had almost crushed his legs at the park. Both men deadpanned Will and his friends alarmingly before smirking at each other. The scarred man suddenly held up his hand with his thumb up like he was aiming a pistol.

"Bang, you're dead," he said, looking at the Baja captain and laughing.

The captain opened the throttle on the muscle boat and it roared away. The wake almost swamped the Sundance again. As quickly as they had appeared, the men were gone.

Chapter 26

*E*veryone grabbed anything that might fall as the Sundance pitched and rolled when the Outlaw shot down the river. Who? Why?

Betsy looked at Will. "The thug from the park?"

"Yep!" Will replied. "A real suga booga, ain't he?"

"A nightmare! And did you see the rough character with him? He was as bad if not worse."

Guy and Penny asked simultaneously, "You know these people?"

"No, but Dave Tressler did," Will said. "I haven't had a chance to tell you about them."

Will then told Guy and Penny everything he had found out about Dave Tressler's side ventures. He told them about the unexpected phone call from an investor at the office, and the details of Macadamia and Spoonbill Partners, beginning with finding the mysterious lists of names. He noted the puzzling memos from Al/Adolfo. He related to them Betsy's Internet research and the discovery of Superior Holdings L.L.C. He told them about his "customer service" calls to names on Dave's list and Omar Perillo's touchy response. He then told them about the encounter at the city park that morning.

"You've been a busy little twosome, and you've uncovered a little shit somebody wants to keep covered up," Guy said.

"But what do we really know?" Betsy asked.

"Enough to know there may be more to the honorable Mr. Tressler's death than anyone thought," Penny added.

"So what do we do? Tell what we think we know to the police or plow on?" asked Will.

"I vote to plow on. The message I got from the cops is their plate is full; that all they can concentrate on is getting this town back on its feet," said Guy.

"So is everyone in? If so, what do we do next?" Will asked.

The response was a unanimous yes. It was also unanimous that no one had a clue as to what the newly founded group's next move should be, but they had a purpose. One out of two ain't bad!

Chapter 27

Guy tried to phone Will at his office before the market opening Monday morning. Will hadn't arrived in Stuart yet. He had gotten delayed on Highway 1. A crew with a crane was trying to pick up a forty-two-foot catamaran sailboat that had somehow been deposited west of the highway. Cars were at a standstill in both directions. When the bottleneck had gone on for about fifteen minutes, Will got out of his car and started a conversation with the person behind him.

"We're not even close to the river. I read in the paper that one marina was completely leveled, and the authorities have not been able to account for any of the boats. I wonder if that is where this boat came from," Will said to the sweating, well-dressed driver. "But you've got to wonder how a huge boat like that got way over here? The river's got to be half a mile away."

"Could be," the man replied. "It certainly doesn't look like the kind of boat you would store on a trailer."

Finally, the boat was hoisted with the crane, and people began getting in their cars again. Traffic started slowly moving.

Will turned on the radio. Creedance rocked.

I see the bad moon arising

I see trouble on the way

Will turned up the volume.

I hear hurricanes a blowing

I know the end is coming soon

I fear rivers over flowing

Will laughed. "John Fogerty, you're a day late and a dollar short."

When Will got to the office there was a stack of telephone messages to return so it was almost lunchtime when he finally returned Guy's call.

"Thanks for calling back," Guy opened. "The other day, after you told us about Superior Holdings, I kept thinking how that name sounded familiar. When I got in this morning I found out why – we used to have that account. It transferred out several years ago."

"Do you remember why it went away?" Will asked.

"When I opened the file this morning, the whole situation started coming back to me. There were always questions from our compliance people because this account appeared to be a money-laundering risk. Operations also hinted it might be guilty of check-kiting a couple of times. I used to have to call my contact at Superior and quiz him about compliance's suspicions. I remember now the first few times I called him he was nice but evasive. Then we went through a period in which I had a hard time getting him to return my phone calls. The last few times I called him he acted real touchy. One day out of the complete blue the ACATS form came in moving the whole thing to another custodian. The bastard never even gave me the courtesy of a call. I just got the notice one day that it was leaving. I remember being relieved. I never made any money off of it. It was just a source of periodic aggravation – all service, no revenue."

"Do your notes show who your contact was?" Will asked.

"Sure do! An Adolfo Soltero. He was Colombian. They called him Al. Even still have a phone number for him."

"I've run into that name recently in Tressler's records," Will said.

Guy continued, "I remember Al never wanted to play by the rules. Rules were always for other people. Everything he did was an exception. Depositing third-party checks. He was always wanting checks made out to some third party. Never had the appropriate LOA on file. Always wanted you to do it now, and would say that he'd bring the LOA to you later. Most of the time I'd end up having to badger him for it. Always asking for checks to be sent to places other than the address of record. He wrote checks on uncleared funds that had just been deposited in his account. Then he would run people by the office to pick up checks; people we had never seen before. I remember they always seemed to be some grease bag with gold chains. He always said he was going to make all the aggravation worth my while, but he never did. Just kind of a general pain in the ass. And he wasn't even nice about it unless he really wanted something."

"Do you think the phone number is still valid?" Will asked.

"It is. I called it this morning. Some wetback-sounding guy answered the phone – a real snarler. I used the excuse I was the former broker following up to see if his current broker was living up to his expectations. He barked yeah. I told who-ever answered the phone that if things didn't work out and he ever needed to change brokers again to please keep us in mind. Whoever I was talking to slammed down the phone. Like I'd take the account back on a bet! About five minutes later I got a call back from him demanding my name. He said he wanted to keep it in case he ever did need it. Must have gotten my number from caller ID. Scared the shit out of me especially since we had that little Latino encounter on the river Saturday."

"I've been thinking about that all weekend. As bad as it scared me, I don't mind telling you it really scared Betsy."

"Penny felt the same way. She didn't sleep well Saturday night."

"Another lead going back to Dave. I'm going to check our system. I bet you a beer the account went from you to Tressler."

"I'll talk to you later."

After Will hung up, he pulled up the screen that listed Dave's accounts. Since Will was Rooney's assistant manager he had universal access to the accounts in everyone else's production number. He tapped in Superior Holdings under broker number 036 and up popped "Superior Holdings."

He hit the positions screen. The account had a value of $2,156,960 until just recently. Several big checks had been written out of it since the hurricane. It now had a balance of $129.

"Wow, there was some real money there, but where'd it go? Let's check the deposits."

The deposits were mostly in even $50,000 and $100,000 increments though there was a couple for $200,000. Will wrote down the names of the people writing the checks.

"I think I'll check the list I got out of Dave's filing cabinet and see if any of these names are on there," Will said to himself.

He got out a highlighter pen to check off the names in case he ran into familiar ones. A surprising number of the names were identical to those on Dave's list.

"This can't be a coincidence," he said, congratulating himself.

He decided to check disbursements from Superior Holdings' account. All of the checks were made out to either Macadamia Partners or Spoonbill Partners. Check amounts were much larger than the deposit checks had been.

"My, My," Will murmured. "This is looking more and more inbred. Wait'll the group hears this."

Chapter 28

*W*ill arrived at his office and saw the familiar car belonging to his sales assistant, Barbara, in the parking lot. They had worked together for more than fifteen years. He had not seen her, only talked to her on the phone, in the confusion since Clarice. Barbara had taken some time off. She had lost her house in the storm. Barbara had an older house that had been built before hurricane straps were part of the building code. The hurricane had lifted the roof off her house and flooded it. She and her husband, John, had lost virtually everything.

Will had sorely missed Barbara. She was the person who kept things running smoothly for him at the office. Barbara was also Dave Tressler's sales assistant.

"Barb," Will said. "You sure are a sight for sore eyes."

"You miss me?" Barbara replied playfully as they hugged.

"Does a dog get fleas? Do you and John have everything under control?" Will asked.

"Not really, but we're making headway. You just don't know how lucky you are your house came through the storm. Good Lord this has been a mess! I bet it'll be two years until life is normal again."

Barbara spent most of the morning catching up on all the work that had been piling up while she had been out.

"You would not believe how many e-mails I've erased," she told Will shortly before lunch.

"Oh yes, I would," Will said, shaking his head. "By the way, I've got a quick question to ask you."

"Gimme a sec. Actually, ask me in the kitchen while we make a sandwich. I'm starving. Let's grab a bite before the phone rings again."

"You were handling Tressler's clients," Will said when they got in the kitchen. "Do you remember an account named Superior Holdings?"

"Uh huh! Nasty man! He used to come in to see Dave all the time. Dave called him Al or something. Everything was always hush-hush with him. Don't you remember? He always shut the door for everything. And if I ever had to go in Dave's office while he was there he'd sit there silently giving me the evil eye until I left. Once or twice there were papers out when I went in. He'd always grab them and cover them up like I was going to see something I wasn't supposed to see. He gave me the creeps."

"I don't think I remember him, but I didn't have a reason to either," Will said, as he put mayonnaise on his bread.

"I'm surprised. He liked body jewelry. This joker was foreign. Always had cigarettes in his pocket and nicotine stains on his fingers," Barbara continued. "Some kind of Latino. Cuban?"

"Try Colombian. Al is short for Adolfo," Will said.

"Really! I wouldn't have guessed that one," Barbara said. "I know you probably think I'm nuts, but I swear one time when I went in there he had a lump under his sport jacket that looked like a gun. I told myself at the time it was probably just a cell phone or pager. I tell you something else not for publication; whenever he came around, Dave would drop everything to make time for him. Even though they joked around with each other, he also seemed to make Dave very nervous."

"You still got the file on Superior?"

"Dave always kept that file himself. I can't tell you how many times Al wanted something done, and Dave magically came up with the LOA he needed. Why do you want to know about Superior anyway?"

"Just between us, I think Dave and Al had some illegal shit going on. Did Al have a personal account?"

"No! Everything was done in the name of the Superior Holdings account. I do remember a lot of the LOA's going to a Macadamia Partners and a Spoonbill Partners. Al raised hell when the cage asked for picture ID before giving him the checks."

Will decided to let the matter drop with Barbara, but he was determined to search Dave's files one more time to see what he could find about Superior Holdings.

About the middle of the afternoon Will got a call from a shaken Guy Walsh.

"Penny just called me from the house. She just had to rush our dog Duke to the vet. Somebody left some poisoned meat in our yard. Duke ate some of it but not enough to kill him. She just happened to walk outside at the right time and take it away from him. She saw some Mexican or something driving away. What shitty bastard would do something like that to an innocent dog?"

"Mexican or Colombian? Guy, I hate to be paranoid but you make one phone call about Adolfo and a few hours later someone tries to poison your dog. I make one call last week and somebody sics the dogs on me via the dump truck in the park and then the boat incident on the river last Saturday. The Superior Holdings account did move over here under Tressler's number. This morning Barbara just told me a little about your old buddy Adolfo that really didn't give me any warm and fuzzy feelings. I hope we're not in over our heads."

"No joke!"

Chapter 29

*W*ill and Betsy talked that night about the incidents of the last few days and concluded if what they suspected was correct they were amateurs out of their league. They decided that Will would tell everything they knew to Lieutenant Mallette the following morning before he went to Stuart. Will phoned the police department and got a 9:30 appointment.

Will tossed and turned all night rehearsing in his mind what he wanted to tell Mallette. Finally about daybreak he told Betsy, "I didn't sleep worth a damn worrying about this mess."

"I know! You kept me awake all night," she said.

Will drove to town. When he went into the police station he was told that Mallette was there.

"Lieutenant," Will said, greeting the policeman and shaking his hand.

"Good to see you again, Will," Mallette replied. "The last time I saw you, you were with Guy Walsh. Did he ever get his office electrical problems ironed out?"

"Yeah, thank goodness. Anything new on Dave Tressler?"

"No, far as we're concerned it's a closed case. He died accidentally in the storm."

"If you've got a few minutes I've got a few incidents that may make you reconsider the Tressler case."

"I really don't have a lot of time but will make time for this. I hope it's good. We're up to our eyeballs with stuff that needed taking care of yesterday."

"I'm telling you, you're going to feel like an idiot if there's something to the information I have and you find out about it from your superior. I'm giving you the scoop free. All it's going to cost you is a few minutes of your time."

"OK! Shoot!"

Will told the lieutenant about the phone call from Tressler's client, and his discovery of Spoonbill Partners and Macadamia Partners. He then related his discovery of these entities relationship to Superior Holdings and the mysterious Adolfo Soltero. He told about his phone call to Omar Perillo that led to the bullying tactics at the park as he attempted to unload his garbage. He told about the frightening encounter with the Baja Outlaw on the river, and Guy's curt phone call with Adolfo Soltero. Finally, he related the close call Guy's dog had with the poisoned meat and his debriefing of Barbara at the office.

Lieutenant Mallette listened silently and took notes.

"Sounds like these are some pretty unsavory characters, but they haven't done anything they can be arrested for," he said. "In the only incident in which you had witnesses they merely exhibited bad boating etiquette. They never came right out and threatened you. They never exhibited a gun and pointed it at you. He may have been rude, but they are not constantly stalking you. At the moment all I can do about this is make note of the names and check to see if they are former felons.

I hope you understand. So far from what you have described, no laws have been broken."

"Well, at least I've gone on record about these creeps. If something happens to me you'll at least have a suspect."

"Will, you've been reading too many whodunits. Nothing is going to happen to you, but, if this pattern continues, promise you will keep me in the loop. They may do something at some point that does cross over the line. I don't want you to feel reluctant to call. Here's my cell phone number. I will look and see if we have either of these two in our database. Call me in a few days."

Chapter 30

Will called Betsy at the bank. "Darling, just thought I would check in and tell you what happened at the police department."

"Surely you got their attention after worrying about it all night."

"Oh, I got their attention all right, but Mallette said there wasn't a damned thing he could do at this point but make a note to the file. They haven't really done anything but intimidate us a bit, and the police department's attitude is that it might just be something we're overreacting to with all the stress we've had recently. He did say they would look and see if these were known bad guys and get back to me."

"Bottom line is we're no safer than before you went down there."

"Well, I guess if something happens to us the police will be one leg up on a lead to find out who did it.'

"That'll be a comfort for me from my hospital bed or my grave," said Betsy.

"You sure know how to make me feel secure."

About an hour later Betsy had to go out to the bank lobby to talk to one of her colleagues. When she did she was shocked to see one of the men who had been on the Baja standing in the teller line with another menacing looking Hispanic. Betsy tried to turn her head and duck in a cubicle, but the man saw her. He motioned to his associate to hold his place in line and walked over to where Betsy was standing. He gave her what she thought was a disarming but slippery looking smile.

"Aren't you the lady who was on the Grady-White this week-end out on the river?" he asked. "Twenty-two footer with the UM decal on the windshield, wasn't it? Sundance was the name, I believe?"

"Yes," she stammered. Her heart stopped – this sleaze-ball knows where my baby's going to school!"

"Nice boat! Sorry if we almost swamped you," he said, showing false concern. "Isn't your husband a stock broker?"

"Yes," she stammered again.

"Is he accepting new clients?" he asked.

"I guess so," she said.

"Where did you say his office is?"

"He doesn't have one right now – hurricane damage," Betsy said.

"I'll make it a point to look him up when he does." The man grinned, exposing a gold molar. His eyes were piercing and serious. When he turned to rejoin his associate in the teller line, Betsy also noted for the first time an old scar on his left cheek. She grabbed the first papers within reach and fled back to her office.

When she was sure he had left the building, Betsy came back down to the lobby and approached the teller at the window who had serviced the Hispanics.

"Diane, those swarthy men who were at your window about fifteen minutes ago. Who are they?"

"You mean Mr. Valdes? I don't know who the other man was, but he kept looking around like he was some kind of bodyguard or something. Even with that coat on he sure looked like he had muscles."

"Do they come in here much?"

"Pretty much! At least Valdes does. There's always someone with him and not always the same person. I've noticed his cohort of the day is usually carrying car keys. Maybe his various associates are drivers. Raul Rojas in consumer brought the account in. They seem to put a lot of money through it. No one has said anything to me about anything being irregular. I think he owns that Colombian restaurant, Casa Camilio, over near Kmart."

Betsy continued to probe the teller. "When you say a 'lot of money,' do you mean cash?"

"No," Diane said. "They never even get close to the daily federal limits for cash, but they always put in about three to four thousand dollars a day. The 'big money' they deposit comes in via large denominated checks – usually $10,000 or more – and there are a lot of them."

Betsy thought to herself, "If their prices are that steep, I will remember not to eat at Casa Camilio."

"Anything wrong?"

"No – just curious. Will and I just met him last weekend. What's his first name?"

"Miguel. His restaurant must have been going full speed almost immediately after the power came back on. He sure kept bringing us substantial money on a regular basis. He must have a good business, and he must have connections. You know he drives a Rolls. I've heard the girls in the drive-up talk about it."

When Betsy went back up to her office, she found the account numbers she was looking for in the computer – Valdes Enterprises L.L.C. dba Casa Camilio. Betsy observed that the average balance on this account was substantial by any standards and out of the ballpark for a restaurant. The address on file did not correspond to the street address on the restaurant. There was no personal account for Miguel Valdes.

As she paged through the history of the L.L.C. account she saw that Diane's assessment was right. Quite a bit of money did pass through this account. Six figure amounts were common. Normal she thought for a successful restaurant until she noticed wire transfers of funds out, many going to South and Central American countries.

Later in the morning Betsy pulled up the new account documentation on Valdes Enterprises on the computer. The authorized signers on the account included not only Miguel Valdes but also Omar Perillo and Adolfo Soltero.

"Small world," she commented to herself.

Betsy wrote down all relevant useful information the file could yield including addresses and phone numbers of the principals.

Chapter 31

*J*oe Rooney managed to borrow the conference room in Stuart to hold the first office-wide meeting the Vero Beach office had had since Hurricane Clarice. As he waited for the meeting to start, Will Black saw staff members he had not seen since the storm. RST's Stuart office had not had enough empty offices to house all of the displaced Vero Beach staff. Some employees had been reporting to Stuart each day. Others had been working out of their homes. Some had even been working out of other offices. A few who had had their homes severely damaged or destroyed had not been working at all.

When everyone was present, Rooney called the meeting to order.

"It's really great to see all of you back together. I wish we were in our office, but this beats nothing. I know some of you had extensive house damage, but, thank the good lord, no one other than Dave Tressler was killed or hurt. We still don't know exactly what happened there. Maybe we never will. As horrible as that was I guess we should be thankful the rest of us lived to fight another day.

"First let's talk about the office. It looks like we won't be back in our building until at least Thanksgiving. For those of you who want to continue coming here we'll pay mileage. If you would rather hook up a remote connection at home we'll help with the necessary technical support. We have finally located a general contractor, but he can't replace anything in the building anyway until all the damaged material is ripped out and disposed of by a properly certified mold remediation contractor. You all know that every room in our building has mold problems. This will be addressed after the roof is replaced. We do finally have plywood on the broken windows so the building should start drying out. If you need files in the building, you'd better get them out now. The firm's official position is they do not want you in the building and will not be responsible if you get injured. This is a tough situation, and we're just going to have to make the best of it. It's just going to take time. Our office will return to normal. Your homes will also return to normal. You've done a yeoman's job so far. You now know pretty much what I do. New York is negotiating for the contractors for the interior work. Our landlord is taking care of the rest.

"Now let's move on to Dave Tressler. I can't imagine why he chose to remain in his office to ride out the storm. The police have officially declared his death as the accidental result of his being at the wrong place at the wrong time. As far as they are concerned the case is closed. I hope you will extend not only your condolences to Connie and the kids but offer to help them if you can. I saw most of you at Dave's funeral. The office did send flowers. I know Connie was glad to see Dave's co-workers cared enough to come even though their lives also were in upheaval. Believe me when I tell you every effort will be made by the firm to make sure she gets everything she is entitled to.

"We have an obligation to make sure that Dave's clients are serviced properly. I am going to reassign Dave's accounts today so you can begin to call them and make sure we are meeting their financial needs. I've tried to talk to each of you in private to see if there were some of his clients you might have had a previous relationship with. As you know the firm has a standardized system for reassigning accounts. Each of you has a power index determined by the firm's assessment of your contribution and importance to the office. We all know this system favors larger producers. I'm not going to debate the merits of firm policy in this regard. That's simply the way things are. I do not have complete files on Dave's clients – the files are in various locations in our old building. Since Dave's office took a bigger hit than anyone's in the whole building, it's possible some files may be in bad shape or may not even exist. Call everyone that I assign you today if possible and start to get to know these people. Take notes when you talk to them. If you don't take notes, by tomorrow a lot of what people tell you will start to run together. Let these people know that you and the firm care. And for God's sake, be sensitive to their feelings when it comes to matters regarding Dave. Some of these people have dealt with him for a long time. Operations and I will be here to help you anyway we can.

"When I call your name come up and get your list. These accounts should have already been put in your number. If they haven't, let me know about it. I've tried to keep one family with one broker by coordinating things with Dave's sales assistant. If you have a problem with an assignment, don't take it to her. Bring it to me.

"That's all I have unless you have something for the group. If not – good to see you, and let's get to work."

Will retreated to his office after the meeting to examine the list that he had just received from Rooney. Before he could even look at it Rooney came in his office and shut the door.

"Just so you'll know, I gave you anything I suspected of being related to the Superior situation."

"Gee, thanks. You're a pal," Will replied sarcastically.

"I did it on purpose. I want to keep a lid on this whole situation if possible and not have it all over the office. Definitely don't want our business all over town. But don't worry – I don't think I shafted you. There are some good sized assets in some of these accounts. I jimmied the system to give you what you would have gotten with your normal power index. Then I added these on top of that. So if they blow up or go away entirely, you're going to be at the same place you would have been anyway, and if some of them work out, you'll be way ahead of the game. If there's some compliance issues they'll get laid off on Tressler. I'll help you where I can. If it turns out to be a honey pot instead of a latrine, it'll all belong to you."

"I hope you're right."

"Don't worry. Trust me on this one. Worst case scenario is you end up where you would have ended up anyway. It's a win-win."

Chapter 32

*W*ill dialed the phone number listed on the account summary page of his computer for Superior Holdings.

No answer. He pulled out the folder he had spirited away from Dave's filing cabinet and started searching it. Good thing I didn't return this, he thought. On a pink Post-it with the name Al written beside it he found a different phone number.

He dialed and a man answered gruffly. "Servicios Temporales Superiores."

"Oh, excuse me I was calling for Al Soltero at Superior Holdings. I must have dialed a wrong number," Will blurted out.

"Who wants him."

"Wilson Black."

"Who's Wilson Black?"

"Will Black with Reynolds Smathers and Thompson. He has an account here."

"I'll see if he's here. Wait."

"Mr. Soltero? Will Black – Reynolds Smathers and Thompson."

"I know who you are."

"My manager assigned me the Superior Holdings account. I'm calling to introduce myself and to see if I can set up an appointment to learn more about your needs so we can make sure your account is serviced properly. I assume you know about Dave Tressler."

"I know."

"We will certainly miss him. He was a valued employee. When would it be convenient for us to get together?"

"I don't know what I'm going to do with that account."

"May I ask just exactly what type of business Superior is in?"

"Investments."

"Exactly what kind of investments?"

"Various."

"Oh! I see. I couldn't help but notice this account carries pretty substantial balances at times but the balance is very low right now comparatively speaking. We certainly hope you will give us the opportunity to earn your business," Will plowed on nervously.

"Send me your card. If I need you, I'll get back to you."

"Is there any information or research that I can include with my card?"

"No."

"Thank you for your time."

Will saw Rooney and motioned for him to come into his office. "I just had the most one way conversation with Señor Soltero I've had with anyone in a long time. You talk about playing things close to the vest. I don't know if I know one more thing about him than when I called except he exists and he doesn't use the phone number on our computer. And you ought to talk to his receptionist. This guy sounds like something left over from *On The Waterfront*."

"So how'd you leave it?" Rooney asked.

"I am to send him my business card so, who the hell knows. I may have an account, or he may come over here and cut my throat."

Chapter 33

Things were quiet for the next week. Will sent out his business card attached to a handwritten note on his company scratch pad, but he didn't try to follow up on the mailing. One day he got a copy of a receipt in his mail slot that a check made out to Superior Holdings had been hand-delivered earlier that morning. The check was drawn on Valdes Enterprises' bank account. The amount was $50,000. The "for" line simply said "payment in full for services rendered." There was no further contact with Soltero.

Two days later another check was delivered for $25,000 written from the same account with the same "for" line. There had still been no contact. He started watching for the courier.

Checks then started arriving daily. The courier was a Spanish looking man he had never seen before. Amounts varied – the "for" line always read the same. Still no attempted contact.

When Will pulled up the account, it now had a net worth of half a million dollars.

He didn't know what to do. Should he just let things rock along or should he attempt to contact Soltero? It seemed obvious that Soltero knew what was going on. He finally worked up the nerve to call.

"Señor Soltero..."

"Please call me Mr. Soltero."

"Mr. Soltero, I've noticed the deposits coming into your account since our last conversation..."

"I know."

"Should I expect this to be a trend? If so, it's a really nice trend. We really appreciate your business. The value of the account is now large enough we might consider diversifying it into some of the many investment options offered by our firm. As I told you last time we talked, I would welcome the opportunity to meet with you and determine how we can best serve your investment needs."

"Don't waste that line on me. Save the standard crap for your little old ladies. I'll let you know when I want something different."

"Yessir."

"Have a nice day. You'll hear from me. You'll know when I want something."

Will mulled over the curt conversation until lunch. He then decided he would investigate and see just where Señor Soltero was located. He printed out the address and told his sales assistant he had some errands to run in Vero Beach.

The address was on a nondescript gravel farm road on the west end of town. There were orange groves on both sides of the long straight road that ran parallel to State Road 60. There was an occasional house or barn, but the road consisted mostly of acre after acre of groves. A canal ran down one side of the road. After driving a couple of miles, Will came to an intersection developed into a commercial corner. There was a country store and gas station on the southwest corner. Cattycorner from this was a little independent used car lot. To the north of it was a house that appeared to be a residence surrounded by a chain link fence. The number on the mailbox was the one on his printout.

That's a strange place to sell cars, Will thought. *Out here in the middle of absolutely frigging nowhere.*

He went into the convenience store to buy a Diet Pepsi. The majority of the customers were Hispanic, as was the clerk. The store had a security guard.

Weird! Will thought. *Why would a little pissant store in the middle of nowhere that looks like it sells to migrant workers need a security guard?*

The store also had security cameras.

Either the owner is paranoid, or this place is rougher than it looks, Will said to himself.

Then he noticed a man sitting on a resin lawn chair on one side of the building. Standing behind him was another Latino who appeared to be a lookout and guard for him. Manual-labor-looking men would approach him with checks. He would do a quick calculation on a hand calculator and give them cash in return. It reminded Will of the shade tree money changing services he used to see in Jamaica.

I'll be damned, Will said to himself. *They're running an outdoor check cashing service.*

Will bought his drink, and sat in his car sipping it. He observed that maybe he had been wrong. There were customers at the car lot. As he sat and watched something else bothered him. Most people were not talking to car salesmen or doing window shopping; they were using the used car lot as a parking lot and going through the gate in the chain link fence up to the adjacent house. A tough-looking Latino was admitting people into the house.

There was a big barn-like structure adjacent to the house. Occasionally, another man dressed in khakis and a knit shirt would open a large gate for a car to drive through and then close it.

On a whim Will decided to get a closer look at the car lot. He locked his car door and walked over to the dealership. Will expected a salesman to descend on him, but he strolled around and peeked in car windows no one approached. Most of the salesmen were standing around smoking.

Will noticed the security guard had walked out of the store and was jotting down his car tag number so he figured maybe it was time to leave.

Chapter 34

*W*ednesday morning arrived. Will had gotten a notice Betsy's car was overdue for servicing. He made an appointment at the GM dealership late that morning. This was the first time Will had seen the dealership since the storm. He was shocked by what he saw. Entire showroom windows had imploded. The acoustical ceiling tiles were completely missing, exposing the building's metal superstructure above. Water damage was apparent everywhere. The only things in place were the mounted billfish trophies on the walls.

Will checked the car in at the service desk. He was told the job would take probably an hour or so. Before starting to kill time reading a dog-eared-magazine in the half-lit waiting room, Will decided he would wander around the car lot and see what other damage Clarice had done to the property. Oak trees planted to beautify the dealership were now having the opposite effect. They gave the premises a Transylvanian look. Acorns crunched and popped under his feet.

The shopping center across the street looked no better. Plywood was still nailed to most windows. Plastic signs looked like vandals had been hitting them with a hammer. There were "open" signs, however.

He noticed a sign for Casa Camilio on one of the out parcels.

"Well, I'll be damned! There's the restaurant that belongs to Miguel Valdes. Maybe I'll go in there and get a bite."

Will told the service manager where he was going and then went across to Casa Camilio.

It seemed to be doing a brisk lunch business. An attractive olive-complexioned girl who appeared to be in her early twenties asked Will if he preferred a booth or table. He chose a booth. The restaurant was decorated with semi-abstract brightly colored original pictures. Many were primitive portraits painted with acrylics by the same artist. These were interspersed with landscape paintings of tropical locations and more abstract equally colorful paintings. He noticed one picture with a familiar style. It had butterball overweight figures staring in a deadpan manner at the viewer. Will detoured over to look at the picture closer. It was signed Fernando Botero.

"I've seen this painter in art books," he commented to the hostess. "Do you think this is an original?"

She looked blankly at him and placed his menu on the table. Will ordered a cup of coffee. He looked at an abstract painting over his booth. It was an oil signed Alejandro Obregon. He wasn't sure who Obregon was, but he made a note to himself to pull the name up on the Internet when he had a few minutes.

Will glanced at the menu. It was definitely exotic to him. He saw arepas, empanadas paisas, plantains, and ají. Beef and beans were popular ingredients. There was yucca and cactus. He finally settled on a breaded beef dish and ordered it when the waitress returned.

While waiting for his food, Will looked around the restaurant. There were few Anglos. Must be good food he thought since the Latinos dine here. The restaurant's patrons seemed to be enjoying a leisurely lunch.

There was a door leading to a back room. Men came and went in a businesslike manner. That must be the office, Will thought.

Will's lunch was finally served. The portions were extremely generous.Will finished over half of the massive meal. As he waited for his check, Will thought maybe this would be a good excuse to meet Miguel Valdes if he happened to be at the restaurant.

When the waitress brought his check he asked, "Doesn't Señor Valdes own this restaurant?"

She looked uncertain.

"Would you check and see if he is here? Will Black would like to speak to him."

He gave the waitress one of his Reynolds Smathers and Thompson business cards.

Will waited for about five minutes. The waitress continued to serve other diners. Finally, a man came out of the door and addressed the waitress in a low voice. She then came back to Will's table.

"Señor Valdes will see you now," she said.

The waitress led him through the closed door Will had seen other people entering and exiting. They walked down a hall with doors on both sides. These doors were all closed and appeared to be locked. About midway down the hall a door opened and a man exited. Will noticed while the door was open, this office had a window. Outside the window, trailered behind the building, Will saw the Baja Outlaw they had encountered on the river. He shuddered .

Will was shown into a small office. Sitting at the desk was the same man Will had seen at Dave Tressler's wake. He also recognized the same two toughs who had accompanied Valdes to the funeral home. They nodded and eyed Will suspiciously but without recognition. This was definitely the same man who had made the rude comment about "how my money is being spent" to a nervous Connie Tressler at Blue Horizons Funeral Home. What claim did he have on Connie? Why was Connie being pressured to give him some or all of Dave's insurance?

"Maria says you want to see me?"

"Yes, Señor Valdes. I was having lunch in your restaurant while my car is being serviced across the street and thought I'd take the opportunity to introduce myself," Will prattled nervously.

"Why would you want to see me – you get a bad meal?"

"No, sir. Actually it was quite delicious," Will plowed on. "I apologize for being presumptuous. I thought possibly you might recognize my name. I saw you at Dave Tressler's wake. I also took over Señor Soltero's account at Reynolds Smathers and Thompson."

"So you're taking over where Tressler left off?"

"Yes, sir. I will do everything I can do to manage the investment portfolio as well as Dave did."

"So you're our new investment man?"

"For your Reynolds Smathers and Thompson portfolio."

"And for Macadamia and Spoonbill?"

"I'm not sure what you're referring to," Will lied.

"Soltero didn't send you over? Forget you ever heard those names. Understand?

If we need you we'll call you."

Before Will could respond, one of the men opened the door for him to leave.

Chapter 35

*L*ife in Vero Beach continued toward normal. Will and Betsy even invited Guy and Penny over for a Saturday cookout. It seemed the perfect way to end the week to watch the big Florida-LSU football game, and cook some steaks. Penny made slaw and potato salad; Will and Betsy provided the ribeyes, and Publix provided the key lime pie. It was the first big test of the season matching two SEC teams.

Will put a Terry Cassidy album on the stereo that he had brought back from the Keys the previous year. Terry sang,

> *I'm hooked on the easy life*
> *down here in the lower Keys*
> *I guess I'll stay forever*
> *It's the only life for me*

"We got to know Terry when we were staying at Dolphin Marina in Little Torch," Will told the Walshes. "Really nice fellow. He sure makes you want to go there."

Despite everyone's best intentions, there was no avoiding shop talk. As they hung out in the kitchen snacking on a veggie tray and ranch dip, Guy unfolded two newspaper ads he had in his pocket.

"Has the stock market been especially bad?" he began.

"Not especially," Will said. "Up about six and half percent year-to-date plus dividends, and that's after the give-back we had in July. It's been in a sideways trend since then, but it didn't use September as an excuse to go in the tank."

"Exactly! The naysayers are naysayers, but we have bears every year. By historical standards, stocks are not over-priced. But since the fear mentality in the wake of Hurricane Clarice, look at how this bank is trying to milk a scared, unsophisticated public."

He spread one of the ads on the counter.

STOCKS ARE DIVING FAST

DON'T LET YOUR SAVINGS SINK TOO!

The stock market is in a volatile cycle with millions being lost daily and slim prospects for a quick recovery. First Federal Bank can rescue you from sinking investments with a variety of safe, secure and insured savings products...

Don't let your investments sink lower, Move your money to a First Federal Bank High-Yield Savings account today!

Safe. Secure. Insured

FIRST FEDERAL BANK

The ad showed a drawing of a skin diver holding a downward pointing arrow that said "STOCK MARKET." On the diver's scuba tank was printed, FDIC.

"Can you believe this shit?" Guy was so agitated that he was almost yelling. "We could never get away with printing lies like this. And they're doing it not because the stock market has been crappy but because the public has had the piss scared out of them in a hurricane."

"Number one – we wouldn't want to," Will agreed. "Number two – thank God we don't have to."

"Can you imagine what kind of compliance department one of these little pissant banks has to have?" Guy said as he laughed. "Six months ago I couldn't spell compliance and now I is one."

"You hit it right on the head. What's the other article you have?" Betsy asked.

"You're gonna love this one." Guy giggled.

The ad said,

Who's Approving Your Mortgage Loans?

Since when did a bank's ability to approve and close a mortgage loan depend on some unnamed, unknown "investor"? At Atlantic Bank we serve our communities, which include funding long-term mortgages in-house at a competitive rate...

WE WANT TO BE **YOUR** BANK

The ad showed a huge color picture of Bozo the Clown wearing a funky bow tie, smoking a giant cigar, with his oversized feet on top of his desk.

Betsy now looked like she was the one who wanted to go for the jugular.

"I thought you'd feel like that," Guy added with a chuckle.

"We would never, never run a tasteless ad like that," Betsy said, her face red. "I can't believe these small local banks run inappropriate garbage like this."

"Don't you love the financial services industry? And for years you bankers thought we brokers were sacrilegious scumbags," Guy teased. "Note, Lady Macbeth, both of these ads were run by banks."

"Ok! Ok! You made your point," Penny said, as she playfully chastised her husband.

"Changing the subject, who needs a drink?" Will asked. "I've got some information on the late Mr. Tressler to bring you guys up to date on. Ever heard of the Casa Camilio on Highway 1?" How about Miguel Valdes?"

"The restaurant, no. Miguel Valdes, I think so," Guy said. "Seems like I remember that name in relation to Adolfo Soltero."

"Good memory! I don't think I've had a chance to tell you I had lunch at the Casa Camilio one day."

"Oh, Yeah? Interesting?"

"Lunch was good, but there were other things a lot more interesting. First of all, this is no Denny's. The owners obviously have money. Every heard of the painter, Fernando Botero? The artist that draws unusual pictures of obese people?"

"Oh, sure," Penny replied. "I read in The New York Times that those paintings bring a lot of money."

Betsy added, "I've read about Botero also. Critics say his subjects aren't fat but baroquely inflated."

"Bingo – high end stuff – I'm positive these were not prints. And that ain't all," Will continued. "I wrote down the name at the bottom of this really strange looking original abstract. I'm sure it was an oil. It was signed by an Alejandro Obregon..."

Penny excitedly interrupted. "He was in the same Times article as Botero. The article called him the Picasso of Colombian art. That wasn't some hash house you were in if the owners can afford artwork like that. Museums collect works by both of those guys."

"I figured as much," Will continued. "And you're not going to believe what else I saw there – the same Baja that bushwhacked us on the river was on a trailer behind this place."

"Small world," Guy said. "The Tressler affair just keeps getting more interesting."

"Let's kick this thing around for a second before the game comes on. Just what do we know?" Will proposed.

"Well, we know for sure that Dave had some involvement with these Colombians and it was not something sanctioned by RST," Betsy said.

"Yeah, he was an agent for them, or he was letting them use their RST account in a questionable manner or something," Penny continued.

"And we know these Colombians are very sensitive about strangers nosing into their affairs," Will said.

"Plus they don't hesitate to go on the offensive when they are riled."

"And we know that seemingly unrelated accounts at my bank are somehow related," Betsy added.

"And the car lot west of town is probably not what it seems..." Will said.

"We know they can put their hands on big money pretty easily," said Penny.

"And don't forget that their presence seemed to intimidate Connie at Dave's wake," Betsy said.

"And Connie hinting that Dave's income has been going up when I know damned well his RST income has been flat," Will said.

"So where does all this leave us?" Penny asked.

"It sounds like to me we need to learn more about Valdes and Soltero," Guy said. "Why don't you and I mosey out one day and take another look at that used car lot?"

"I also think we need to consider some of the other people Tressler financially victimized," said Betsy.

Will added the names of Tommy Tressler, Ralph Ness, Wally Beach and even Dave's father-in-law, Mike Pollard.

The game turned out to be a honey. Some called it "the greatest game ever played." Florida began the fourth quarter with a 24-14 lead, but the Tigers made five fourth-down conversions, took the lead with 1:06 remaining and LSU won, 28-24.

Chapter 36

Will called Guy Sunday morning and suggested they go to the car lot.

"Why don't we go out there after lunch?" Guy said. "And I've got an even better idea. Since I've got bike racks on my car, I'll pick you up. We'll park my car a mile or so away from the convenience store and ride our bikes there instead."

Will liked the idea.

Guy picked Will up after lunch, and they headed out State Road 60. They turned north on the county road and soon found a good place next to a country produce stand to park. Guy and Will unloaded their bikes and started peddling up the asphalt road. The weather was gorgeous. They began to experience that first nip of fall. Will and Guy talked as they rode.

"Do you have a plan when we get to the car lot?"

"To be very honest, no I don't. Since it is Sunday I thought maybe we could just poke around and play it by ear."

"If nothing worse we can say we got some exercise and got out of the house," Guy agreed. "I see the store about three hundred yards up."

Will and Guy approached the Stop and Go. Instead of the parking lot being empty as they had expected, there was a crowd of about ten Hispanic men hanging out and chatting in Spanish. Some were drinking beer and wine coolers. Most appeared blue-collar. There were two cars that stood out from the rest. Both were new black Mercedes – one a sedan, and the other an SUV. Each had a driver leaning against the door who was talking to some of the men in the crowd. The drivers stood out because they were better dressed than the other men mingling in the parking lot. Will and Guy noticed Omar Perillo, who appeared to be in charge. He was holding discussions with men in the crowd one at a time. Others seemed to be patiently waiting for their turn to talk to him. As Perillo would finish with each man, he would sometimes give the man a slip of paper. Sometimes money would change hands. Some were dismissed with a gentle slap on the shoulder; others received a squeeze on the shoulder blades or arm. The men never returned the gesture but deferentially moved on to make a place for the next person.

Guy whispered to Will, "I know you're not a car nut, but you're looking at a quarter of a million dollars worth of cars there. That S 600 has a V-12 with 510 horses that can go zero to sixty in four and a half seconds. That ML 550 SUV has a V-8 with 382 horses. It has five-speed four-wheel-drive."

"I'm impressed," Will replied.

"Let's not stop here," Guy suggested. "Let's peddle on a little farther and then pull our bikes over on the edge of the road and sit there like we're resting."

"I need a drink of water anyway."

As Will and Guy sat on the side of the road and watched, cars were brought out of the barn up by the house and men from the Stop and Go got in them and drove away. Other cars were then driven from the used car lot into the garage to replace them. The crowd gradually disbursed.

Guy and Will got back on their bikes and rode back to where their car was parked. They loaded the bikes and started the drive home.

A red light caught them about half way back into town. Will noticed Guy kept looking out of his rear view mirror.

"Anything wrong?" Will asked.

"That ML 550 SUV – it's behind us."

When they got back over to Will's subdivision the black SUV didn't try to enter the gated neighborhood. Instead it kept going south on A1A.

Guy dropped Will off and headed to his house.

Once Guy got back on A1A he noticed the SUV behind him again. It followed him all the way to his house. When Guy pulled in his driveway it pulled up behind him. With their car idling, two burly Hispanic men got out. Guy recognized them from the Stop and Go.

"My employer thought he recognized the man with you," one said in a heavy Spanish accent. The other man glared at Guy. "He was wondering if he might help you with something. Asked us to find out your name and where you live in case he ever needed to mail you anything."

"Guy...Guy Walsh," Guy said. He felt a knot in his stomach. He couldn't believe these two thugs had followed him to his house. "I can't think of anything I need."

As soon as he said it, Guy thought that was a stupid statement, but he was too dumbfounded and scared to know what else to say.

The thugs said nothing. They just gave him the once-over again, got back in the SUV and left. Guy felt cold sweat on his brow.

"Who was that?" Penny asked when he came in the house.

"Someone who I wish didn't have our address," Guy replied.

"I think I'll call Will and give him a heads up."

Chapter 37

*M*onday morning started pleasantly for Will. He decided to drive down A1A to Stuart instead of taking Highway 1. He opened the sun roof on his car to take advantage of the cool early morning fall air. Will could smell the salty air blowing in from the Atlantic. Traffic was nonexistent as he passed condo after condo. He could almost pretend the condos didn't exist since most appeared empty, the snowbirds having delayed their winter trip back to Florida because of Clarice. Will came over the inlet, and got that view he never tired of from the top of the bridge of both the river and the ocean. He passed the power plant, and then there were wide open spaces that stretched several miles until he approached the Martin County line. The vegetation still looked raggedy and butchered from the storm, but the road was marvelously clear and his alone. On his left he could enjoy the calm Atlantic, on his right the intercoastal. Once he got into Martin County traffic picked up slightly, but all the bridges were down, and he continued to make excellent time and soon scooted into Stuart on East Ocean Boulevard. The only thing that nagged at him on the idyllic drive down the coast was Guy's phone call the night before.

Will listened to the pre-opening research call. There was an upgrade on Williams Companies and underweight calls on both Cablevision and Eli Lilly. The large pharma analyst predicted the Merck pipeline of new products was finally improving and upgraded the stock. The price target for John Deere was raised. The economist called for a mixed environment for the bond market, and pronounced the stock market to be valued fairly. There seemed to be nothing especially frightening on the horizon. Looked like the week would be low stress and uneventful. Uneventful is sometimes good, Will thought, and he started perusing his e-mails to see if there was anything that needed his immediate attention. The market opened steady, confirming the prediction that the strategist had made on the call earlier. Will thought about the scene he and Guy had witnessed on Sunday. He wondered why the cars were taken to and from the barn and then driven away by the men hanging around the Stop and Go. He wondered also about the godfather-like scene happening simultaneously. He wondered if these cars were being used to traffic drugs or if they were a source of a getaway for illegal aliens. Maybe he was reading too much into the whole damned thing. Why were the Colombians so protective of their turf? And just what the hell were they protecting?

About mid-morning Will left his desk to go to the copying machine. When he returned to his desk, Omar Perillo was sitting in his office. Barbara apparently had been away from her desk and had found him sitting there when she returned.

"Señor Perillo! What a nice surprise to see you! What brings you to Stuart? Have you met my assistant Barbara?" Will blurted, trying not to sound nervous, holding out his right hand. "What can I do to help you this morning?"

"May we talk in private?" Perillo said.

"Sure, let me close my door."

"Mr. Black," Perillo began, "Why have you recently taken an interest in me and my colleagues?"

"If you mean yesterday," Will alibied, "It was purely coincidence that my friend and I decided to ride our bikes yesterday out by your store."

"If that were the only time a coincidence had occurred recently I might believe you, but there have been multiple coincidences," Perillo said. "Many coincidences often are not coincidences. Do you follow my drift?"

"Señor Perillo, I felt if we at RST were going to be able to continue to serve your needs with the same efficiency as Dave Tressler, I needed to understand your affairs better," Will lied.

"Please understand. I am not here to be argumentative. I do not want to doubt your word, but, as we both know, I don't have an account with you. It is my friend Adolfo Soltero who has a relationship with your firm, not me. Now tell me what is going on. Why are you shadowing me and my friends?"

"Señor, first let me make my apologies. My seemingly intrusive behavior has not been restricted to you or your associates. As you may or may not know, my wife, a friend, and I found Dave Tressler's body after the hurricane. It was a very unnerving experience. It was especially distressing since we knew him. Maybe we overreacted to a gruesome situation, but we all thought there was more to the misfortune than what appeared on the surface. Since that time we tried to familiarize ourselves with Dave's contacts and associates. We felt like we owed this to his widow and children. I am sorry if it seemed like we singled you out. The official version of Dave's death just didn't all add up in our minds."

"What do you think really happened?" Perillo asked.

"We really don't know. I guess we're just amateur sleuths with active imaginations, in over our heads."

"But why us?"

"OK, Señor Perillo, I'll level with you. We know that Dave was selling some partnerships not sanctioned by RST for some of your friends."

"How do you know that?"

"We found documentation Dave left behind in his office."

"Have you turned these documents over to anyone else?"

"No, we haven't."

"If Dave were our agent, as you allege, we would not have a reason to wish him harm. He would be an asset that my associates and our firm would prize highly."

"Asset?"

"Excuse me, I should have said employee. It would be a relationship that we would want to either nourish or dissolve, but dissolving it in a manner such as you are suggesting would be a little bit extreme. Don't you agree?"

"It certainly would be extreme in my eyes."

"And therefore illogical... Don't you agree? Our association with him would have been mutually profitable – the same kind of profitable relationship we might be in a position to offer to another qualified individual... such as yourself."

"Is that an offer?"

"Everything I say is hypothetical. And as long as we are on hypothetical statements I might suggest that it could behoove you and your friends to look more closely at Mr. Tressler's private habits."

"Private habits?"

"Yes, his private habits such as his attitudes on taking chance."

"Taking chances?"

"Lady Luck. Mind you, all I know is possibly small town gossip, but what I hear is Mr. Tressler was no stranger to games of chance."

"Has the rumor mill been specific about which lady might be most familiar?"

"No," Perillo said. "But I have been told that a good place to research matters might be the Internet. It offers a myriad of possibilities for a venturesome person. But let's talk about the other reason for my visit. Señor Soltero has been very satisfied with your services and gave you as a referral."

"What kind of RST account would you like to gather information about?" Will asked.

"Why don't you tell me what RST can do for me? By the way your friends, Guy and Penny Walsh, have a lovely home on Seagrape Lane."

Chapter 38

"*D*arling," Will said, as he stood in his bathrobe shaving, "Why don't you call the Walshes and see if they want to try to make happy hour at the Quail Valley tonight?"

"Happy hour, or happy hour and dinner?" Betsy asked.

"I don't care. Whatever the group wants to do. And make it whatever time suits the group. I'll bug out of Stuart as soon as the market closes. Just call me down there some time during the day and let me know what to expect."

"I think I can manage that, your majesty," Betsy replied, as Will climbed in the shower.

That evening, Will and Betsy arrived at the club before the Walshes. They ordered a drink and relaxed. Five minutes later, Guy and Penny walked into the club lounge.

"Sorry, we're running a few minutes late," Guy said.

"Hey, we just got here ourselves," Will said. "We're about half a drink ahead of you, but I'm confident you'll catch up."

After chatting about the stock market for a while, Will described Perillo's visit.

"He popped down to Stuart Monday unannounced and wanted to know why my sudden and intense interest in him and his associates. I tried being evasive, but that didn't work. He saw right through me, and demanded that I be candid."

"Wow!" Guy and Penny said.

"So I leveled with him, more or less. I told him that we were the ones – and I never used your name..."

"Thank God," Penny said with a sigh.

"...who found Dave Tressler's body, and the official version of the story didn't add up to us. I also admitted to him we knew about Dave's involvement with selling limited partnerships that were not sanctioned RST products."

"And then?"

"He wanted to know who we had turned the info over to."

"I told him no one."

"OK?"

"Then we started playing a cat-and-mouse game. He did not deny the limited partnership relationship. We started talking in hypotheticals. He said if such a relationship existed Dave would have been an important asset to his organization."

"Asset?"

"It's funny! I said the same thing. Then he changed the term to employee and said an employee was a relationship to be expanded upon if things were going well and terminated if things weren't, but there were less radical ways to terminate a failed relationship other than complete elimination."

"This is getting to be a deep hypothetical managerial discussion."

"Ummm Huh! He then hinted, hypothetically of course, that Dave's position in the organization would need to be replaced and wondered if I might be interested in learning more."

"And you said?"

"I sidestepped the issue."

"Go on."

"He then suggested that possibly Dave's personal interest in chance taking might have played a part in the picture. I asked, 'as in Lady Luck.' He responded affirmatively."

"This is really getting interesting."

"Then I went out on a limb and went fishing for what kind of gambling. Do you know what he suggested? He continued to stress that he was speaking hypothetically. He suggested a place to possibly start might be the Internet."

"Whoaa! Do you think he's in a position to know something?"

"I do. I think you shouldn't take these people lightly. And now are you ready for this – he opened an account with me – said Soltero had given my name as a referral."

"I don't know if I'd like that or not. It could get dicey."

"No shit! And not to worry you – he knew your name and where you live. He dropped a hint by saying you had a nice home on Seagrape. I swear I never used your name. I have rehashed my conversation with him every day this week. I never disclosed any facts on you. The only thing I ever said was that a friend was with me the day we found Dave's body."

"Gimme another drink!" Guy said. "Make it a double. All of a sudden I have a knot in my stomach. All this certainly puts a different light on things. What do you think?"

"Guy, I believe these people are dangerous and into some bad shit, but we don't really know exactly what. Could they have killed Tressler? I think they are capable, but I'm not sure of their motive!"

"I don't know what to think. We need to mull this over for a few days, and I guess we need to learn more about Internet gambling."

"I don't know whether to panic or not," Penny said, her voice shaking.

"I don't either. We thought we had picked up a hot ash, but maybe we've had our hand in the fire."

After another round of drinks, Guy and Will started talking shop. Suddenly Will remembered what he had to face the next day and sighed.

"As bad as I hate to break up this marvelous evening, we need to get on home," he said, draining his drink. "We've got to get up early in the morning."

"But tomorrow's Saturday," Penny said.

"We've got to go to Orlando for the continuing education test I've been grandfathered out of taking all these years. Well, they finally caught up with me. Under the new rules I now have to take it every three years," Will said with a grimace.

"I was notified that I've got to get that done before April," Guy added.

"Betsy's going with me. After the test we thought we'd have lunch in Orlando."

"Good idea! If you've got to go anyway, might as well have a little fun while you're there," Guy agreed. "Drive safely."

Chapter 39

*W*ill and Betsy got up at 5:30. Will had to be at the testing center by 8:30. They grabbed a cup of coffee at Dunkin Donuts on their way out of town. Will reminded Betsy this was close to the State Road 60 turnoff to the Stop and Go.

I-95 had very little traffic. The same was true of State Road 60. It was no different on the Beeline. Finding the center turned out to be a simple matter. It was a nondescript square, glass office building.

Will and Betsy took the elevator to the third floor and found Suite 300. An attractive black woman was waiting at the reception desk. Next to her was an elderly white woman.

"I am here for the ethics exam," Will announced to the receptionist, handing her his online test confirmation.

"When your guest leaves the building," the woman announced, "I will check you in."

The receptionist waited until Betsy left and then asked for Will's picture ID.

Will handed the black lady his driver's license and waited while she examined it and compared it to Will's face. The white woman continued to say nothing but watched as Will's identity was verified.

"Please put your right index finger on this screen," the black lady then said.

Will complied.

"Please put your right index finger on the screen again."

Will complied again.

"Please put your right index finger on the screen one more time."

Will looked at her quizzically but once again complied.

"Now please put your left index finger on the screen."

Will continued to cooperate.

"Now please sit in this chair so that I may take your picture."

Will did as told.

"May I see your picture ID again?"

The woman compared it to the picture that she had just taken.

"Yes it's still me," Will couldn't resist saying.

The white lady who had said nothing up to this point finally spoke.

"Please come with me," she said in a deep Southern drawl.

She led Will to a door not five feet from the black woman's desk and asked, "May I see your right index finger?"

She held Will's finger on the screen which compared it to the results from his previous fingerprinting.

"May I see your picture ID?" she asked.

Will couldn't resist commenting, "But I just showed it to the other lady and we've never left her sight."

"I'm sorry. I don't make the rules."

Will and the white lady were standing next to a steel door. The remaining portion of the wall was dominated by a large plate-glass picture window."

"Please look through this window and pick out your work station."

Virtually all were empty.

"I'll take number eight," Will quickly decided.

"When you enter this room you will be monitored by a camera at all times," the woman continued. "You will also be observed through this window. No one is allowed to talk once we pass through this door. I will log you into work station eight. If you need to leave the room during the exam, hold up your hand and I will escort you out."

She took Will to a machine and motioned to him with hand signals as to what she expected of him. She then left the room.

Will looked over his shoulder. The woman was watching him from the other side of the window.

"Sheeit!" Will mumbled to himself. "What is this business coming to?"

He glanced back over his shoulder guiltily.

The elder woman was looking right at him. Will could have sworn she could read his mind.

He hit the enter button.

Two actors filled the screen. One was a broker, obviously a big hitter from the size of her office. She was telling her manager about an international attorney named Sheila Rothenstein, an important international attorney who lived in Geneva and was her client. The client was giving a cocktail party for VIPs at her U.S. condo and had invited the broker and a guest to attend. The broker had chosen to take her manager as her guest. The actors went on to portray these and other associates of the attorney, introducing legal and ethical dilemmas for the broker and her manager that Will was expected to resolve. After thirty minutes Will had successfully completed the minefield-loaded exercise.

Will needed to go to the restroom. Without thinking he started to stand up. The elderly woman waved at Will in sweeping motions from the picture window to remind him he was only allowed to raise his hand and silently streaked into the room to prevent further infractions.

With no words being spoken, the woman quickly logged Will off his computer and led him to the door. Once out of the room she compared his fingerprints with those already on the computer monitor. She then led him the five steps to the black receptionist's desk where they once again repeated the procedure. He was then informed that the restroom was down the hall.

Within two minutes Will was back from the restroom and once again stood before the receptionist. She looked up and once again requested he present her with his picture ID and to place his hand again on the screen to check his fingerprints.

Will was incredulous, but gut instinct told him it would be best not to comment.

He passed the inspection. At this point he couldn't restrain himself from a sarcastic fake "Whew!"

Both women looked at Will humorlessly as the white one walked him the five steps to the testing room door and once again repeated the procedure before leading Will back to his work station.

Case number two. An investment banker busily at work on a big deal received an unannounced visit from her retiree uncle who wanted her to help him with an investment club proposal. She was called out of her office by her boss, and her uncle looked at some of the confidential information on her desk, mistaking it for a research report. A story continued to unfold as the situation escalated into the closest thing possible to an international investment crisis. Once again Will successfully negotiated the minefield-loaded situations, thereby saving the world. When finished he held up his fist in a mock gesture of victory.

The elderly woman merely looked at him from behind the picture window like he had lost his mind. Will quickly pulled down his arm and pretended he had just been stretching. His monitor looked relieved and satisfied.

On to the third case. Champ and still champ. Will had saved the world twice in one hour. A broker gets an e-mail meant for the head of his firm's research department giving him vital inside information on a public company.

Once again, Will met the challenge.

"Superbroker," he almost uttered before he noticed his shadow peering at him through the window.

Two hours later, Will was recertified and certain that he was in line for a citation for bravery and staggering deductive reasoning ability. It was time to sign off.

As he pushed his chair back from the work station, his monitor raised her hand as a reminder and came back into the room.

She motioned to Will he was not finished yet. She hit a button and Will saw he was expected to fill out an exit interview.

"How would you rate the testing center – one to five?"

Will diligently answered all their questions and rose to leave. As if by magic another set of questions appeared. Will answered them.

"What the hell," he said to himself. "I'm too close to the end to not finish the game."

Another set of questions appeared. After five sets of questions, Will was free to leave. As he left his fingerprints were checked one last time.

In the lobby Will was given a cell phone to call Betsy.

When he saw her outside, he only had one comment, "You ain't going to believe it. What a 'security system' process I have been through over the past few hours! Since nine eleven the world has changed more than I ever imagined! If this security process was applied to the rest of the world, we would have no terrorism or crime. Let's get the hell out of here."

Chapter 40

*T*hat following Monday Betsy checked to see if the Tresslers had an account at her bank, and it turned out they did. Dave's RST commission checks were direct deposited each month into an account that was in Dave's name only, and then a fixed lesser amount was transferred over to a joint account he kept with his wife Connie. The vast majority of the time this left funds behind. The statements on this single account went to a box at the beach post office. The statements on the joint account went to their home address. Betsy was virtually positive that Connie probably didn't even know the single account in Dave's name existed. When she looked at the activity in the joint account she saw what looked like normal expenses to run a household. There were checks to Publix, the house note, the utility bills, school-related expenses, car notes. Nothing that seemed out of the ordinary for a married couple with two kids. There was an occasional deposit when the account was low from Connie's father, Mike Pollard. Then Betsy looked at the single account that Dave did not seem to want Connie to know about. Not only were his paychecks being deposited there, but there were occasionally large deposits from other sources. These deposits were not direct deposited but resulted from checks made out to Dave. Despite the periodic large influx of cash, the average balance for the most part stayed modest. Then she noted some interesting outgoing activity. Dave cashed checks made out to cash several times a month that were over a thousand dollars each. That's a lot of walking-around money, Betsy thought. "Will's stash of petty cash isn't anywhere near that. Dave really must have been living large."

Then the name "Forex" caught her attention. Finally, there were multiple ongoing debit-card charges to something called BETUS.com.

What's a betus? she thought.

Then it hit her – "betus" –Bet Us! Of course. An online betting service! I'm not going to gather that information on my bank computer. If someone finds that on my office computer, I could be in a lot of trouble. I'll look this up at home."

She did however Google the word "Forex." Wikipedia had a listing.

The foreign exchange (currency or forex or FX) market exists wherever one currency is traded for another. It is by far the largest financial market in the world, and includes trading between large banks, central banks, currency speculators, multinational corporations, governments, and other financial institutions. The average daily trade in the global forex and related markets currently is over US $3 trillion. Retail traders (individuals) are a small fraction of this market and may only participate indirectly through brokers or banks, and are subject to forex scams.

There were eleven pages of information. Betsy printed them to show to Will when she got home.

"What in the devil was Dave doing having debit charges to Forex?" Betsy wondered.

She then hit "back" on her computer and other Web sites popped up.

Practice Forex trading. Free $100,000 Practice Account With Real-Time Charts...

Online currency trading with Forex club. Forex education for beginners and Advanced Forex tools for experienced traders. $50,000 practice account for new accounts...

Free Forex Forecasts...

Learning Forex Trading? Free Books, Guides, CDs and Demo accounts. Did we mention FREE? Plus 24 hr support.

There were 37 million Google entries for forex. The list of Web sites that offered to make you an immediate currency specialist with the lure of big profits went on and on. Betsy dialed Will at his office to tell him she had looked up Forex and inform him of the outflow of funds from Dave's account to BETUS.com. She told Will of her misgivings about accessing this possible hot potato on the computer at the bank.

"I agree," Will said.

That evening, Will and Betsy typed BETUS.com into their computer.

BETUS.com We've got your game.

Up to an Incredible 145% in bonuses!

50% Sign-up Bonus 25% Referral Bonus 10% Extra In Casino Chips

50% Reload Bonus 10% Gambler's Insurance

PLAY FOR FREE PLAY FOR MILLIONS IN THE BAHAMAS

Train with poker legend Daniel Negreanu

NFL Daily Lines

Boxing

"Boy," Will exclaimed. "They do it all."

"They've got more ways to lose money than Carter has little liver pills," Betsy agreed, "and I think Dave may have found them all. You wouldn't believe how many times a month his debit card transferred money to these people."

"And Connie thought Dave just lost a little money playing golf and betting football with his buddies," Will said with a sneer.

"Many months, more money went to BETUS and the Forex broker than they kept as an average balance in their household account," Betsy added.

"You know that as an employee of a NYSE member firm, Dave was not supposed to have any accounts other than his RST accounts without full disclosure and then, only after getting permission. He would never have been given permission to trade currencies on line, and if anyone had found out what he was doing on the sly he would have been fired, no questions asked," Will said.

"Why would he take that kind of risk?" Betsy said.

"He was obviously a very sick puppy," Will said. "He had to be hooked."

"Or maybe he dabbled and got behind and was trying to play catch up," Betsy said.

"And the harder you try to climb out of a hole, the deeper it can get."

"Poor Connie!" Betsy said.

"Good grief! What a goddamned fool! Let's call Guy and Penny and tell them what you have found out. Guy wanted me to tell him about my Orlando session anyway."

Chapter 41

*"H*aving a cocktail party at your office for the Christmas parade?" Will asked Guy, as they relaxed in Will and Betsy's swimming pool.

"You thinking about Christmas already? You gotta love Florida! You're thinking about Christmas and here we are chilling in a swimming pool, drink in hand."

"I'm thinking about that pony keg of ice cold Amber Bock draft you always have at the party," Will said. "Besides, it's closer to the holidays than you think. It's November. Hell, we're staring down the barrel of Thanksgiving."

"You're assuming that the city will have a Christmas parade this year, Guy said. "Did you burn a Christmas CD to give away this year?"

"Yes, I did. It was done before Clarice, and yes, I read in the paper there will be a parade this year. City officials believe people especially need for our local traditions to stay intact."

"By the way, I forgot to tell any of you, guess who called me at the office yesterday? Connie Tressler!" Will said.

"What did she want?" interrupted Betsy. "I hope you went out of your way to be nice. I really feel for her and the children."

"You know I did. She asked when the office was going to reopen. She also wanted to know if I would meet her down there so she could get Dave's personal effects. She asked if Dave's office had been cleaned up yet. I told her not really. His office was one of the worst hit and since no one needed to use it, it had been left pretty much alone except when the police were in it. I told her everything in it had, for all practical purposes, been trashed by the storm."

"So are you?" Penny asked.

"I told her I'd do it one Wednesday after work."

"Wonder why she suddenly is interested?" Betsy asked.

"I wondered that too," Will added. "I finally got her to admit that she's looking for Dave's good watch."

"Hmmm!" Guy said. "I'm really surprised she wasn't looking for that before now. Dave sure loved flashing that Rolex around so prospects would think he was a successful investment counselor."

"And everyone else he encountered would believe the mighty Mr. Tressler had arrived on the Vero Beach scene with style and panache," Will added sarcastically.

"Now don't be tacky, Will. Which reminds me, we haven't talked about Dave Tressler lately," Betsy added.

"That's because there's been nothing new to talk about."

"Why don't we summarize what we do know," Betsy continued. "Maybe lightning will strike one of us."

"Who wants to go first?"

"Dave Tressler's life was not as transparent as it seemed," Guy said.

196

"Or his death either," Penny added.

"That's for certain," Will said. "And Dave certainly wouldn't have satisfied Diogenes' quest to find one honest man."

"C'mon fellows, let's get serious," Betsy said. She began by summarizing Dave's online betting habits; she also mentioned his stupidity in selling limited partnerships not authorized by RST.

"Dave was the kind of guy that you either could easily like or hate," Guy continued.

"Yeah, hate. Like from even way back – like Wally Beach," Will said pensively.

"Why Wally?"

"According to Wally he was a major college prospect. Bobby Bowden recruited him. Dave ruined his chance to play major college ball with a cheap shot in practice when they were teammates at the high school. Took out his knee. He's held a grudge ever since," Will replied.

"Or a client like Ralph Ness. Will, remember the day we ran into Ralph at the convenience store?"

"Do I ever!"

"That's the first time I think I had ever seen how venomous a person could become when he feels like his broker had not been operating with his best interest at heart."

"People forget that we have a fiduciary responsibility to our clients, and these clients get very upset when that trust is breeched – real or imagined," Guy added. "I'm not sure you told me about this."

"Ralph was a client of Dave's who lost a sizeable chunk of money on naked options Dave had recommended," Will said.

"It's coming back to me. Also don't forget you told me about Dave's brother, Tommy."

"I absolutely cannot imagine treating my brother that way, or on the other hand him doing me that way either. Can you imagine selling your own mother an insurance policy, leading her to believe all her children will be equal beneficiaries, and then going behind her back and making yourself the sole beneficiary? What a sleaze! Why that stunt alone would be grounds enough to make someone want to kill him."

"You don't think Connie is a suspect, do you?" Penny asked.

"No way!" the remainder of the group said in unison.

"Let's not forget Mike Pollard," Betsy added.

"Mike's a great guy, but he sure got the shaft!"

"He did everything for that scum bucket except make his cold calls for him. Dave would never have even been granted an initial interview at Smith Barney if Mike hadn't sponsored him. The job description calls for a college graduate. This guy was lucky he graduated from high school. Talk about lucky in love. If he hadn't been Mike's son-in-law, Dave Tressler would have been selling aluminum siding or working in a retail store at the mall. And how did Dave pay Mike's generosity back? Mike had to keep bailing him out on compliance matters, and Dave tried to raid his customer base," Betsy said.

"Y'all have any thoughts on the Colombians?" Penny added.

"Yep, I don't think there's a soul here who isn't convinced they're scary SOBs who will do whatever it takes to make money," Will said. "I believe they'll lie, steal, or manipulate a situation in a heartbeat with no remorse, as long as it promotes business. They may or may not be our prime suspects. You had to be there when Omar Perillo came to visit me. He can be pretty convincing. These Colombians aren't saints, and they're obviously into a lot of questionable and illegal ventures. I'm also sure what we've been exposed to is just the tip of their iceberg. My gut feel is we don't want to know too much about their affairs. It could be dangerous to our health, but I'm not convinced that doing Dave Tressler in is going to go down on their resumé of accomplishments. Not that they gave a damn about Dave. I would suspect it strictly depends on whether on balance he was more useful to them dead or alive. We all know they were using Dave's services. But he was an outsider providing a service to them. It's entirely possible they could have been as surprised as any of the rest of us at his sudden demise. But if that is the case they're not going to admit it to us unless it becomes in their best interest to throw us a bone."

"So bottom line," Betsy said, "we still don't know any more now than we did. Let's talk about something more pleasant. Things like when do you think your office will reopen? Or when our girls are coming home from school for the holidays? Do you think many people will come to the parade? And, maybe one of us should write a letter to Santa and ask him to put a break in our stocking for this cold and apparently getting colder case."

Chapter 42

*R*ooney called a staff meeting Tuesday morning in the Stuart conference room. "We plan to be back in our office next Monday," he said. "I'm sure you're as sick of driving as I am. The office is not finished. We will have workmen under foot for who knows how long. Make up your minds you're going to live with things not being perfect for a while. I'm just going to shut Tressler's door for the time being. We'll tell the contractor to save his office for last. No one is using that office now anyway.

"On to something more pleasant. I want to let our clients know we're back in town. I'm going to plan a wine-and-cheese reception Thursday week so our clients can see the progress we've made. We'll start it when the market closes that afternoon. People can stop by on their way home from work. The bar's going to be in the parking lot. We'll put some tables and chairs down. It will be catered. You'll get a chance to see clients you haven't seen since the storm. We'll open the parts of the building that are presentable. Start deciding who you want to invite. This is going to be kind of an end to hurricane season; Thanksgiving; early Christmas; welcome back snowbirds; we appreciate your business; we're sorry you've been inconvenienced; we're back in town celebration; all rolled up in one. It's not going to cost you a dime."

The response was unanimously enthusiastic. Various people had ideas on decorations, choice of wines, whether there should be a full bar and so on.

Will rushed back to his office and called Connie Tressler.

"Will, I'm so glad you called. I was sitting here thinking about you."

"You must have ESP. I was thinking about you too. Since you wanted to get Dave's personal effects out of his office, we need to schedule a time. Rooney just announced the office will reopen next Monday and he's planning on having an open house for clients Thursday week. How about tomorrow?"

"Tomorrow would be perfect." Connie said. "I'd really rather not haul out Dave's things in front of everyone. I still feel funny talking about Dave to other people and having to answer questions. And. Will, thanks for thinking of me. Sometimes I feel so alone."

"I'll tell Rooney I'll meet you there after work tomorrow," Will said. It'll just be the two of us. You're going to need to bring some boxes. Dave's office is still just like the storm and the police left it."

"Will, forgive me if I act like a silly girl when I get there and start crying. I still can't believe all this has really happened. Tragedies like this are supposed to happen in some stranger's family, not your own."

"Connie I'm not going to say I know what you're going through because I don't. I really don't know how I'd react if Betsy were suddenly taken from me. I'd probably be the biggest baby in the world."

They agreed to meet at 5:30.

Chapter 43

*W*hen Will and Betsy rode into his office driveway at 5:30 Wednesday, Connie was waiting with the boxes she had brought. They hugged, and Will unlocked the door.

"Well, let's go see what kind of mess we're facing," Connie said.

The door to Dave's office was still marked with yellow police tape. Will tore it loose so they could enter. Very little inside had changed. The windows had plywood over them, but the rest was still in shambles. When Will looked at Dave's chair he got flashbacks of the day they had found Dave's body. He could almost see Dave sitting in his chair, and he could still swear there was a smell of the rotting corpse. He shuddered but tried to make sure the girls didn't see his reaction.

Connie just stood there as if in a trance. When she saw Betsy glance at her she pulled out of it. "I...I...I don't know where to start," she said.

"Let's try to do this in an organized manner," Betsy said. "Will, go get a couple of boxes and a trash can while Connie and I decide where to begin."

"I've made an executive decision," Betsy said, when Will walked back in. "We'll start with his desk."

Betsy opened the top drawer and Connie started going through it. Connie handed Will throwaway items for the trash can he had brought in. Other articles she put in the box to go home. Soon the first box was full.

Connie went through the desk drawers. When the last one was empty, she looked a little disappointed.

"Is there something you thought was here you didn't find?" Will asked.

"Yes. Remember the other day when I mentioned Dave's Rolex. We've never found it. I thought it might be here. Dave spent more on that Rolex than I paid for all the jewelry I own. He loved it. I ransacked the house and everywhere else I could think it might be. It's just vanished."

"Maybe it'll turn up somewhere else here. I'll keep my eyes open for it now you've reminded me of it," Will replied."

"Ouch!" Connie gasped. "I just stubbed my toe on something."

"Oh, you just kicked Dave's crystal ball," Betsy said.

"I'd forgotten all about that," Connie said. "Look! It has a red smear on it. I wonder if it's blood."

"I didn't notice that before," Will said. "Tell you what, let's leave it alone. I'll call Tom Mallette at the police department in the morning and see if he will stop by and pick it up. He can get his lab to analyze it."

"This is getting creepy," Connie said. "Let's try to get this job finished."

They worked for another hour, but the watch wasn't found.

"I guess I'll just have to keep looking," Connie murmured.

As they locked the door after Connie's car had been loaded, Will said, "I told you about the reception a week from Thursday. Please try to come. Everyone would love to see you."

"Let me think about it," Connie said. "I'll call you and let you know."

They all hugged one final time.

"Connie, please don't be a stranger, and please don't hesitate to ask us if you need anything," Betsy said. "You know we love you. Promise?"

"I promise."

Chapter 44

The first thing the following morning Will dialed Lieutenant Mallette at the Vero Beach Police Department.

"How is your DICK TRACY HOME STUDY COURSE coming along?" Mallette said. "Ready to graduate and join us full time? We're always looking for good men."

Will laughed and said, "As soon as my 2-Way Wrist Radio comes in, but it looks like I'm going to need more than that. We've learned some interesting things, but we're a long way from being able to draw any conclusions, much less prove anything. We still can't prove a crime was committed and Dave's death was not an accident."

"Welcome to the world of detective work," Mallette said. "As you can see it's not as easy as Agatha Christie makes it look. So what do I owe the honor...?"

"Tom, may I ask a big favor? Yesterday when I was trying to help Dave's wife gather up some of his personal effects in his office, we came across a decorative crystal ball in the rubble. It appeared to possibly have blood on it. Needless to say this upset Connie Tressler greatly. I left it where we found it. Would you send someone from the crime lab over to pick it up and analyze it?"

"I don't see why I couldn't do that for you, Will," Tom offered. "Since there's no open investigation, I can't press them to put the project on the top of their priority list, but we should be able to get back to you in a few weeks with the results."

"You're a pal. I owe you one. It may turn out to be nothing, but then again it may turn out to be something important."

"One thing I've learned in my twenty years plus of police work, you never know where an important clue is coming from. Sometimes something just drops out of the sky and is what we end up building an entire case around."

"Yeah, I think they mentioned that tidbit in my Dick Tracy manual. Before I forget it, remember the missing Rolex we mentioned? That was what Connie was most interested in recovering when she came over here. It was extremely expensive. Gold with diamonds all over the face. I do remember he wasn't wearing it the day we found the body. It stood out in my mind because it was probably the first time I'd ever seen him without that watch on."

"I can't say I blame her. If I had a piece of jewelry that expensive I would certainly be preoccupied with getting it back," Tom agreed.

"One last thing that has been bothering me is Dave's Harley," Will said. "It's really strange he had no transportation at the office the day we found the body. When my wife and I drove in the parking lot that day, no vehicle was there. That's one reason we were so surprised when we found him in the building. We knew from Dave's wife he was probably riding his Harley the night of the storm, but it wasn't in the parking lot. Do you think the storm washed it away, and we'll never find it? Or did he get to the office some other way?"

"Yes, funny you should ask, there is new information. And I mean I just got it. We called Tressler's widow to tell her we've recovered the bike. A Harley answering that description was reported by an elderly lady who lives near your office. I assume it's the one you're talking about. Anyway, I'll get someone over to your office today to pick up the crystal ball. Then as soon as I get a lab report I'll get back to you. In return I expect you to keep me posted on the watch situation."

"Sounds like I'm getting the best of the deals," Will said. "Just give me time to drive back up from Stuart, and I'll meet your man there whenever."

Chapter 45

Guy poked his head in Penny's door about mid-morning.

"You remember Angela Mauri, the wholesaler from Metropolitan in Tampa? She called about a week ago and wanted to do a product update and walk-through at ten. I told her fine, but now I have a client who wants to come in at the same time. Would you mind seeing Angela when she comes in?"

"Sure," Penny agreed.

"Good! If she sees I have a client in the office she'll be on him like a piranha. You know, according to Angela, everybody's a prospect for insurance or an annuity. In the meantime I'm going to close my door. That way I know she won't catch me."

"Don't worry. You're safe. I'll tell the receptionist to send her to me when she comes in," Penny said.

Soon Penny overheard a loud exchange with the receptionist.

"Angela Mauri, regional vice president, Metropolitan, howareyou? I brought some bagels for the office. Also how would you like a Metropolitan Snoopy doll?"

"I'm doing great. Thank you. I'll put the bagels in the kitchen," the receptionist replied.

"It's a good thing you're well because if you weren't no one would care anyway," Mauri said with a laugh. "May I see Guy?"

"Guy has a client. He'll be tied up for a while. He told me take you to Penny's office."

"Wonderful!" Angela said overenthusiastically but looking slightly disappointed. "I know where her office is."

"Penny!" the wholesaler beamed as she approached Penny's office. "Howareyou!"

"Great, Angela. It's good to see you."

"It's a good thing you're well because if you weren't no one would care anyway." The wholesaler grinned at her own joke as she stuck out her hand.

Angela Mauri was the prototypical young, well-educated, aggressive new generation of sales person. An incredibly fast-talking Bostonian with all the current buzz words and a light-bulb smile. You had the feeling if you pulled a secret cord the smile would automatically switch on. She appeared thirtyish and was dressed in a Brooks Brothers suit, subtle gold jewelry, and sensible navy business pumps.

Security wholesalers were the industry road warriors. Often their territory consisted of several states. Penny could visualize Angela returning to her low-maintenance condo on the weekends when she was not attending broker due diligence meetings in a fancy hotel.

Angela's wedding band stood out as she clutched her burgundy Coach briefcase. Her hairdo was designed to be done quickly in a motel room before the workday. Penny guessed she was married to someone similar to herself who traveled as well. Two clean-cut, well dressed ships that passed each other on weekends. They drove expensive cars, most likely leased. Her trunk was full of sales material. She had no children yet. She and her husband were too busy getting ahead. Angela never hesitated when traveling to have a drink after work or to go out for dinner with the boys. She always picked up the check. Her cell phone was constantly ringing; her Blackberry was never out of use as she waited impatiently in someone's lobby for the opportunity to sell her product. Her head was filled with sales quotas and always thinking ahead to her next stop.

"Come on in, Ang. Guy's going to be tied up for a while."

"How's biz? Other brokers in this region are selling a lot of our products. Anyone who isn't is missing an opportunity."

"Business is still a little slow. We had the hurricane back in September, and the town's still recovering," Penny said. "What can I do for you today?"

"Well, your business is about to take an upturn. The Met is on the cutting edge of the insurance industry. We have listened to what people in the field want, and we have designed the products to satisfy those needs. With these products you will earn the easiest five percent you've ever made. I don't see how your clients can say no. Being the one to introduce them to the Met will segue you from being just another advisor to being the client's primary or only advisor. When you see these progressive products you may even want to buy a Met product for yourself."

Penny wondered if the wholesaler owned her own products.

"Come on in and we'll talk about it. You won't need to see Guy because I'll relay everything you tell me. Here, I'll close the door."

"Penny, I know you guys are not insurance specialists, but you are doing your clients and yourself a disservice if you don't at least let them know you are in the life insurance business. If you don't mention insurance, I can guarantee you someone else will. Life insurance products have been dramatically improved over the last several years. The mortality tables being used permit insurance to be issued with lower premiums than in the past. The internal expenses of the products have been declining. The policies have more options and increased flexibility. Our policies have some of the most innovative riders in the industry. The future is available today. As you can tell, with products this good I'm pumped.

"And the best thing is you don't have to go through the learning curve on these products. You know why?"

She barged ahead without waiting for an answer.

"Because you have me! I'll do all the work. All you have to do is to get your clients to give you their existing policies for analysis. Get either the policies or copies of them to my internal and wait for a few days. Get me in front of the prospects, and I'll take it from there. You find 'em; I'll close 'em. You just made yourself the easiest five percent you ever made. I'll help your clients fill out the apps; my internal will make arrangements for them to get a physical. You'll be doing your clients a service as well as yourself. And I don't have to tell you, some of these can be really nice tickets – the kind of tickets that can make your month and kick you up to the next production level. Now, let me show you what the Met has to offer. You will be selling them the best, issued by one of the most widely known insurance companies in the world. By the way, you'll never get the objection the client is reluctant to deal with Metropolitan. *Everyone* knows the Met."

Angela reached in her rolling brief case and pulled out a sales brochure. As Angela barreled on, Penny's mind began to drift. She zoned out and found herself nodding zombie like at the appropriate times. How many times had she and Guy heard a similar story?

"...Mike Pollard over at Smith Barney bought..."

Penny suddenly zoned back in.

"I'm sorry. What did you say about Mike Pollard?"

"Well, you know Mike is a member of Smith Barney's Chairman's Club. He's Chairman's Club because he knows a winning product when he sees one. Mike has really become a believer in our variable life product. He fell in love with our variable policy which guarantees the cash values to grow by at least seven percent for the first ten years but gives you all the upside of the market. He also liked the long term care feature. He even bought some for a member of his family."

"Oh yeah! How do you know it was for his own family?"

"Because he asked me to get him the forms he needed to get the load waived on the policy. We do that for brokers with whom we have a relationship. If you ever need any insurance let me know, and I'll show you how it's done to really save you some money. You know what Mike said about this policy? Some products are made for selling, and some are made for smelling. This one was made for smelling."

"Cute! You mind if I ask how big the policy was?"

"Penny, much as I would like to, you know I can't disclose that. If it ever got back to Mike, he and I would be finished. Plus he could get me in trouble with my boss. I'll just say this though; it was the biggest ticket I've seen come out of his office for a long time."

"Angela, let's talk. You want our business, don't you?"

"Of course I do! We could really be good for each other. Everybody knows Guy is capable of throwing some really nice tickets to a company if he believes in their product."

"Well, I've got a proposition for you, and I promise you, hand on the Bible, I'll keep the information confidential. Who was the insured on the policy Mike bought?"

"I don't know, Penny! I could get in trouble."

"If you do me this favor, I'll tell Guy maybe he should consider Metropolitan products for appropriate clients. He will never go on a campaign on your product and slam dunk it into accounts. He doesn't do that, but he will consider you favorably when he thinks your product is appropriate for a particular account. I can't promise you results. That's up to Guy, but your products could well become part of his recommended product mix."

"I get the message. Our chances of doing business will increase dramatically if I do you this favor. And you're not going to dump me in the creek?"

"I think we understand each other."

"May I use your phone? By the way, I have a Metropolitan Snoopy doll for you. And oh, just for the record, that policy meant a $50,000 ticket for Mike. Made his month and mine too."

Chapter 46

*L*ater, Penny summarized her meeting with Angela for Guy. They decided it was their turn to treat Will and Betsy to a lunch. The group agreed to meet at Vincent's, an Italian restaurant and popular local hangout.

Vincent's was a well known restaurant to long time Vero Beach residents. It was in an unassuming storefront in a shopping center, so discreet that snowbirds often never found it until a local told them of its existence. The décor was understated. It had a counter as well as booths and tables. Some people who didn't want or like to cook ate virtually every meal at the restaurant and could be seen at the same time in the same seats almost every day. If you were truly local, it was almost impossible to go to Vincent's without seeing at least one person you knew.

The Walshes and the Blacks arrived at Vincent's about the same time and walked into the building together from the crowded parking lot. The owner, Guy Amato, was spinning pizza dough in the front.

"Hi, Guy," Guy Amato said.

"How's it going, Guy," Guy Walsh said in return.

"You guys feel like pizza?" Penny asked.

"Whatever you guys want," Will responded.

"I feel like I"m trapped in a time warp of 'who's on first'," Betsy said.

"No, Guy's not first. He'll order second," Will said.

They all laughed, and their favorite waitress, Elaine, showed them in. "Booth or table?" Elaine asked. "Is this a beer or tea day? Do you need menus?"

"Booth and tea. We have to go back to work."

"We have wedding soup today and pasta fagioli. The special is clams over linguine. The catch is dolphin – fried, broiled or blackened."

The group quickly decided on their choices – pizza slices to salad with calamari.

"Have I told you our office is reopening next Monday?" Will said. "We just want to be back here even if the office is still a mess. Our clients want that too. One nice thing is RST has authorized us to have an open house in our parking lot Thursday week for clients and friends."

"That's a fantastic idea," Guy said. "I'm sure clients will turn out in droves. It really doesn't matter if the building still looks like shit, clients just want to see what you're been going through and tell you and have you sympathize about their own hurricane experiences."

"Which leads me to something I wanted to tell you," Will continued. "Called Connie Tressler. I made arrangements with her to meet Betsy and me at the office to pack up Dave's belongings."

"It took us several hours, but we got everything packed up. The main thing Connie was looking for was Dave's Rolex.

Said she has looked everywhere for it. We couldn't find it in the office debris either. I'm starting to wonder if whoever killed him stole it."

"It sure wasn't there when you and I brought the police in to bag the body. Remember we talked about that at the time," Guy added.

"Connie pointed out a red stain on the crystal ball that was usually a focal point of Dave's desk. The next morning I called your friend Tom Mallette at the police station. He was nice enough to send someone over from the police lab to retrieve it. They're studying it right now trying to see if the red is dried blood. I don't know if they'll do a DNA analysis or not. Tom said the lab would check it for fingerprints, but that would take a little time."

"Great!" Guy said. "Isn't it nice to know someone at city hall. I'm sure otherwise there's no way in hell it would have ever gotten done, period end of it. Good job!"

Things got quiet as they ate their lunch.

When everyone had finished, Guy continued. "Now we've got something to report to you. I'll let Penny tell you since she was the one who had the moxie to make things pop."

Penny began her update about her visit from the Metropolitan insurance wholesaler.

"I know Angela Mauri. Talk about a piranaha!" Will added. "She's hungry, climbing mountains like she wants to be president of the Met. You picked the right one to put the squeeze on. She would crawl over five miles of broken glass for an order."

"It's funny you chose that word to describe her," Penny said. "Guy snaps his index finger and his thumb together every time her name is mentioned. It took her about thirty seconds to think my proposition over. Ethics were never an issue. She just wanted to be satisfied she wasn't going to get into any trouble, and Guy and I would be indebted enough to throw her some tickets in return."

Penny finished her story.

"Well, well, well," Betsy said. "This certainly puts a new perspective on things. I wonder if Connie knows about the insurance policy. It sure explains why the Colombians were hanging around the wake like a pack of hungry dogs. I wonder how they knew about it."

"Maybe they didn't," said Will. "Maybe they just figured they'd lean on her and see what happened. I'm sure they figured he was on RST's group life insurance. But why did they think they were entitled to any of the proceeds? They were paying Dave money not the other way around. Let's face it, he was peddling their 'golden opportunities' for them."

"You're right! We've missed something somewhere," Guy added.

"So Mike Pollard insured Dave's life – very, very interesting."

"Then Angela gave me a bonus I didn't ask for," Penny continued. "I still don't know if she gave it to me on purpose or if it was an accident. She told me how much commission Mike made on the policy. We all know what the commish rate is, so then it became a simple math problem to figure out the face value of the policy – one million smackers."

"Super job, Penny. I always knew there was a devious side to your personality," Will said.

"I've been trying to tell you for years that I didn't marry just another pretty face," Guy added with a chuckle.

217

"So we know Mike bought a million dollar life insurance policy on his son-in-law. I'm pretty sure Connie doesn't know about it. What do we do with this information?"

"We need to find out for sure. I vote for Penny to call Connie and try to find out."

"But what do I say to her?"

"When all else fails sort of tell her the truth, just don't tell her who gave out the info. Put the spin on it your supposition is based on second hand knowledge that came to you by accident. After all we do owe it to our source to protect her."

"I'm not so sure the story will fly and keep her from hyperventilating. So tell me, why should Connie want to talk to me about it at all?"

"You're an insurance specialist. Offer to help her file the beneficiary paperwork."

"OK, that makes sense. I'll do it."

"I'm confident you'll know how to handle it. It's our turn to pick up the check."

"Nah! We invited you," said Guy.

Chapter 47

*T*he answering machine clicked on.

This is the residence of Connie, Davie and Elizabeth Tressler. We're out gallivanting around and can't take your phone call. After the beep leave your name, and your phone number, and we'll return it when we get home.

"Connie, this is Penny Walsh at 234-0909 when you get a chance. I'll be at the office all day."

Penny received a return call after lunch.

"Penny, it's Connie. Sorry I missed you. I've been over at my mom's house all morning."

"I hope it was just for a visit. I hope nothing's wrong with her?"

"No. I think we're both just down from stress. She wanted me to come over, and I just needed to get out of this house. Everything in here reminds me of Dave. It's funny the stages of life you go through. When you're a child you want to be around your parents all the time. Then when you're a teenager, it's an imposition to have them around any time. Then you get married, and you have a lukewarm relationship with your parents and take them for granted. Then a tragedy like this happens and you find out just how much you depend on them after all. When all is said and done, you're twenty years older, and you've come full circle."

"Connie, I don't want to be nosy and tell me if I'm out of line, but as you may or may not know, I handle all the insurance matters for Guy's office. He sells the policies, but it's pretty much up to me to see they are serviced properly. I bring this up as a friend. Did Dave leave you any life insurance? If so, I'll be glad to help you file the paperwork."

"I appreciate the offer," Connie said. All this paperwork is so intimidating to me. This is all new territory to me. Dave did have a group life policy through work, but I don't know how to file for benefits. I know I really need to do this, but I've been putting it off."

"Is that the only insurance policy – the group policy?"

"The only one I know anything about," Connie replied.

"Are you sure?"

"I think I am. Why do you ask?"

"Well, you know the insurance community is a pretty small one in this town. I heard your father had taken out a policy on Dave."

"If he did, he never told me about it."

"You might want to check. It won't hurt to ask."

"I'll do that. Thanks for the tip. I wonder why Daddy would do that."

"Let me know the particulars, and I'll start getting the paperwork together. We'll fill it out together over at my office one day. If there's more than one policy, we can do them all at the same time."

"You're a friend, Penny. I've really found out who my friends are since Dave died."

Chapter 48

*C*onnie called her mother and asked if Mike had bought any life insurance on Dave. "Not that I know anything about," Constance said. "Why do you ask?"

"I just heard from someone who talked like she knew Daddy had purchased a policy on Dave. I thought if he had, you'd know about it."

"It sure would be manna from heaven if he had that type of foresight, but, darling, we both know your father is smart, but he doesn't have a crystal ball," Constance said. "Not one person in a million would have thought Dave would have died at his young age. Who was telling you this?"

"Mama, I'd rather not say. I don't want to cause any friction."

"Do you know which insurance company?" asked her mother.

"I don't know that either."

"Well, the whole thing sounds very puzzling to me. I wouldn't get my hopes up, sweetheart. I believe if that policy existed, I'd know about it. Your father and I don't keep secrets from each other."

"I guess that kind of luck would be too much to hope for. Luck is something I haven't had a whole lot of lately," said Connie.

✦✦✦✦

Connie immediately phoned her father.

"Connie, darling!" he answered. "Good to hear from you. When can we expect you over for dinner so I can see my favorite grandchildren?'

"Daddy, you're always such a kidder! They're your only grandchildren. I'll try to bring them by this weekend."

"Well, that automatically makes them my favorites, doesn't it? So what do I owe the pleasure? You rarely call me here at the office."

"Daddy, did you buy a life insurance policy on Dave?"

"Uh! Uh!"

"Daddy, is something wrong?"

"No, darling, of course not! It's just my sinuses acting up. What makes you ask me about insurance?"

"Something I heard."

"Maybe we ought to have lunch."

"How about 11:30 at Waldo's?"

"That's fine. I'll just meet you there."

Chapter 49

*C*onnie arrived at Waldo's at 11:15. She knew she was early. She was anxious. Was there something going on that she wasn't being made aware of? Was her father treating her as if she were still a child? Was her mother privy to knowledge she was not sharing with Connie? Or had she just jumped to conclusions with incomplete information? Connie knew deep within her that whatever her father's involvement it was only because he had the best of intentions and loved her. These questions and issues had bounced back and forth in her brain all morning.

Connie approached the front door of Waldo's but changed her mind about entering. Waldo's was the restaurant concession attached to a time-share beachfront hotel called The Driftwood Resort. It was one of those places locals loved to show tourists and then watch their reaction to the eclectic nature of the property.

The Driftwood had begun as a private residence that had been completed in 1937. The original home was called the *Breezeway* because it had a large opening in the central portion of the first floor. Before many years had passed the family started to use the residence as a hotel. It was eye catching with its board and batten walls, wood-shingled gables, decorative truss work and rustic balconies. Two ancient rusty cannons were embedded in one wall. Assorted ceramic tiles were incorporated in the design of the concrete floors. On one wall was a small mural of a Spanish explorer landing in the new world. The grounds contained a portion of Waldo's collection of more than two hundred mostly rusty bells. There was also a huge copper boiler, broken concrete pedestals, relief sculptures, an old buoy, a replica of a lighthouse, and other assorted accumulated objects of every description. The rooms were not merely numbered but had names like Flounder, Tarpon, Marlin, Snapper and Sailfish.

The restaurant was added after World War II and was equally eccentric. Posts were tree trunks. Some had wooden barrels surrounding the base. The doors were massive and unpainted. The floor alternated between concrete and odd ceramic tiles. The walls were covered with objects Waldo had collected in his world travels. The restaurant was dominated by three massive outrigger type wood timbers that decorated the south end of the building. Locals patronized the restaurant, but during the season snowbirds abounded.

While waiting for her father, Connie peeked in some of the stores that flanked Waldo's to see if she might get some ideas for Christmas presents.

Mike suddenly appeared, and they hugged.

"Let's not sit inside," he said. "Let's get one of the tables out by the boardwalk."

They walked through the restaurant, out a massive back door, and through the pool area. Soon they were seated at an umbrella-covered table, breathing the salt air and watching sandpipers walk the beach.

Connie waited for a raspberry tea; her father waited for a coffee. She ordered a BLT and cole slaw; Mike ordered an artichoke omelet with toast.

"Now tell me the truth, how are you adjusting," her father led off. "If you need some tranquilizers, my doctor will prescribe them for you."

"Daddy, things are fine. Tranquilizers! Honestly! I just need time to adjust. I just need time and some space."

"If you say so, darling. I just wanted you to know your mother and I are here if you need us."

"Daddy, there is one thing I want to ask you about. Did you take out any life insurance on Dave?"

"Yes, sweetheart, I did."

"Why didn't you ever tell us about it?"

"Well, I thought it was something best kept quiet. I own the policy. Dave was merely the insured. I didn't want you to misinterpret my intentions. Like I might be hinting your husband couldn't afford premiums. Also I'm in a position to evaluate policies and tell a good one from one that may not be so good. The one I bought for you guarantees the cash values to grow by at least seven percent a year for the first ten years and also gives you any market rates of return above that. They also sold it to me on favorable terms as a professional courtesy since I'm in the business. Darling, I also didn't want you to feel guilty or think you had to take over the premiums at some point. I had a lot of reasons I suppose. Mostly it was because I love you.

"Wow, Daddy. I don't know what to say."

"Connie, I didn't want you or Dave to think I was interfering in your affairs, but it has worried me for a long time y'all seemed to live up to every dime Dave made. Also I have been worried Dave might lose his job. You've got to remember I knew Dave sometimes took liberties and chances in how he dealt with his clients. I never told you because I didn't want to put undue stress on you, but I bailed him out of some tight situations. It also worried me watching him zip around town on that Harley-Davidson. He never wore a helmet. I have to be concerned not only for you, but after all, I do have two grandchildren at risk. I was going to tell you soon. I really was. How did you find out about it?"

"Well, I didn't know for sure until this moment. The subject came up when I was talking to Penny Walsh about filing the beneficiary paperwork on Dave's group policy. She offered to help me file for benefits. You know she does that for a living. She was trying to be a friend."

"How would she have known?"

"I don't know. You know I don't know much about these things. It doesn't matter, I guess. The fact is she was right. What's the death benefit on the policy?"

"A million dollars."

"Wow! Does Mom know about this?"

"No, Connie. I guess it was my little secret. I am sure it's certainly going to be timely. You probably need money now."

"Especially now I know that a large piece of Dave's other policy will have to go to pay off some debts he incurred."

"What debts?"

"That's just it, Daddy. I don't know for sure. Some people Dave was doing business with have told me he owed them money. They were kind of frightening. Latin gentlemen. I had met them through Dave a few times. To tell you the truth I'm a little bit scared of them, but I'd don't know exactly why."

"I think I might. Sweetheart, I hate to be the one to tell you, but Dave had a gambling habit. These people wanted me to stand good for some of his debts, but I threw them out of my office. That was another thing that concerned me. Have these people ever threatened you? If they have I'll call my friend the police chief and..."

"No, Daddy. It's nothing you can put your finger on. They just scare me. One made a comment at Dave's wake about being there to see how his money was being spent. It made me start thinking I really didn't know much about Dave's business affairs."

"Why didn't you tell me about these people, Connie?"

"They scare me, that's why. I didn't want to give you anything more to worry about."

"I knew you and Dave were having a hard time of it."

"How'd you know that? I thought I was careful to keep my differences with Dave from you and Mom."

"Connie, we may be old, but we're not blind. We can recognize a problem when we see one. You can't keep things from us any more than you could when you were a child."

"Daddy, I love you!"

"I guess we just don't tell each other enough, but, you know, I'd kill for you, darling."

"Oh, Daddy! Don't talk like that."

Chapter 50

Connie returned home shell-shocked. She didn't know what to think. She was surprised at the windfall of money that was close to coming her way. She was stunned at how transparent her marriage had been. She truly thought she had gone to great lengths to cover up her marriage's deficiencies. And what else had her parents observed they didn't want to confront her about? She started to wonder about how many other people around town had seen through the happy domestic smoke and mirrors.

Was she the only one who didn't see how much Dave lived on the edge? Were people going out of their way to be extra nice to her just because they knew too much and felt sorry for her, or because they really liked her for herself? And how deep was Dave into these Latinos? It was one thing for them to drop hints to her at the wake but to visit her father? And what would they have said to him that upset him to the point he threw them out of his office? How much of a threat were these people to her children and herself?

Connie was preoccupied with questions for the rest of the day and didn't sleep well that night. Even her children said she seemed to be in a fog. Connie was relieved on one hand she would receive this money, but then concerned about managing it. Thank goodness her father was an investment professional. She really didn't want to think about it. She just wanted to know the money was there for her and her kids when she needed it.

Connie's mind was still a muddle of unanswered questions when she finally called Penny the following week. Connie knew her father would help her file the beneficiary claim forms, but she knew Mike was a busy man and felt guilty about bothering him. After all Penny had made the offer and if there was a charge involved she wanted Penny to get it. Besides, Penny was the one who had told her of the windfall policy.

"You were right Penny about a life insurance policy," she said. "I'm not sure how you knew exactly, but my father confirmed he was paying for an insurance policy on Dave's life. This has got to be just about the sweetest thing he has ever done for me, but it's almost scary he could be so intuitive. Were Dave and I that much of an open book? If we were, I'm not sure I can face people around town."

"No. I am not aware of people gossiping about you behind your back," Penny said.

"Penny, I'd like to take you up on your offer to help me with the paperwork. And please charge me for your time. It's only right."

"Don't be ridiculous. If I hadn't wanted to help out I wouldn't have made the offer. Now let me tell you what you're going to need. When you get these things together, call me and we'll get it done. Shouldn't take long. It'll also give us an excuse to have lunch."

Chapter 51

*T*he next week was a flurry of activity at Will's office as everyone mailed their open-house invitations, tried to clean their areas, and sort through hurricane-damaged-files to see what was retrievable and what should be shredded. Rooney hired a company to haul dangerous debris and got the building owner to rehire the lawn service in an attempt to make the premises look as presentable as possible. A rental company could not be found to provide fold-up tables and chairs, but a broker's church agreed to loan theirs for the evening. The caterer agreed to make hors d'oeuvres.

Barbara, Will's sales assistant, suggested creating life size cardboard figures like those used at carnivals and beach resorts. The cartoon-like figures had the heads cut out so fun memento pictures could be taken of clients attending the party. The caricature was a combination Santa and Mrs. Santa hanging on to a Christmas tree as a hurricane attempted to blow them away. The art teacher at Saint Edwards, an RST client, drew the whimsical figures with acrylic paints and highlighted them with colored chalk. Ray, one of the brokers who happened to be a camera buff, agreed to bring his printer the day of the party and set it up in the parking lot so clients could be given their souvenir photos immediately after the pictures were taken.

Jim bought the booze and Davis found a pan group in Stuart that jumped at the chance to play a gig in Vero Beach.

Little by little, the details of Thursday's party started to come together. Not only were clients excited about attending, but the buzz with the staff ratcheted up daily. Rooney had the parking lot pressure-washed and then watched over it like a hawk to make sure it stayed clean.

Tuesday, on the way to work, Will remembered he had forgotten to remind Connie Tressler of her invitation.

"Do you think I should go?"

"Connie, you have no reason to duck people. It'll only make people ask questions about things that otherwise probably wouldn't cross their minds. You've known a lot of these people for your whole life. They're not going to bite you. They're either your friends or Dave's former clients. They want to say 'I'm sorry.'"

Connie said she'd bring a girlfriend.

Thursday morning, Christmas decorations – a wreath and garland – were added to the building. Warren Lewis went to the Methodist church to get the tables and chairs. Disposable tablecloths and flowers were added. The other tables and chairs were strategically placed on the parking lot. Ice chests were unloaded. The area under the building overhang was reserved for the food tables, the pan player, and the bar. At the back of the parking lot, where there was sure to be plenty of sun, the headless cutouts were set up for photo making.

The festive office was a distinct contrast to the hotel and condo directly across Ocean Drive. Both of these buildings had been a total hurricane blow-through. A visitor could clearly see the ocean through some floors of the hotel.

Plywood had been nailed over the sliding glass doors on the condo units. Roofing material instead of Christmas decorations adorned the bushes around both buildings. Mountains of rubble continued to dominate the front parking lots of each building. The whole scene was one of abandonment. Jim joked to Warren whereas they were sprucing up as if it were the night before Christmas, directly across the street looked like the nightmare before Christmas. By 4:30 droves of people – some in shorts, some in shirts and ties – walked down the street and up the parking lot to join the party which was now well under way. The pan player showed his versatility: *Yellow Bird, Roll Out The Barrel, Jingle Bells.*

Guests munched assorted cheeses, crackers, chicken wings, pastries and other goodies. Waitresses kept glasses filled. There was a short but steady line of clients getting their pictures made with the cutouts. Brokers were taking clients, drink in hand, to tour the damaged building.

Even after two months everyone seemed to have a storm story they wanted to share. They were now hurricane veterans, with the battle scars needed to be inducted into an exclusive Florida fraternity.

Betsy spotted Joan and another couple in the crowd. Betsy had not seen Mrs. Terwilliger since before the storm but knew her home had survived without much damage. Will had made it a point to stop by her home on his first trip to RST's Stuart office to make sure she was all right since telephone service had been spotty and cell phones had been down completely. Joan was a very special client of Will's and more importantly, she was a close family friend, in fact like family. As a retired banker from New York, she and Betsy found much in common through the years. Mrs. Terwilliger had watched Lexie grow into a young woman and had joined

Will and Betsy for Christmas and other holidays as well as Lexie's school events.

The crowd grew. By six-thirty the parking lot was elbow to elbow.

Will was talking with Betsy, Connie, and Joan after getting the ladies a drink when Omar Perillo joined them.

"Nice affair, Mr. Black," Perillo said as they shook hands. He had on linen slacks, expensive loafers and a white guayabera shirt. Two other silent Latins stood a few steps behind him. "Is this an early holiday party?"

"Señor Perillo, good of you to come. Actually we thought of it as a holiday, end-of-hurricane-season, sorry-you-were-inconvenienced, welcome-back-seasonal-clients, we're-back-in-Vero Beach, RST-appreciates-your-business party, all rolled up into one."

"I wish our restaurant investment attracted a loyal crowd of this magnitude."

"Oh, I know how you can do it," Will said facetiously. "Give away free food and booze like we're doing."

"Excellent point, Mr. Black, it would be enjoyable I agree, but I'm not sure how long we'd remain in business."

He turned to Connie. "Mrs. Tressler, I believe. It is good to see you again. You are looking especially beautiful tonight. Once again my condolences over the death of your husband."

"Mr. Perillo, you are too kind," she nervously said.

"I hope chance will smile on us and we shall meet again in the near future." Perillo said with a smile. "Will you pardon me? I see someone I had hoped to speak with."

After Perillo eased into another foursome, Will went to refill Connie's glass of wine. Betsy asked Connie, "Did that guy make you nervous?"

"Yes, I guess he did. I didn't expect to run into him here."

"Perillo is now one of Will's clients."

"I'm just making a big deal out of nothing. I guess I'm just not as good holding my own in social situations as Dave was. Dave always knew what to say when he met a stranger. It seems like I never do. Besides it's just been an upsetting day."

"How's that, Connie?"

"When my mom came over to baby-sit Davie and Elizabeth this afternoon she told me that she and my dad have separated. Daddy's taken an apartment."

"My God!" Betsy said. "No wonder you're a nervous wreck. You poor thing! They've been married forever."

"I've rarely even seen them fight," Connie said. "I always wished my marriage was as stable as my parents' marriage. I've often felt guilty my marriage had not worked as well as theirs. It was almost as if I had let them down. I started not to come tonight. It upset me so much, but I had promised Will I would, and Mama was already there to baby-sit, and I don't want anyone else mad at me."

"C'mon, Connie, please stop it. You don't owe anyone an apology. We wouldn't have been mad at you if you hadn't come. We just want to see you move on with your life. You've got your kids to live for and being a recluse is not going to help them since you're now their only parent."

"You're right. I've just got to pull myself together. It's just every time I think I have, something else seems to happen."

"Enough of this! Smile!" said Betsy. Here comes Will with your wine. I'll get with Penny, and we'll plan a girls only outing next week. We'll knock some tennis balls around and some lunch. OK?"

"It sounds like fun."

Chapter 52

*T*he Friday after Thanksgiving was set for the girls' outing. Betsy took the day off since the day traditionally was a dead one at the bank. And for Penny, even though the markets were open, most people fully expected it to be a slow day. Clients would probably be at the mall on Black Friday; many brokers used it as an excuse to take a four day weekend. When she called to confirm their appointment Penny suggested that it would be a wonderful day to fill out paperwork on the insurance policies. She reminded Connie what she would need to bring with her: details about the policies, copies of Dave's certified death certificate, the affidavits of domicile, and any death claim forms she had.

Penny told Connie since it was a slow business day they should be able to get any missing forms from the processing clerks at the insurance companies without staying on hold for extended periods of time and these clerks would have time to walk them through the forms on the phone, virtually insuring they would be filled out correctly. "You're really smart," Connie said. "I never would have thought of all that. I'll be sure to be at your office by ten."

Connie noticed as she drove that the city of Vero Beach was starting to look festive. The city had decorated the light posts. There was a municipal Christmas tree in the median on State Road 60. Businesses were starting to decorate. One car dealership had added an elaborate lighted sleigh and reindeer on its roof. Wreaths were attached to the light poles on the bridge. One home was decorated even though it had been totaled. A discarded couch waiting by the street to be picked up wore a bow. When Connie got to the beach, city workers were unloading barriers in preparation for the Christmas parade planned for the following Saturday evening.

When Connie arrived at Penny's office, Guy was trying to wrestle the office Christmas tree onto its stand.

"Ho, ho, ho! Give me a hug," Guy grinned when he saw Connie come in the door. "And what do you want for Christmas this year, young lady."

"You don't want to know," Connie replied dryly.

Penny walked into the lobby with a box of ornaments. She saw Connie and smiled. "I told you this is always a slow day," she said.

"You look so busy. Maybe we should do this another day. I don't want to intrude and be a distraction."

"Nonsense. There's plenty of hands available for putting out decorations. The parade will go right in front of this building. We always open the office for clients and friends to give people a place to watch it. We'd love to have you join us, and bring the kids," she said, smiling sincerely.

"You're so kind, but I'm really not in a joyful mood."

"You really ought to reconsider for the kids' sake – the parade is sure to bring at least some holiday joy to all of you. Anyway, let's look at the paperwork. We'll spread it out on the conference room table. We've got an hour or so before Betsy gets here."

When they got in the conference room, Penny closed the door and separated Connie's papers into piles and briefly examined the forms they were about to fill out.

The girls filled out forms. As they finished each one, Penny would gather the needed substantiating documents and preprinted envelopes and paper-clip them to the forms she would mail them in. Penny did virtually all the work; Connie just watched and signed what Penny told her to sign.

"You've done in thirty minutes what would have over-whelmed me for the whole day," Connie said, when the last of the paperwork had been matched to the proper form.

"You know, Connie, you're really going to be in very good shape. You're not going to be able to go out and blow money like there's no tomorrow, but you're not going to be a pauper either. You have a million dollars from Dave's supplemental group life insurance plus another million coming from the policy your dad bought. You also will continue to get medical insurance at employee rates. Then you'll get a lump sum settlement from Dave's retirement program. That will get rolled over into an IRA in your name. Plus you'll be vested on his productivity bonuses which you'll get each year for the next five years, and then there was his stock purchase program."

"My gosh! That sounds like a lot."

"It is! Oh, I forgot his 401(k). Oh yeah! You do know you need to apply for Social Security survivor and dependent benefits?"

"No, I didn't! How do I get Social Security? I'm not 65."

"Doesn't make any difference! You're a widow with minor children. You've got money coming to you," said Penny.

"You make it sound like I'll have more money than when Dave was alive and working – and one less bill, his bookie bill."

"Connie, you should be ecstatic, but you don't seem to be."

"I guess I'm just overwhelmed," Connie said sadly. "I just don't know what to do next."

"If I were you, I'd call the Social Security Administration first. You'll probably have to go down there. It's out on State Road 60 around 20th. Then I'd get hold of RST and see what you've got coming from them. I'm sure Will or Joe Rooney will do everything they can to get things rolling. And don't forget your dad's in the business."

The receptionist stuck her head in the door and said Betsy Black had arrived. "Why don't you talk to her for a second," Connie said, looking almost like she was going to cry. "I'm going to the powder room, and then I'll catch up with you. And do you mind if we skip tennis? I'm really not in the mood. Why don't we just have lunch instead? I want to treat. It's the least I can do."

"If it'll make you feel better," Penny said. "Smile, you're a wealthy woman."

"Funny, I don't feel rich. I'll join you in a second."

Connie walked into Penny's office a few minutes later. Her eyes were red.

"Betsy," she said. "It's so nice to see you again. And you have your tennis shorts on. Do you mind if I take a rain check? I had a cold earlier in the week, and I still don't think I've recovered completely. Do you mind if we just do lunch?"

"Why don't we sit outside at The Patio? I definitely wouldn't want to get near the mall today," Penny said.

"Good idea, and we'll take two cars since The Patio is near my house anyway," Connie replied.

The Patio was a ramshackle old building that had been a landmark in Vero Beach since the Depression. It was another legacy of the same Vero Beach pioneer who had built Waldo's. It looked like an old barn.

"Let's eat outside," Connie suggested. "It's too pretty to be indoors."

They ordered bloody Marys, and as they sipped them talk turned to children, homes and Christmas shopping. For the most part the conversation was between Betsy and Penny. The bloody Mary wasn't lightening Connie's sober mood. She ordered a rum and Diet Coke.

The waitress brought their lunches, but Connie just picked at hers.

"You must not have liked your lunch, Connie. My flounder was great," Betsy said.

"Oh, I'm sorry, Betsy. I hope I haven't been a downer. I guess I wasn't as hungry as I thought."

"You should be celebrating," Penny joked. "We're going to have to start calling you Connie Rockefeller soon."

But Connie choked back a sob and said, "I'm just sitting here thinking about Mama and Daddy being separated. Daddy's moved into an apartment on Dahlia. I can't believe it's happening. Not to my parents. They love each other. Mama is the one who wants it. She told me so. I just can't imagine why."

"Have you tried talking to her about it?" Betsy asked.

"I'm going to do it this afternoon. I have a knot in my stomach," she said, as she gulped back tears. "I just don't know if I can take much more. Six months ago all I had to worry about was Dave's spendthrift habits. That looks minor now. Much more and I'll be at the breaking point. It certainly doesn't feel like Christmas."

Chapter 53

*C*onnie left The Patio in a fog. She was vaguely aware Penny had told her she was financially well fixed for someone her age, but it really hadn't sunk in. Her mind was on what lay ahead. She felt she must have a serious heart-to-heart with her father before she saw her mother. She wondered how she was going to tell her children, who were still trying to get used to the fact they would never see their father again, now Grandma and Grandpa would no longer be the couple who lived at 211 Atocha Way, who always were there to make them feel loved and secure. But why? And why now of all times? Was God punishing her for some unknown transgression? Was he trying to test her like he did Abraham? Was she having a belated Sunday school guilt trip?

Connie drove over the bridge to her father's office going 65 and continued to speed up A1A.

She arrived at Smith Barney and entered the lobby like a robot. Mike was on the phone. Since he was a Chairman's Club producer, he had the largest office in the building. It was a corner office with two glass walls affording a view extending down and across Ocean Drive. His office had a mahogany conference table and chairs as well as a small couch. Announcing his status was bright brass lettering outside his door that said MICHAEL L. POLLARD SENIOR

VICE PRESIDENT OF INVESTMENTS. Her father saw her through his open door and motioned her in.

"Mrs. Hawthorn, don't let one down day upset you, he said over the phone. "Markets are volatile. They don't move in a straight line. That's why you make more money in the market than you do with a CD. We have had up markets now for five months in a row. This market is overdue to settle back some. In fact it's healthy. I don't care what CNBC said. Yes, Mrs. Hawthorn, I'll call you if I think the market is really going down. I won't forget. I promise. Goodbye now."

When he hung up, Connie said, "Problem?"

"Naw! Just the usual handholding. It comes with the territory. I guess it does sound serious to the casual listener, but it's how I make my living. This is what put you through school, me handholding little old ladies who have boocoodles of money and even more time on their hands."

"I don't think I could do it."

"Most people can't. That's why those of us who can, make a good living." Mike nodded. "Now what can I do for my favorite girl?"

"Daddy, what's happening between you and mama?"

"Let's just say we have chosen to disagree on some important subjects, he said. "I don't want to worry your pretty little head. You've got enough on your mind."

"Daddy, don't treat me like an airhead."

"I'm not, sweetheart. This is something your mother and I have to work through."

"Daddy, would you take that kind of answer from me?"

Mike was silent.

"Daddy!"

"Connie, please don't push me on this. I don't want to say anything I'll regret. Please?"

"Daddy, you're not being fair with me." Connie said, starting to cry.

Mike looked guilty.

"It's funny you can handhold old ladies, but you can't or won't do the same thing for your own daughter."

Connie turned around and left.

Chapter 54

*C*onnie drove straight to her mother's house. At the gate to the restricted subdivision the guard waved her through.

The area brought back a lot of memories. This is the house where her first date had come to pick her up and where a few years later her date had arrived in a rented limo to take her to the prom. This was the house where she had played on the dock or fished with her father so many times. It was in this neighborhood she had gone trick-or-treating. She still remembered getting her senior picture made in the front yard by a huge hibiscus bush. She also remembered her mom crying as they packed her belongings for college. This was home, but whose home would it be in the future? She couldn't imagine strangers living in her home and making their own memories.

The garage door was up and her mom's car was in the garage. Constance's house was the only one on the block with no Christmas decorations. Connie almost dreaded the conversation that lay ahead, but she had to find out what was going on.

Connie went into the house though the garage.

"Mom, it's me," she said loudly.

Constance was wearing some old clothes. She would never have worn them out, even to go to the grocery store. She wore very little makeup and her hair was tied up in a scarf. She looked worn, tired and old. Her expression reflected a defeated attitude.

"Hi, mom," Connie said, and kissed her mom on the cheek. Connie's voice cracked as she made small talk in spite of her effort to seem chipper. "Had lunch with Penny Walsh and Betsy Black today. The Patio had some really good specials."

"They usually do," Constance said.

"Mom, Penny helped me start to file some of the paperwork on Dave."

Constance nodded.

"Mama, what's happening between you and Daddy?"

"Darling, I really don't want to talk about it."

"Mama, I'm not a child anymore. You're the one who told me he had gotten an apartment. I think you owe it to me to level with me and tell me the truth. You and Daddy have been so happy."

"I told you because you were going to find out anyway. Why can't you just let me retain some dignity and privacy?" Constance said, a tear rolling down her cheek.

"Mama, we've never kept secrets from each other. I love you both, and I need you both more than ever since Dave died. Please don't shut me out and make me think the worst. After everything that has happened I just don't think I can take much more."

Constance sighed. "Connie, you were right when you said we have never had secrets in this family. I thought we never would. Recently, I misplaced my prescription sunglasses. I started thinking maybe I had left them in the glove compartment in your dad's car. When I went out to check I found Dave's expensive Rolex. I know that watch, and I know you've been looking for it."

"I know I have. I've looked everywhere."

"Your father has told me repeatedly he hasn't seen Dave for months. Not since they had that disagreement back in the spring. When I asked your father how the watch got there he just acted like he had no idea. I have never seen him react in such shock. I almost believed him. At first he said maybe it was a watch belonging to one of his golf buddies that got left in there by accident. Then he said someone must have put it there. Your dad has never been any good at lying to me. He gets this guilty look I can see through in a Yankee second. He had that look."

"Maybe he was telling the truth."

"I gave him the benefit of the doubt for a few minutes too. Then I remembered Mike got home from work late the day the storm hit. I remember it well because I had been calling him all afternoon trying to get him to leave the office. He kept putting me off, saying he had an important appointment. Your father finally admitted to me the important matter he had to take care of the day of the storm was Dave. Some Hispanic men had called on him a few days before thinking he should pay back some money they claimed Dave owed them. He told me he refused and asked them to leave his office. He called Dave, but Dave didn't return his phone calls. He finally was able to corner Dave the day of the storm. Apparently, they had quite a brouhaha. He accused Dave of jeopardizing his grandchildren's future and not being a good husband to you. Dave called him an interfering old man and told him he was capable of running his own life. Your father said it was quite a scene. He told me when he left Dave's office, Dave was in an absolute rage."

"That sounds logical. Dave did not like to be told what to do. When I tried to tell him what to do we had some of our most dreadful fights."

"Well, if Dave was fine when your father left, how did he get Dave's watch? We went round and round. It was the worst argument we have ever had. When it was over, I told him until he could give me the truth it would be best if he moved out. Now you know what's going on."

"Oh, Mama," Connie said before crying uncontrollably. "Please don't tell me you're thinking what I believe you are!"

Constance's face turned ashen, "I don't know what to think, darling, and your father is not helping matters any. He says the watch is as much of a surprise to him as it is a mystery to me. I will say this – his story has stayed consistent. He finally got to the point where he wouldn't even talk about it. He seemed frozen with fear. The more I pried, the more he clammed up. That's why I told him until he decided to level with me it would be best if he just moved out. Darling, you know I've never been a bluffer. I'm the worst card player in the world because I can't hide my feelings. This mess has been the biggest bluff of my life...with everything at stake... and he called me on it. I hope to God he was telling the truth...I also hope he'll forgive me...I pray I haven't thrown away everything we've ever had."

Chapter 55

*S*aturday was gorgeous. Decembers in Florida, more often than not, are enviably superb. Temperatures formerly in the upper eighties drop to a delicious range of highs from the high seventies to the low to mid-eighties and lows in the sixties to low seventies.

Will and Betsy decided it would be a wonderful day for their annual quest for the perfect Christmas tree. They wanted to surprise Lexie when she arrived home for Christmas break, endowing the house with a gaudy, cheesy look that makes a house cheery and festive during the holiday season.

Will was playing Kenny Chesney's popular Christmas CD on the car stereo. Holiday music always made his mood soar. He couldn't help but sing along with Kenny's rendition of *All I Want For Christmas Is A Real Good Tan.*

"Your enthusiasm is contagious, but Kenny you aren't and you're never going to be," Betsy said.

"Like I've told you before, honey, it's not the voice; it's the spirit. So where do you think we should go to look for a tree?" Will asked.

"Well, there's the Exchange Club lot, Home Depot, Lowes. And don't forget, there's a lot in front of the mall."

"Let's try the Exchange Club then. They usually have good trees, and it does go for a good cause. Besides Warren Lewis is in The Exchange Club."

"Works for me! The other day, Connie was severely depressed when we had lunch, but I guess I would be too if my parents hit me with the fact they were separating."

"Well, she's more vulnerable than she normally would be. There's nothing about Dave's death that hasn't been traumatic. Sure ought to make you appreciate me."

"Believe me, I do, Will. More than you know. I know I don't tell you enough but..."

Then Betsy continued, "We're both guilty of taking each other for granted. Something like this Dave situation sure reminds you that you can't and shouldn't take anything for granted. You know what they say, 'There but for the grace of God go I...' By the way, do you think Connie really will come over to Guy's office for the Christmas parade?"

"I hope so. Not only would it be just what the doctor ordered for her, but this is something she can share with her kids they will truly enjoy. Didn't you promise Penny you'd help her get set up for tonight?"

"Yep! That's not work though; it's fun. It gives us a chance to sample the wine to make sure it is going to be acceptable for company," she said, laughing.

Will and Betsy found an eight-foot spruce, full and green with a heavenly evergreen aroma. They took it home, put it in a water filled-bucket on the patio, and decided it would be decorated when Lexie got home from the University of Miami. Will then dropped Betsy at the Walshes.

On the way to the Walshes, Will had cranked up the stereo again to listen to one of his perennial favorites, the Drifters' timeless doo-wop version of *White Christmas*.

Later in the afternoon Will joined them at Guy's office. Ocean Drive seemed to exude a sense of anticipation for the parade soon to be transforming it into a joyous wonderland for a few hours. Saw horse barriers had been set up by the city. Early birds had set up lawn chairs to stake out a front row seat along the curb. A beachside jeweler on the west side of the street had put up a large open tent on aluminum poles. Other people started arriving with ice chests on wheels loaded with their special goodies. Soon people were jockeying for space.

Will and Guy stood on the second-floor balcony of Guy's office building. Guy was drinking merlot out of a stemmed glass; Will had his usual bourbon on the rocks. Guy had the office doors open and the stereo was playing Mannheim Steamroller's *Joy To The World*.

"Now this is the only way to watch a parade," Will said. "It is too bad our building does not have a balcony."

"Look who I see coming down the street, Connie, Davie and Elizabeth."

Guy pointed at the outside staircase and motioned for them to come up and join them. He then yelled at Penny and Betsy that Connie and the kids had arrived.

By the time the parade started at six o'clock, Guy's office was filled with clients and friends. Noisy revelers happily ate the party munchies and crowded one another trying to get to the self serve-bar. From this vantage point, Guy's guests could see the parade approach two blocks away.

The police patrol cars drove down the street, sirens blaring. They were followed by the local charter school band that marched smartly, playing *It's Beginning To Look A Lot Like Christmas*. The parade had begun. Soon, floats and other attractions entertained the enthusiastic crowd that was now four-to-six-people deep. Polished antique cars blew their horns. The children's ballet class cavorted. The local martial arts school students dressed in their karate gi's marched in formation. Decorated fire trucks, city utility vehicles, cherry pickers, ambulances, plumbers' and electricians' trucks, and every other imaginable vehicle joined in the festivities. Then the Vero Beach High School marching band blared *Jingle Bells*. It stopped right in front of Guy's building so the majorettes could put on their show. Colorful floats rolled into sight lighting up the night sky. From their birds-eye perch, the parade stretched all the way down Ocean Drive to the horizon.

Proud parade participants waved at the crowd, which waved back. As each component of the spectacle approached inevitably someone would yell, "Oh look, there's …" and then frantically wave to attract the current VIP for a moment. Often the participants would then reach into their bags of throws and let fly a shower of candy. For two hours, it went on. This may not be the Macy's Thanksgiving parade, the Rose Bowl parade, or a Mardi Gras parade, it was something far better – friends, neighbors, teachers, kids, business associates, people who responded to your needs every day of the year, the heart, soul and backbone of Vero Beach, the people who really counted.

Guy's guests drifted back and forth from the balcony to small chat groups inside. Down on the street, the kids played with other kids and competed for the candy being thrown. Parents occasionally went down to make sure their children stayed under control. Connie was in and out of Guy's office as needs dictated. Even when she was upstairs talking to other adults she didn't relax and enjoy the parade but had one eye on the street. She, like most concerned parents in Vero Beach, didn't worry about some pervert taking their child; their concern was more in the line of being available in a hurry if a skinned knee or elbow were to occur.

Betsy thought maybe she could draw Connie out and get her to shake her melancholy mood.

"Connie, look! Did you see the United Way float? It had a giant black hand shaking a giant white hand. Not exactly a Christmas theme. What do you want to bet that float was left over from another parade?"

"You're probably right," Connie said.

"Aw, c'mon, girl! You don't seem to have caught the spirit. Hey, it's Christmas! It's the time to be happy even if it's only for the kids!"

"Is it that apparent I'm not into this? I thought I'd masked it pretty well."

"I hate to tell you, but you're transparent as hell."

"That bad! You know, I haven't felt this low in a couple of months. With Dave and my parents and all... But you don't want to hear this. Let's watch the parade and have fun."

"Maybe your parents will work through this rough period. I can't imagine what could be so bad they would break up permanently."

"Oh, Betsy," Connie said as, she started crying. "It's awful! It's absolutely awful! Dave's watch...well, it turned up. My mother found it in my dad's glove compartment. Not only does he claim he doesn't know how it got there, he refuses to talk about it. He just stonewalls everyone when the topic is brought up. That's not like him. How did he get that watch? He and Dave hadn't spoken civilly to each other for months. He may have been the last person to see Dave alive. Mom said he came home from work late that day and wouldn't tell her where he had been. He's never kept secrets from Mom. They went round and round. It finally upset Mama so much she told him to move out until he was willing to tell her the truth. Why would he jeopardize his marriage unless he had something to hide? Betsy, I just don't think I can take much more. I tried to get him to talk about it. He told me the same thing as he did Mama – it was none of my business. Forgive me for telling you all this and spoiling your evening. I shouldn't have. It's not your problem."

Chapter 56

*W*ill Black was returning to his office when Barbara looked up and motioned to him.

"Will, did you find any Christmas presents for Lexie or Betsy?"

"Not really. I went to four different stores, and nothing jumped off the shelf at me as something either one of them couldn't live without. It's really hard to buy something for someone who really doesn't need anything, and I've never been much of a shopper anyway. Maybe I'll just look in some of the catalogues that come to the house and see what I can find there."

"If you're going to order stuff you better get off your duff and do it," Barbara said. "You're going to run out of time in another week or so. By the way, before I forget, a Lieutenant Mallette just called here looking for you."

Will's call to Mallette was answered on the second ring.

"Thought I'd let you know I haven't forgotten about your request, Mallette said. "I have not gotten an answer back on the fingerprints and the stain on the crystal ball."

Tom continued, "I just wanted to let you know that our lab has been doing double duty since the crime lab in Fort Pierce was severely damaged in the storm."

"I remember reading about that in the newspaper," Will said.

With sincerity and concern Tom added, "I am really sorry it is taking so long, but there is a valid reason. They promised me something within the next two weeks."

"Tom, I understand your situation. The Fort Pierce crime lab is just one of many services disrupted by the storm." Will continued, "You were doing me a favor and I'm not holding you to a schedule for results."

Chapter 57

As they often did, Will and Betsy were relaxing in the pool after work listening to the Fab 5 of Jamaica sing Christmas carols on the stereo.

Down in Jamaica there's hot, sunny weather

And people are warm and friendly all the time

Now it's the Christmas season

And the fun shall come

Have a joyful erie Christmas in the sun

"I love that album. That was some of the best music you ever found in Jamaica. I'll never forget it was in July..."

"And hot as hell," added Will.

"You had asked Henry Davis if he knew how to find any interesting record stores in Montego Bay. Henry took us down this narrow, rough looking alley full of pot holes and pointed the store out to you. Remember it was up on a landing at the top of some rickety wooden steps."

"I'll never forget the look you gave me – like let's get the hell out of here."

"As I recall, it didn't look anything like a reputable store. Looked more like some place that fenced stolen goods or made bootlegs. No sign. No nothing. Just a door, like a delivery door on the second floor of the back of the building. Kirk and Nancy were with us. Kirk had an ice chest full of beer. You went up the stairs. We had the sliding door to Henry's van open because it was so stinking hot, and this wino or crazy street person came up and demanded a beer. I was never so scared in my life. Lexie was sitting on the seat right by the open door. She was only five years old. I just knew by the time you got back, we were all going to be dead. I'll never forget Henry walking up to the filthy creature and telling him to get the hell out of there and quite bothering us or he'd call the police. The guy was screaming obscenities at us when Henry approached him. I always thought he could have knifed Henry since he was acting so weird and violent. If something like that had happened, I don't know what I would have done. Kirk just sat there drinking beer the whole time in shock, not knowing what to do. He was afraid if he got confrontational, the lunatic might harm Lexie." said Betsy.

"But the drunk didn't call Henry's bluff! He knew Henry was a Jamaican and Henry meant business. He did just what Henry told him to do. He yelled some threats and said unintelligible things about Americans, but he got the hell out of there," Betsy continued.

"I was upstairs. Probably good I couldn't hear a thing. I'm sure I would have panicked. I didn't even know y'all had a problem 'til I got back. Anyway, I asked the store clerk if he had any Christmas records. He got out a Marcia Griffiths, a John Holt, and this raggedy looking vinyl album by the Fab 5 called *Christmas In The Sun*. I consider myself pretty well-versed on Jamaican music, but I had never heard of the Fab 5. It was obvious this album had been played to death as a demo in the store. Little did I know it was going to become one of our all time favorite Christmas albums. Also, remember on another trip a few years later when I wanted to see if it had been released on CD? I called the Kingston phone number on the back of the album's cover and the Fab 5's bass player, Frankie Campbell, answered the phone. He told me it was in print and where I could buy it. Really a nice guy! I didn't know who he was until later. I thought he was just a receptionist."

"We've had some good memories, haven't we? You know, I miss Henry and Rose," Betsy said with a sigh. "I guess that's one reason I feel so sorry for Connie Tressler. So many of her memories have been permanently tarnished by what's happened to her this year."

"On a happier subject," Will said. "I'm always so glad we go to Vero Beach's Christmas parade every year. The parade is when I usually first get in the mood for Christmas. I was kind of afraid we might miss Christmas this year. Things seemed so bleak after Clarice, but here we are just like every other year, chilling in the pool listening to the Fab 5. Our life truly has been good! Unpredictable, but good!"

"And while we're talking about Connie, I really need to update our friend at the police department and keep him in the loop. He didn't have to let us have access to their lab, you know."

"You're right!" Betsy said. "Why don't you call him in the morning? Tom's the pro. He should be the judge of what should be done next – if anything. Oh, here's another one of my favorites."

Welcome back to Jamaica one more time again,
Welcome to Jamaica, ladies and gentlemen!
Welcome to Jamaica, boyfriend and galfriend,
Welcome to Jamaica, all de pickney dem

Suddenly, the wireless phone Betsy had taken out to the pool rang. Will reached over to answer it.

He heard a gruff voice on the other end of the line.

"Mr. Black?"

"Yes, this is Will Black."

"Señor Valdes. You got something that belongs to me, and I want it back."

"What's that, Señor?"

"You got my papers you got out of that loser Tressler's office, and I want them back. And I mean everything. Comprende," Valdes growled.

"I certainly don't want to keep anything that belongs to you," Will said. "I keep all business related matters at my office, not my home."

"I'll send someone by tomorrow. Have them ready."

Valdes' tone chilled Will to the bone. He hung up with no goodbyes.

♦♦♦♦

Will went into his office early the next morning and copied everything he had taken from Tressler's office he thought he might want down the road. At eight thirty, he called Mallette.

"Tom, we need to talk ASAP. Some things have happened that I need to bring you up to date on."

"You sound frightened. No one's been hurt have they? Where are you – at your office? I can be there in fifteen minutes."

"No. I just received a little scare, that's all. The sooner you can get here the better. I may be getting a visitor."

"I'm on my way."

♦ ♦ ♦ ♦

At Will's office Will told Mallette about the call from Valdes.

"He made it clear in no uncertain terms he thought I had gotten papers out of Dave Tressler's office that belonged to him relating to Spoonbill Partners and Macadamia Partners, and he wants them back. He's sending someone by here today. He made it clear that he meant business."

"Give 'em what they want," Mallette said. "I'm sure there's nothing in there worth getting hurt over."

"Oh, I plan to." Will said nothing about the copies he'd made. "Hope you realize there's some other things I have to be vague about – you understand – client privacy. If it seems like I'm rambling, I am. I don't know what may be important and what isn't. I'll probably bring matters up randomly as I think of them."

"I'm all ears. You told me about Spoonbill and Macadamia."

"Let me start with this. If you go out State Road 60 to the address I wrote on this piece of paper, you'll find a used car lot where most people wouldn't expect a used car lot to be. I got the address off one of Tressler's accounts. The contact person on the account is Adolfo Soltero."

He tore a page with the address off his scratch pad and slid it across the desk to Mallette.

"This address is on a gravel road that runs parallel to State Road 60, to the north of it. There's a country store with gas pumps. The name is Stop and Go. The last time I was there, under the shade tree to the side of the building it appeared some guy was running an outdoor check-cashing service.

Will continued, "Cattycorner across the street is the used car lot with a chain link fence around it. Lots of Hispanics were hanging around both times I was there. It's almost like a compound – the store, a used car lot, a big house with a barn or workshop or something attached to it. The fence goes around both the car lot and house. I went in the store and bought a soft drink. There was a guard in the store's parking lot. The store also had security cameras. I took my drink and walked over to the car lot to browse, and I can tell you I was one of the few genuine looking customers they had."

Tom nodded.

"Most of them, quite frankly, didn't look like they had the money to buy a used roller skate. They didn't seem to give a damn whether they showed me a car or not. People were coming and going from the house through a guarded gate. When I got back to my car the guard at the store was writing down my tag number. That whole scene was bizarre."

Will plowed on.

"Guy Walsh and I went out there again to ride our bikes one Sunday. Guess who seemed to be in charge that day? Omar Perillo. He was holding court in the parking lot of the store. I wish you could have seen it. He and his henchmen were in two big black Mercedes. Everyone seemed to be catering to him. The scene reminded me of the wedding scene at the beginning of *The Godfather*. Cars were being taken out of a big barn-like-structure and then systematically assigned to these lowlife looking wetbacks who then would drive off in them. There must have been twenty of them waiting subserviently to see him that day. I'm not sure if the cars were illegal or the drivers were illegal or both, but something abnormal was going on. When we left, two of his men followed us back to town in the SUV. After Guy dropped me off, they followed him to his house. They blatantly drove into Guy's driveway, asked him his name, and wrote down his address. Scared the shit out of him. The next morning I got a visit from Perillo himself at my office in Stuart wanting to know why I insisted on continuing to involve myself in his affairs. He managed to drop into the conversation for no reason what Guy's address was and what a nice house Guy had. I got the message."

"Will, I told you once before, you watch out," Mallette said. "You're messing with fire. What'd you tell him?"

"I tried to blow smoke up his ass, but he saw through me instantly. I was finally forced to tell him the truth. I know this sounds crazy, but Perillo ended up opening an account with me. Said Soltero had given me a good recommendation. You could have knocked me over with a feather. I would have been less surprised if he had come there to, as they say in the crime movies, 'take me out.'"

"You've definitely been watching too many hoodlum shows," Tom said.

"Maybe he opened the account so he could keep an eye on me in the future. You've heard the old story about keeping your enemies close where you can see them."

"OK, so the greaseball is probably into some shady stuff, and he has enough money to open a brokerage account. To be honest, Will, I have heard his name mentioned before, but technically he's clean. He does not have a rap sheet I've been able to find. But what does all this have to do with Tressler's death?"

"On the surface nothing, I guess. It just reinforces in my mind what kind of people Tressler was in bed with. My mama always told me where there's smoke there's fire."

"Let me tell you something off the record. I don't want my comments to leave this room. Do we understand each other?"

Will nodded.

"We know this address. We've had surveillance on it for some time in a cooperative effort with the Border Patrol and FBI. We first became aware of it when an illegal alien had a car accident on I-95. The car he was driving was traced back to the lot you just described. There was artwork we suspect might possibly be stolen in the trunk. We haven't been able to nail this bunch on anything yet, but it's just a matter of time," Tom said.

"One more thing," Will added. "Perillo told me subtly I should be spending more of my time investigating Dave's attitudes on risk taking. I didn't know what he was talking about, but when I got Betsy to check Dave's bank accounts, she found out what he had been alluding to. She found pretty conclusive evidence that Dave was an active Internet gambler – he used a company called BETUS and also Forex – a lot."

"What's BETUS and Forex?" Tom asked.

"BETUS does mostly sports, you know, the usual bookie stuff. Forex is an Internet vehicle for trading currencies. Foreign currencies are a hot dot now-a-days for traders. The leverage used to trade currencies is unbelievable. You can either hit it big in a hurry or lose your ass real quick. There's always action. The personality profile of the people attracted to it is very similar to the profile of people who are hooked on

265

trading commodities. It's the new frontier for adrenalin-junkies who think they've found the easy way to get rich without working."

"Now you're starting to get my attention. And Perillo gave you this tip? Interesting. Tell me more."

"Betsy also discovered Dave had a special bank account in his name only. His paycheck was always direct deposited into that account. It was also the account he deposited his limited partnership moonlighting money in. He then would move money to his joint account so his wife would have money to run the household. I don't think she had a clue about all the razzle dazzle going on. The single account statement went to a PO box instead of his house. This is how Dave always kept some trading money for himself. You'd think his single account would really build up with part of his paycheck going in there on a regular basis, but the balance was up and down like a yo-yo. What made the balance so volatile were scads of debits as money constantly went out of the single account to both Forex and BETUS. He was using a debit card to move money to them as needed. As out of touch as his wife was, she still knew they were always robbing Peter to pay Paul. She just didn't know why. She told Betsy and me that money caused ongoing stress in her marriage."

"We see marriages all the time where the wife doesn't have a clue, but some of them surprise you on what they really know," Tom said.

"Yeah, I know what you mean. See how this story grabs you. It makes me wonder even more about what Connie Tressler knows and doesn't know, and when she knew it. There was a Miguel Valdes at Dave Tressler's wake. My wife and I heard him make an inappropriate comment to Connie Tressler. He told her he was there to check and see how his money was being spent. Connie turned white. Betsy and I both were horrified. Anyway, I found out that this dude owns a restaurant over on Highway 1 called Casa Camilio. So I went there one day."

"It doesn't look like much on the outside. Just another shopping center hash house, but when you go in it's a whole different story. The clientele was almost exclusively Latin. Even the menu was in Spanish. And the owner spent lots of money decorating the joint. Ever heard of the artist named Fernando Botero?"

"Can't say that I have."

"He's the one who always paints fat people. I've read that his paintings sell for a fortune. Well, they had original Boteros hanging on the wall. After I saw those I wrote down the name of another artist that they had on the wall. His name was Alejandro Obregon. I had never heard of him, but I later found that he's considered to be the grandfather of Colombian abstract art. His stuff trades for even more than a Botero. They had a fortune just hanging on the walls."

"So where is this leading?" asked Tom.

"After lunch I decided to do a little snooping and prospecting after I saw a constant procession of Latin men going in and out of this unmarked door into the back. The door led to a hallway that went into the back end of the building. I gave the waitress my business card and asked if I might see Valdes. About five minutes later a big tough looking man came back out of the door and whispered to the waitress to inform me that Señor Valdes would see me. When I went into the back all the doors off the hallway were closed except one.

Through its window I saw the same Baja Outlaw that accosted us on the river one Saturday and scared the shit out of us."

"I remember."

"I almost crapped when I saw it there, but I'm getting away from the purpose of this story. I told Valdes that I had taken over Dave's Tressler's accounts. He misunderstood me and thought that I was going to be the new salesman peddling Spoonbill and Macadamia partnerships for their organization. He thought Soltero had sent me over. When I told him that I was only talking about RST business his attitude got very hostile. He warned me that I had better forget I had ever heard him mention the names Spoonbill and Macadamia. Then I got escorted out."

"Will, I've tried to tell you to walk lightly around these people," Mallette said. "You don't know who or what you're dealing with. I can't stress it enough. You fuck with the bull, you'll get the horn. Anything else?"

"Tom, remember when I told you that Dave Tressler's super expensive Rolex was missing? Well, it's turned up. Mike Pollard's wife found it in Mike's glove compartment."

"She kicked him out of the house because he couldn't give her an adequate explanation why it was there. He and his son-in-law weren't on speaking terms. Also, Mike was out of touch for a time the day of the storm which he refused to discuss with his wife. His daughter, Connie, tried later to reason with him. He stonewalled her too. Now do you think maybe the police department ought to reopen this case?"

"Whew! You've given me a big cud to chew. Let me think about it and kick it around with some other people downtown. I'll get back to you."

"That's all I can ask," Will said. "I promised you as this story evolved I would keep you up-to-date. I hope this information will be of value."

Chapter 58

*C*onnie Tressler was rushing around trying to get ready to leave the house. She needed to go the dry cleaners and to Publix. She had to get gas and she wanted to go by the veggie market and Davie needed a piece of construction paper for a school project and she had to be on time to pick up the kids after school. Connie did one last fluff on her hair, checked her makeup and left the house. Just as she got to the car she remembered she had left the grocery list in the house and dashed back in to get it.

When she returned to the garage there was a gleaming black Mercedes S600 behind her car in the driveway. In the front seat were two Latin men. It took her a second to recognize them. It then hit her like a ton of bricks that they were men Dave had had dealings with. She remembered them from Dave's wake. One had made the nasty comment about spending "my money" she hadn't quite understood at the time. The other one had been at the Reynolds Smathers and Thompson open house. Connie's stomach knotted.

The men got out of their car and slowly walked up the driveway. One smiled and held out his hand.

"Mrs. Tressler, Omar Perillo. I hope you remember me. And I think you've met my associate Miguel Valdes. It's a pleasure to meet you again. May we have a moment of your time?"

"Of course I remember both of you. It's good to see you again. Is there something I can do to help you? I was just leaving, and I'm really in quite a hurry."

"We will be brief. May we come in?"

"Uh, Uh, Uh, sure! I guess so. Would you mind coming into the house through the garage door so I don't have to go around and unlock the front door?"

"That would be fine. We don't mean to inconvenience you. I promise we will only take a moment of your time."

Perillo held the door open for Connie to enter. She showed them into the living room.

"Mrs. Tressler, I hate to have to bring up an indelicate matter with you this soon after your husband's death, but there's a matter of some money."

"Money? I don't know what you are referring to."

"Your husband owed us a fairly large sum. We came to see what arrangements you had planned to repay the debt."

"I don't have the foggiest idea what you are talking about," Connie replied.

The two Latin men looked at each other. Perillo reached in his pocket and took out a piece of paper. He handed it to Connie.

"Mrs. Tressler, that is a promissory note for $250,000. As you can see, it has been signed and dated by your deceased husband. The reason for our visit today is to ask you what arrangements you are making to repay our generous loan."

"Oh, my God! Mr. Perillo, you have to believe me I know nothing about this loan."

"Do you not agree you are looking at your husband's signature?"

"I don't have that kind of money," Connie said, starting to hyperventilate. "I simply don't have that kind of money! You've got to believe me! Please!"

"You don't seem to understand. We want our money," Valdes rasped.

"I realize perhaps we have caught you unawares," Perillo said more gently. "But you also have to understand we are businessmen, and as businessmen, we expect people to meet their obligations. We gave your husband credit on good faith. We expect to be treated fairly in return. Now what arrangements can we expect from you to fulfill his obligation?"

"Please understand me! It's not that I don't want to pay you back. I just don't have the money."

Connie started to shake and then cry.

"He should a thought of that before he made the bets. If you can't afford to lose, you shouldn't be in the game," Valdes said cruelly.

"Did I understand you right this is money Dave lost gambling?"

"I didn't talk Japanese or nothin', did I? That's exactly what it is," Valdes looked at Perillo as if he expected him to laugh at the sadistic joke.

"Once again not to seem indelicate, Mrs. Tressler, I need to remind you the loan is not interest free."

"Interest?"

"The interest your husband agreed to is $2,000 a week. And that is if he is current. If he is not, we are forced to assess penalties. Considering his unfortunate circumstances my associates and I have not visited you until now out of respect to your loss. We are not without heart. I hope you understand we do not enjoy having to make this visit now, but we are after all businessmen. We are in the business of making a profit on our investments."

"Yeah, we want our fuckin' money."

"Enough said," Perillo added and gave a momentary silencing glance at his ill mannered companion.

"Believe me when I say I don't have any money. My husband and I were not living together when he died. He only gave me enough money to run the household."

"We will visit again in a week – say about this time next Thursday. That should give you time to make arrangements. We would prefer to not have any unpleasantries. Lovely picture of your children, by the way. You are a most attractive family."

"Please don't make me worry about my children. They are all I have. I'm going to be getting some insurance money. I will repay what Dave owed. I promise."

"I don't wish to push, but when may I ask?"

"I don't know, but I swear I'll find out. Just leave me and my children alone."

"It is not our wish to frighten anyone," Perillo said. "I hope you understand our intention is to conduct business in an efficient, businesslike manner. We will call again in a week. If you can make arrangements before next Thursday feel free to call this number."

Perillo handed Connie an engraved business card.

Chapter 59

*C*onnie showed the men out and went back in her house. Through the front window she could see the Mercedes drive away. She sat in the Queen Anne chair short of breath, unable to control the spasms that wracked her body.

"$250,000! How could Dave get in so deeply with men like that?" She shuddered as she expressed herself. "I was telling them the truth. I don't have that kind of money. Penny told me that I'll have that and more soon. I'll just have to give it to them."

Then came a wave of anger. "God damn you, Dave Tressler! I can't believe you were so selfish and so stupid as to put your family at risk like this for utter nonsense. Wherever you are, I hope God is going to punish you for your despicable behavior! I can't believe I loved you – I idolized you – once. I hope you burn in hell, you selfish bastard."

Then she said aloud as if to convince herself, "Connie, you'll get through this. Let's go run our errands. Take your mind off it. You can't let Davie and Elizabeth see you like this."

She balled up her fist and hit the back of the upholstered chair, "Damn you, Dave, you sorry SOB. Why'd you leave me like this? My father never did anything to my mother like this. It's not fair! It's just not fair!"

Her mind in a fog, Connie backed her car down the driveway and drove down the street.

One by one the errands got done though Connie could not have reconstructed her path if someone had put a gun to her head.

One sentence continued to play over and over in her mind.

We want our fuckin' money.

"Dave, I hate you. I wish I had never met you."

Connie dialed Penny's office number, but she was out.

When Connie arrived at Saint Edwards a long line of parents and grandparents had already queued up to pick up their charges. The bell rang, and the tide of children started flooding from the building.

After Connie had picked up Davie and Elizabeth, she drove home in silence. When they arrived, she snapped out of her fog momentarily to tell the children to help bring in the groceries and then get right on their homework because Mommy had some business she needed to take care of.

"Is it about Daddy, Mom?" Davie asked.

We want our fuckin' money resounded again in Connie's brain. "I'm sorry, darling. I was thinking about something. Yes, there's some of your father's business I need to tend to. Go start on your homework. I'll put the groceries up."

No more questions were asked.

Connie went out on the back patio and called Penny. She was put right through.

"Have you heard anything about Dave's insurance money?"

"No, but I wouldn't have," Penny said. "I'm not the agent of record on the policies. Any communications would have gone directly to you. In fact I'd call them, but they won't disclose anything without your permission. You've got the phone numbers for the customer service desk for death claims on the copies of the forms that I gave back to you. Why don't you just call them? If you do it now, their offices will still be open. I am sure they can quickly bring you right up to speed. I feel sure the funds will be out in a few weeks."

"...I don't... know the right questions to ask. ...Are you sure you can't help me?" Connie sniffled. "You know just what to ask. I just get lost."

"Sure, Connie you know I will. Don't let all this fluster you. We'll just get on a three way conference call, and you can authorize them to speak to me. Do you have the files out?"

"I'm calling you from my back patio on my cell phone. I didn't realize I needed the file."

Connie went into the house, spread out the file on Dave's desk and called Penny back. Within ten minutes they had talked to customer service reps from both insurance companies. The story was the same at both places. The claim forms had been sent to legal for review and it would take more time for the distributions to be approved and processed. They were told to call back the following week, and the paperwork's progress would be checked once more. Connie was frantic.

We want our fuckin' money.

We will visit again in a week.

"Penny, you just have to pin these companies down and find out when and if I'm going to be getting some money. You just have to! I'll take less if necessary!"

"Connie, I'm sure that everything is all right."

"Penny, I don't want to be insistent, but you have to make them process my money."

"Is something wrong? If there were something seriously deficient, I'm sure they would have told us when we called."

"Penny, I have to have that money," Connie said. Penny could hear her crying in panic. "Some of Dave's associates are insisting he owes it to them. They had a promissory note proving that he owes them. They scared me. I can't take the risk they might hurt my family. Don't you understand? I just can't."

"I don't understand! Calm down! Take a couple of deep breaths and tell me what you are talking about. What men and what money?"

"They're gamblers, horrid scary people. Dave owes them gambling money. I can't remember their names. It's the same terrible Spanish men who came to Dave's wake. They won't take no for an answer. They will either get what they want or they'll hurt us! You have to help. I need that money."

"Did they threaten you?"

"Not in so many words, but I got the message."

"How much money are we talking about?"

"$250,000... but it goes up $2,000 every week. I'll take less if I have to, but I have to get rid of these people! You had to have been here. One of them gave me this evil look and said 'I want my fuckin' money.' It made my blood run cold! How could Dave do this to me? How could he? My father never did anything like that to my mother. Things like this just don't happen to respectable people like us!"

"Connie, I'll see what I can do, but you really should go to the police. Don't try to deal with these thugs by yourself. Promise me you'll call the police."

"They are coming back next Thursday, and they expect to get paid. Penny, they were looking at a picture of Davie and Elizabeth! Please help me! They terrify me!"

"Connie, I am not sure there is anything we can do to hurry the money. But I will talk to Guy and see if he has any suggestions. You really need to call the police!"

"As bad as I hate to, I'm going to call my father. He'll know how to deal with them. Mama said he got tough with these creeps the last time Dave got into trouble with them. Why did Dave do this to me, Penny? I gave him the best of everything I had. He...he...."

Connie couldn't finish. The phone just went dead. Penny listened to the dial tone not knowing if she should call back.

Chapter 60

*C*onnie brooded all night and slept little. She replayed the events of the previous day over and over in her mind. She watched as the hours ticked off the big digital clock by her bed. She flipped on the bedroom television from time to time, but it didn't help. She alternated between her bedroom and the den. More than once she looked in on the kids. She thought about going out on the back patio but was afraid to unlock the door. I'm not one to have insomnia, she thought. Every time she closed her eyes she could visualize the big black Mercedes turning into her driveway. She continued to see the big burly man and the smaller wiry one getting out, each slamming his door with authority, silently taking in everything around them, and then walking boldly with resolve up her driveway. They had seemed to be making a mental inventory of all that was hers, like it was soon to belong to them.

Your husband owed us a fairly large sum of money.

"$250,000 – $250,000! I've never seen that kind of money before."

Connie's heart palpitated.

We came to see what arrangements you had planned to repay the debt.

Her mind raced.

"Maybe I should call Daddy. He would know what to do, but, God, I don't want to drag my father into this."

We want our fuckin' money.

We are businessmen...and expect people to meet their obligations.

"I don't even gamble on marked down meat in the grocery store. I don't even enjoy buying a lottery ticket. I wouldn't even know how to find the winning numbers in the newspaper. I despise gambling."

If you can't afford to lose, you shouldn't be in the game.

"Gambling on what? I thought he just lost a little money playing golf!"

I didn't talk Japanese or nothin' did I? We want our fuckin' money.

"That horrible man just looked like he would enjoy hurting me and my kids."

The interest your husband agreed to is $2,000 a week. And that is if he is current.

"$2,000 a week! That's $8,000 every month! That's a lot more than I pay for Davie and Elizabeth's school tuition!"

We want our fuckin' money.

Sometime before daybreak Connie decided she was going to call her father. He would know what to do. He always seemed to know what to do.

Connie called as soon as the kids were dropped off at school, but Mike Pollard wasn't at the office. Finally, after 9 she reached him.

"Good morning, darling. I'm sorry I'm running late. Now, what can I do for you on this fine morning?"

"Daddy...," Connie started crying. "Daddy...," she tried again. She sniffled. Her throat closed. She was still not able to get her words out.

"Now just settle down, darling! Take a deep breath and tell me what's wrong. Has something happened to one of the kids?"

"No! The kids are fine. I got this visit from these disgusting, evil men."

"What evil men? Connie, tell me slowly. Organize your thoughts. Start at the beginning. Tell me what you're talking about."

"These men say Dave owes them $250,000. They want their money by next Thursday. If they don't get what they want, they'll hurt Davie and Elizabeth, I know they will! Daddy, I didn't want to call you, but I don't know who else to go to. They had a paper showing Dave owes them the money. They say if they don't get it, they'll want even more money. He was gambling."

Connie again burst into tears.

"Connie, do you know these men's names? Do you know where to find them? What kind of gambling?"

"I don't know. Honest to God, I was too upset to ask. One of them left me a business card. He told me to call him if I got their money before Thursday. One of them glared at me and said some horrible things. He looked like he could slice me up and never think twice about it. He was looking at a picture of Davie and Elizabeth! My babies! Daddy, I don't know what to do! This is the most horrible thing I've ever been through!"

"You did the right thing. You called me. Now, read me the name and phone number on the business card. I'll take care of it. Don't do a thing. Don't talk to anyone about it. Let me take care of it. That bastard...That sorry no-account bastard! Why did you ever marry him and make him part of our family?"

"What did you say, Daddy?"

"Nothing...I was just talking to myself. Now you just calm down. I'll take care of it, I promise. Have I ever let you down?"

"No, Daddy, you haven't."

"And I won't let you down now!"

Connie hung up.

Chapter 61

Mike did not react immediately. He needed to think about what his daughter had just told him. The worst thing he could do was go off half cocked. He had done that before and regretted it.

Mike thought. I have three choices. I can meet with these assholes at my office. I can meet with them on their turf, or I can meet them at some neutral location.

The more he thought the madder he got. He knew as well as he was sitting there that Dave owed them the money. But he'd be God-damned if he was going to bail out that dumb fuck of an ex son-in-law.

When I think of everything I did for that little shit ass. Without my sponsorship he probably would have clerked at the mall for close to minimum wage – if he was lucky. The little turd was too stupid to get a degree. I got him into my business. Then once he got in the door, I helped him get his business off the ground. You would think he would have walked the straight and narrow since he didn't deserve to be there anyway, but he had the morals of an alley cat.

Mike had worked himself into a state. He felt flushed. He could feel his blood pressure was up. He inadvertently snapped the pencil he was holding in two. He looked at it and threw it into the waste basket. Then he thought of his daughter's near hysteria and about his grandchildren, and his head cleared. This was not going to be simple. Getting mad wasn't going to accomplish a thing.

These are not the kind of people you just blow off, and they go away. They pride themselves in not letting the mark come out on top. I've got to let them know they are not dealing with peon Dave Tressler any longer...or my weak daughter. They are talking now to Michael L. Pollard! Michael L. Pollard who knows people in high places, people who can make life very tough on his enemies if they continue to bother my family. These spics think they can be merciless? Well, so can I! They're not going to get blood out of a dead turnip. He's dead and his debts went to the grave with him. That's it – show's over, monkey's dead! I'll choose the meeting place. I'll choose the time. They're about to start learning in a hurry who is really in charge.

"We might as well get this ball rolling." Mike said aloud.

He closed his door and dialed the number Connie had given him.

"Mr. Perillo? This is Mike Pollard. You may remember me. My daughter is Dave Tressler's widow."

"I am aware of who you are, Mr. Pollard. How may I help you?"

"I would like to arrange a meeting to discuss a matter you brought to my daughter's attention. I would prefer for our meeting to be discreet. Would 1 p.m. today at 324 Dahlia, Apartment D-215 suit you?"

"I can fit that time into my schedule."

"Do I need to repeat the address?"

"I got it the first time. Goodbye, Mr. Pollard. I look forward to seeing you at one o'clock."

Chapter 62

Mike went home for lunch that day. He wanted to make damned sure he would be at the apartment well before his guests arrived.

Shortly before one, Mike peered out his front window and saw a black Mercedes drive down Dahlia. It parked in front of the building and three men emerged. Mike recognized Omar Perillo and Miguel Valdes. Perillo was a wiry sophisticated man who walked like he was tightly wound. Valdes was large and burly and walked without the grace of his companion. Each step was heavy and menacing. The third man got out of the back seat. He was young and muscular, with a dark ponytail. Mike figured he must be the bodyguard. He remained standing beside the car as Perillo and Valdes looked for the outside stairwell. A Christmas wreath marked its entrance. The large man noticed it and silently pointed to the stairwell. The wiry man nodded and easily mounted the stairs; the larger man plodded along.

"It's show time!" Mike said to himself.

Moments later the doorbell rang. Mike answered immediately.

"Mr. Pollard, my name is Omar Perillo. My colleague – Miguel Valdes. I hope we have not held you up."

"No, you are right on time. Please come in."

The two men entered the apartment.

"Sirs, please be seated. My daughter tells me her deceased husband incurred some recent debts with you gentlemen just prior to his unfortunate demise."

"Yes, he did. As you know from our last meeting, your son-in-law was a man of many weaknesses," Perillo said.

"And he was a fuckin' poor gambler too," Valdes mumbled with a sneer.

"As I was saying," Perillo continued, "Dave came to us and asked us to finance a streak of bad luck that had plagued him. Since we knew him from working with him in other ways, we agreed to provide the bridge financing he needed. No one in our organization anticipated his early demise, but a loan is a loan and honor is honor. As much as it may be an inconvenience to his family, we expect the loan to be repaid in the same honorable spirit as it was made."

"How much did Dave borrow?"

"$250,000 plus $2,000 per week interest," Perillo said. "We have a promissory note he signed agreeing to the loan terms. He was under no duress. He freely agreed he would repay the loan on these generous terms on a timely basis. Sir, we are not a bank. We are a lender of last resort. We set the terms to compensate us for our risk and to derive a modest return. We are businessmen. We only ask the family to respect the commitment. We held up our end by providing the necessary funds when he needed them. We now ask his family to be equally honorable."

"Yeah, we want our fuckin' money," Valdes mumbled."

"I am sorry my son-in-law had the poor judgment to borrow money at these usurious interest rates," Mike said. "However, your agreement was between you and him. I do not consider this to be a debt of honor my family owes to you and your associates. As unfortunate as his death was, it was one of the risks you incurred when you decided to loan him these funds. It is not my debt or that of my daughter. Your business was between you and Dave Tressler. I am not going to pauperize my family to repay a debt they do not owe or were not even aware of. I am warning you to leave my daughter and her family alone. If you don't heed my warning, I can make the authorities aware of your activities. Do we understand each other?"

"No, Mr. Pollard, let me tell you what we understand," Perillo said. "We expect these funds to be repaid in full. We also have ways of dealing with those who do not cooperate with us fully. I will give you an example. I have been told your son-in-law wore a very distinctive and very expensive watch. I am also told this watch mysteriously disappeared until recently when it was found in the glove compartment of your car. Do you know how his watch came to be in your glove compartment?"

"No, I do not. I wish I did," Mike said.

"Well, I do," Perillo continued. "And I also know other facts, if combined with the mystery of the watch could have the authorities asking questions about your son-in-law's death that no one wants to address. These facts can stay buried, or they can easily surface. The choice is yours. Now, as I told your daughter, we would be grateful if we could resolve these unpleasant matters by next Thursday. We will expect to hear from you. If we don't, you and your family will hear from us. Good day, sir."

288

"Yeah, we want to see the money by next Thursday," Valdes said. "Do we understand each other, partner?"

The two men rose and left Mike's apartment.

Chapter 63

*T*he alarm went off at seven instead of six-thirty since it was Saturday. The weekend routine was soon to begin. Betsy had told Will the night before the errands she had planned for the day. She needed some poinsettias from Home Depot to decorate the house. Betsy was eager to make the house as festive as possible when Lexie got home for the holidays. She wanted to be at Sam's early to try to beat the Saturday crowd. Betsy went to the bathroom to plug in her hair curling irons, then to the kitchen to hit the button on the coffee pot. Will opened the patio door to let the dogs out before going out to retrieve the newspaper. He stripped the plastic wrapper off the paper to take a quick peek at the headlines.

BLIZZARD PARALYZES NORTHEAST

THOUSANDS WITHOUT POWER

"Payback time," he thought groggily. "So many of these people were holier than thou back during hurricane season about why anybody would want to live in Florida. From here until spring we get to laugh our asses off about why anyone would live in the northland. At least we didn't lose power in below freezing weather."

Another headline quickly caught his attention.

MERCHANTS REPORT BRISK CHRISTMAS SALES DESPITE ACTIVE HURRICANE SEASON

Below the fold, another headline jumped out.

PROMINENT BUSINESSMAN KILLED IN ONE-CAR ACCIDENT

He read the first sentence.

"Holy shit! Mike Pollard!" Will yelled out. He made a beeline for the house, losing a flip-flop in the process.

"Betsy," he yelled as soon as he was back in the front door. "Mike Pollard's dead!"

"What do you mean he's dead?"

"Car wreck! According to this article no one knows how it happened. There weren't any witnesses. It was a one-car accident."

"Where?"

"State Road 60, out past the mall. Went off into a grove last night at high speed. He rammed a tree head-on."

"Do they think he was drunk?"

"Not according to this. The deputies investigating the accident couldn't tell exactly what happened."

"Maybe he swerved to avoid an animal. Very strange! And they said he was alone in the car? And there were no witnesses? Very, very strange," Betsy said.

Betsy then told Will about her meeting with Penny the day before.

"Penny told me Connie Tressler called her toward the end of last week. Connie was asking when she might expect Dave's insurance claim to be processed and when she might expect checks. Penny tried to explain to her they really weren't in the loop since Guy's office wasn't the agent of record on the policies. Penny ended up doing a three way call with both insurance companies to see what they could find out. The service reps told them these things just take time and you can't hurry them up. This was not what Connie wanted to hear. Penny told me the longer she talked to Connie the more the tone of the conversation changed from routine to panic. She said Connie began hyperventilating as she admitted why she was desperate for the money. Dave owed the Colombian thugs $250,000 in gambling debts. Can you imagine?

Betsy continued, "Two of the cretins visited Connie at home, subtly hinted her children could be in danger, and then gave her until this Thursday to come up with the money."

"As in day before yesterday? Nothing like a reasonable deadline," said Will."

"Oh, I almost forgot. You know what the vigorish was? Are you sitting down? $2,000 a week – a week!"

"That would clean out the cookie jar in a hurry," said Will.

"Connie was almost incoherent. She told Penny she was so desperate she was going to call her father. Seemed convinced he could handle them. Said he'd gotten Dave off the hook once before with this same motley crew. Do you think they used Dave's weaknesses to compel Dave to work for them? Do you think that's why dumb Dave sold their piece-of-crap limited partnership units? You reckon Mike actually tried to get involved?"

"You have got to ask yourself, how do some people get in so far over their heads?" replied Will.

"You talking about Dave or Mike?" asked Betsy.

"I'm not sure. I guess I could easily be talking about either one of them."

Chapter 64

*T*he church was packed thirty minutes before the service was scheduled to begin. The Pollards were a very well-regarded family in Vero Beach. Mike had been a broker with Smith Barney as long as anyone could remember. He had always run a good, clean business and was highly respected for his financial advice and success. Now he was dead. His wife Constance had actively supported community causes. Their daughter, Connie, had been born at Indian River Memorial Hospital. She had started pre-K at Saint Edwards. When she graduated from there she had been recognized as a "die hard" like Will and Betsy's daughter Lexie. The term was reserved for a student who had never attended any other school. This put her in an enviable minority. Connie was the quintessential hometown girl, and other than a stint away from Vero Beach to go to college, would probably live her entire life right there in Indian River County. Native families of this ilk were shown a particular respect.

Perhaps more sympathy than normal had also been generated because of the nature of Mike's death, magnified because this was the second dramatic death in the same family in less than six months. This fact alone had made some people feel obligated to attend who otherwise might have just sent a sympathy card. Still other people wanted to make sure they were seen attending and would have paid cash to make sure their names were part of the permanent registry. The atmosphere was charged almost as much with social politics as genuine compassion.

Countless hands were shaken in the church parking lot, out on the sidewalk, and in the long line in the vestibule.

Will and Betsy saw Tom Mallette outside the church. Tom indicated he had something he wished to discuss with them later. When they entered the church they saw Guy and Penny had saved two spots for them on the pew they had staked out. As they waited for the service to begin, Will whispered to Guy his brief conversation with Mallette and asked Guy if he knew what it could be about. Guy shrugged.

An urn with Mike's cremated remains sat at the front of the church. His picture sat next to it. Just before eleven, the bereaved family was brought into the church and seated at the front.

At 11, the service began, and the buzz in the sanctuary ceased. After the opening prayer, the minister began his script.

"We are saddened and shocked at the death of Michael Lawrence Pollard and the way in which he died. We offer our sympathy to his wife, Constance, his daughter, his grandchildren, and all of Michael's other relations and friends. Michael's death is a tragedy. For you, his family, I am sure you feel lost. At a time like this we search for something to give us hope and light. A candle, for example. The candle to give you light is Jesus. Turn to Jesus; he will be the candle that will bring hope and light to the darkness of your lives. You should have no doubt that God is with you in the pain and grief you are suffering. Again and again the Bible tells us God is close to those who are suffering.

The Lord is close to the broken hearted.

Blessed are those who mourn; they shall be comforted..."

The minister's baritone voice rose and fell as he got into his well-rehearsed rhythm. Will's mind wandered, and he looked around the room. Connie and her mother looked confused, downcast and overwhelmed. Connie's kids looked bored and fidgety.

The minister went on:

> You have made us for yourself, O Lord
> and our hearts are restless until they rest in Thee...

Five rows in front of him, Will saw Soltero and Valdes. They too seemed to be surveying the crowd.

Will punched Guy in the ribs, held up two fingers, and nodded where he wanted Guy to look.

Guy looked back and mouthed "My, My!" Then Guy shook his head slightly, rolled his eyes back in the same direction as before, but held up three fingers instead of two.

Will glanced again and saw what had drawn Guy's attention – Omar Perillo was sitting there as well.

Betsy and Penny noticed the hand signals and glanced in the same direction. They both nodded.

Soon, the congregation rose to sing *Amazing Grace,* and the service ended. A final prayer was said. The minister announced the reception would be at the Vero Beach Country Club. Out on the sidewalk more hands were shaken. Women exchanged hugs. Standard comments exchanged again.

"It's so tragic..."

"I couldn't believe it when I read it..."

"Isn't it horrible..."

"Such a waste..."

"Poor Constance! What's she going to do now?"

Then, as if the factory whistle had blown, people rushed off in different directions. Some were going to the reception, some were going back to work, some would just go home. It was time for life to resume for the living. Everyone went away with a clear conscience since they had paid their respect to a deserving Vero Beach family.

The Blacks and the Walshes ran into Tom Mallette on the sidewalk.

"Don't forget to come by when you have a chance. We need to talk," Tom said.

"How about tomorrow at two o'clock in my office? OK with you?"

"Works for us. See you at two."

Chapter 65

*T*he club assistant manager at Quail Valley River Club met Will and Betsy when they walked in the front door of the club. A stunning Christmas tree was on the porch. Handmade evergreen wreaths with spray painted glittering pine cones decorated the door. When they entered another tree had been decorated for the lobby. Fresh evergreen garland with expensive blown glass balls had been strung around the gas log fireplace. The fireplace was lit, which heated the garland just enough for it to give the whole room a warm, woodsy, holiday smell. Even the grand piano in the entryway wore a red satin bow.

"Mr. and Mrs. Black, so good to see you. Happy holidays! Two for lunch?"

"Four actually. The Walshes are meeting us here. They should arrive any second."

"It's always good to see them. Porch or the grill? It's really nice outside today."

"Porch will be fine."

Guy and Penny walked in, and the hostess led them all out to the porch, took their drink orders, and left menus.

After some small talk Guy said, "Don't you think it's weird that Mike Pollard would die on a perfectly straight level road, in ideal weather, during a period when traffic was light, with no seeming extenuating circumstances?"

Will added, "After his daughter sought his help to intercede with the spics? One day after the deadline that had been imposed for payment in full for a very large amount of money?"

"I don't understand why they would want to kill him. You can't get money out of a turnip or a dead man. And Connie had money coming. Soon! She just couldn't get her hands on it at the drop of a hat.

"But maybe they didn't know that. Or maybe they didn't believe it when they were told she was coming into serious money."

"Or, maybe they thought it would be easier to tap Connie for the money than her dad," said Guy.

"Or maybe," Betsy added, "maybe it really was an accident. People sometimes just lose control of a car. He could have been using his cell phone. Maybe he dropped something on the floor, tried to pick it up and took his eye off the road. Maybe what Mallette is going to tell you tomorrow afternoon is there was a mechanical problem with the car."

"If there was a problem with the car, I think that would have been disclosed by now," Will replied.

"I hope our meeting will shed some light, not just raise more questions. Questions we got plenty of. I would like some answers."

"Knock on wood...we have less than a day until we find out some answers. Here comes our food. Bon appétit!"

♦ ♦ ♦ ♦

Will dropped Betsy off at the bank and headed for his office. Their after-work plans would be no different than most days – upon arriving home it would be time to fix a drink, slip into their Jacuzzi or pool, and share the day's experiences.

Betsy arrived home before Will that afternoon. Will had a four o'clock conference call after the market close. She gathered the mail from their mailbox at the end of the driveway, opened the garage door, and drove into the garage.

Before fixing their "happy hour" drinks, Betsy went through the mail to see if there were any bills or Christmas cards she needed to separate from the mounds of catalogues and other advertisements. The volume of sales material was staggering most days now that the holiday season was fast approaching. She laughed to herself as she thought about Bob Rivers' parody of *Deck The Halls* entitled *Wreck The Malls* that Will had been playing for her a few days ago. The song seemed caught in her brain and played over and over.

Unexpectedly, she came across a large brown envelope addressed to Will Black. There was no return address. The address label was typed on a small square and had been taped to the envelope. She laid it aside for Will.

By the time Will got home Betsy was already in the pool. As he walked through the house, he noticed his mail and saw the brown envelope. He opened it before heading out to join Betsy.

The contents of the envelope were most unexpected. Will started scanning the letter, but then he started reading it with more attention. Before finishing it, he impulsively tore open the patio door and lurched out to the pool deck in disbelief and puzzlement, waving the document as he ran.

"My God, you're not going to believe this," he said.

"Are you going to read it aloud to me or not?" Betsy asked.

Will was so mesmerized by what he was reading, he didn't even hear Betsy's plea.

"Why? Why was this sent to me?" he asked.

Chapter 66

*T*he following day Guy rode with Will over to the police station to keep their appointment.

"Mrs. Jackson, I really don't think Mr. Joye is butchering your tree just to irritate you. Part of your tree is hanging in his flower bed," they heard Tom Mallette say in a frustrated voice as they entered his office.

He hung up his phone and shut the door for privacy.

"That's the third time today that woman has called. She also called yesterday while I was out."

Guy looked at Will and laughed out loud, "And you thought God chose only brokers to baby-sit cranky old people."

Tom grinned.

"Thanks for coming, guys. I'm glad I ran into both of you at the funeral yesterday. It saves me two phone calls. I've really meant to call you, but it's been pretty hectic around here. We're up to our eyeballs still investigating hurricane complaints."

"What's your main problem?" Will asked.

"The police department's number one problem is investigating contractors who have been hired to do work for people who have taken deposits for jobs and made commitments they can't keep. Some were just stupid or greedy enough to take on more jobs than they could complete. Others honestly fell into this trap by not being able to get materials or find workers, but many are out of town storm chasing fly-by-night opportunists who descended on the town like locusts because they saw a chance to make a quick buck after the storm. Some did a half-ass job; some never showed up at all after people gave them a down payment. Some of these people weren't even properly licensed – just shade tree hammer swingers with a good line and fast feet. These guys figured we had so much on our plate that we'd never catch them. The public's been equally guilty in many cases. You know the old wives' tale – it's hard to scam an honest man. People have not been getting permits and inspections like they should. Others are so desperate to get their houses repaired they're willing to pay cash for the job before it even starts.

"Let's get down to the business at hand. I've thought about the Tressler case a lot over the last couple of months. I've tried more times than you'll ever know to come up with reasons why Dave Tressler's death should be classified as a homicide versus an accident. There's been nothing clear-cut about his death. God knows, I don't have to tell you, of all people, that. The last few weeks things really started moving fast. First, I finally got an answer back from the lab on both the fingerprints and the stain on the crystal ball found in Dave Tressler's office. The results of the examination of the stain showed it was Dave's blood type."

"Not totally unexpected," said Will.

Tom continued, "The lab was able to pull some really good fingerprints. One belonged to a certain Omar Perillo. He is listed as a real estate developer. The other prints belonged to Michael Lawrence Pollard; now he's dead. It has all climaxed with Mike Pollard's death. I'll be honest. I never reopened this case because I haven't known what the hell to do."

Will and Guy nodded.

"I asked you here today to see if you had any intuitive thoughts on Mike Pollard's accident. A pistol was found in the wreck under the driver's seat. Although someone had attempted to remove the serial numbers, our lab was able to identify the gun as being the same one purchased by Mike Pollard a week before his accident. All of the other potential evidence in this car crash appears to have been cleaned up by whoever got to the scene before the police arrived."

Will responded, "You believe someone altered the scene?"

Tom nodded.

Guy said, "I wonder what his plans were for that pistol."

Tom shook his head in a "your guess is as good as mine" look.

Will continued, "I've something to share with you. I want you both to read this letter I received yesterday."

He then handed Mallette what appeared to be a blood-stained letter. Guy sat there silently. Will gave him a copy of the letter, which he began reading at the same time. Will quietly observed both their reactions, saying nothing until they both had finished.

John G. Hadley, Esquire

Dear John,

As I sit here in my office, my memory rolls back through all of the years I spent serving my clients, supporting our community, being a member of my church, enjoying the compa-

ny of friends, and most of all, providing a stable and loving home for my family. I can truthfully say I always approached my work, and in fact treated everyone in my life with honesty, integrity, and had an overriding desire to direct my efforts in the best interest of each.

I was a successful financial advisor for my clients; a loyal, productive employee to my firm; a concerned, involved citizen in the community; a compassionate supporter of friends; and most importantly a faithful husband and loving father and grandfather. I had it all – everything a man could possibly want. I lived with the illusion that if I did the right things to all of the people in my life, the rewards and fulfillment would be multifold. They were, that is, until my daughter married a pompous idiot.

He brought chaos to an otherwise orderly world. The moment I met him I hated him. My initial impression proved to be correct over and over and over again. Little did I know then that Dave's lack of character, illegal actions, constant embarrassing behavior, and infidelity would obsess and magnify my disdain and hatred to the boiling point.

He was a disgrace to the securities industry. The manner in which he chose to invest clients' funds was to benefit his own interests – not theirs. He robbed clients from fellow brokers with deceptive practices and outright lies. A constant compliance nightmare, he always pushed the envelope beyond allowable limits. He even tried to raid my long term portfolio of clients in one of the sneakiest moves I ever saw in my over thirty years as a financial advisor. The sorry bastard even used his fiduciary knowledge to lie to his mother and cheat his own brother out of his inheritance while making a lot of money for himself.

He was a thief, a liar and a compulsive gambler. His character was lacking in the very basics of appropriate behavior. He was not only unfaithful to my daughter, his wife and the mother of his children, but also verbally abused her, even in public settings. His interest in his children and their activities were completely selfish and self serving.

To me and just about everyone that knew him, his incessant disgusting actions were endless. His ethics were nonexistent; he was an embarrassment to humanity – his behavior humiliating. The straw that broke the camel's back came the day he died, when I received a second visit from some of the criminals he was doing business with – he had even stiffed them, refusing to honor a loan commitment. They landed on my doorstep because he suggested I could easily be persuaded to satisfy his debt if they threatened my daughter and grandchildren. For God's sake – his own wife and children he would put in harm's way!

That was it – that was all I could take. I had the thugs thrown out of my office and went to RST to find the little shit. He was sitting at his desk with a smug look on his face. He said he had been expecting me. He knew I would come over to see him after his latest "referral". He laughed and continued laughing this disgusting chuckle. There was a crystal ball on his desk – I picked it up to throw it at him. He just chided me and told me I didn't have the courage to throw it. He snickered so hard he put his head down on his desk. Even then he continued to insult me, calling me a sentimental old simpleton. He said the world was made for the young and that it was past time for old impotent fools like me to make way for the young bucks who still had balls. He said he'd never divorce my daughter; it was too sweet a gravy train. He was completely amused at his ability to totally infuriate and antagonize me. I understood then just how evil he was. My breath started coming in short gasps. I thought that I might black out. But he was right. I did not throw the crystal ball. Instead, I smashed it into his head – the taunting stopped – he slumped back in his chair. Then, I threw the crystal ball down and left his office for the last time.

The hurricane was coming; I needed to get home to help my family prepare. As I drove down A1A in a trance, I realized my activities that afternoon were far more meaningful than merely helping get ready for a storm. After all, I had just given my family a new lease on life – the most help a man could ever provide to his kindred. My guilty conscience was eased. I smiled with the satisfaction that Dave Tressler was out of our lives forever!

May God forgive me. I know he understands.

Michael L. Pollard

"Holy shit!" Guy replied.

"This sure puts a new light on things" Tom said.

"That was my reaction too," Will continued. "I honestly didn't know what to do with it. Other than Betsy, you're the only people I've shown this letter to. This letter was sent to my home address." Each sat silently for a moment.

"What's your gut say, Tom?" Will finally asked.

"You tell me first," Tom replied. "I don't want to influence your response."

Will and Guy looked at each other, unsure how to respond.

"The first thing you have to ask yourself is who will benefit from the disclosure of this letter's contents?" Guy said.

"Or who would be hurt if we just let sleeping dogs lie?" Will quickly added.

"My gut says leave well enough alone," Guy agreed decisively.

"I didn't want to be the first to say it," Tom said. "But that's my gut feel too. I guess I just wanted confirmation."

"This family's been hurt enough – in fact, too much," Will added.

"I agree. Do we have a consensus?" Tom asked.

"As far as I'm concerned, we do," Guy said. "Do you agree, Will?"

"Let's just say this is our way of wishing Merry Christmas to some very deserving people who have been having a very hard time of it."

"While this cleans up the Tressler matter, it seems to leave the Pollard incident in question," said Tom with a sigh.

As Tom started thinking aloud, he added. "Certainly I plan to follow up on the blood stains and any prints that may be on this letter. If the blood is Pollard's and there are no prints on the letter, which was probably wiped clean like the accident scene – well, this case will go nowhere."

You could see the perplexed look on Tom Mallette as he rose from his chair. Then without warning he said, "Gentlemen, this meeting is concluded. I believe we have made the best decision. Some matters don't have a pat textbook answer. Enough said...Thanks for all of your help and support."

EPILOGUE

*C*hristmas Day was picture perfect. The sky looked flawless. The air was calm, and the temperatures moderate. It was an extraordinary day, one where no moment should be squandered. Will woke up with the Ringo Starr lyrics *"Come on Christmas, Christmas come on"* stuck in his brain and found himself singing them as he turned on the tree lights.

The Blacks effortlessly enjoyed once again the traditions that made Christmas so special to them. They opened presents, emptied their stockings, and took pictures. Will embarrassed Lexie by giving her a prolonged affectionate bear hug and reminding her how special these holidays would seem in the future.

Shortly before noon the Walshes arrived to share their turkey dinner.

Guy did a little jig at the door when he heard the soca singer Crazy on Will's stereo.

> *Put Jesus in your Christmas*
> *Jesus in your Christmas*
> *Jesus in your Christmas this year*
> *He came down here to save us*
> *From wickedness and chaos*

Put Jesus in your Christmas this year

Soon bloody Marys and mimosas flowed liberally.

"Look at this perfect day," Guy said. "Things sure are different than they were in the aftermath of Clarice, aren't they?"

Laura and Lexie drifted off to Lexie's room to look at the presents Santa had brought.

As they gathered around the kitchen island, Guy offered a toast.

"To good friends and a wonderful new year!" he said.

"I think you'll all agree it's been one helluva year!" Guy continued.

"You are a master of understatement. I don't know if I can take another one like this," Betsy replied.

"Would you have thought this time last year both Dave Tressler and Mike Pollard would be dead?" asked Penny.

"Not in a zillion years! I also didn't know this was going to be the year when a megastorm was going to roar through Vero Beach. Well, it did and here we are four months later talking about it," said Guy.

"I also never dreamed we would become acquainted with Colombian mobsters..."

"We learned more about them than we wanted to know..." continued Will.

"Who, by the way, are into illegal activities unlike any I ever knew existed in Indian River County," added Betsy.

"You have to admire initiative and creativity," Guy said.

"Riiight!" Will said. "But don't you feel sorry for Connie Tressler? Her Christmas this year sucks."

"I took some Christmas cookies that Lexie and Laura made over to the family. Connie is still a pathetic bundle of nerves. She had the bare minimum of Christmas decorations out," Penny said.

Penny continued, "Do you know what Connie told me? She thinks the Colombians killed both Dave and her father. They called her the other day still demanding their money. She paid them. She's scared to death – was asking me since she paid them off, did I think they would just leave her and the kids alone?"

"That's a lot to deal with," said Betsy. "But telling her the real truth, in my opinion, is not going to lessen the burden."

"All anyone can do is hope time will diminish her fears and sadness. I'd sure hate to have this much sorrow in my life, but maybe she'll meet a nice man and get remarried. She's really a very sweet attractive person," said Guy.

"Maybe she's right. Maybe the Colombians were responsible for Mike's death – we'll probably never know," Betsy said. "I feel sorry for her mom too."

"I'm glad Tom decided to let this matter drop. I think it was the right thing to do," Will said.

"I agree 100 percent," Guy said.

"I think the rest of the family has paid enough for having a self-centered prick in their midst. You know what they say about not being able to pick your relatives," Penny said.

"I guess some people would say Dave got what was coming to him, though I wouldn't wish his fate on anyone. I guess there's some truth to the old adage that says what goes around comes around," said Betsy.

"Yep, one way or another he was brought to justice," Penny said.

"Hey! Enough! This is Christmas. Let's talk about our trip to the Keys. I can't wait. I think we will all want a little R and R before hurricane season returns," Will said.

"We have so much to be thankful for. We shouldn't take it for granted," Betsy said.

"Good friends," said Guy.

"Great company," said Will.

"A nice family," said Penny.

"Profitable businesses," said Guy.

"Terrific children," said Betsy.

"The good life in paradise," said Penny.

"Amen! You know, we're really so lucky!" said Betsy.

"Yes, we are! Someone, turn the stereo up – I like this song," said Will.

If you're worried and you can't sleep
Just count your blessings instead of sheep
And you'll fall asleep counting your blessings